**'What are you going to do with me?'
Beth asked.**

'Oh, do not fret. I have no designs on your person,' he said.

'Then let me go.'

'That, I think, would be considered unchivalrous.'

'No more unchivalrous than holding a lady against her wishes.'

'If the lady has no idea of the danger she is in, then a gentleman has no choice.' He laughed suddenly. 'Whatever made you think you could pass yourself off as a boy? A more feminine figure I have yet to meet.' His eyes roamed appreciatively over her as he spoke. The only slightly masculine thing about her was her cut-down fingernails. He was intrigued by them. 'It is a good thing I intervened when I did.'

Born in Singapore, **Mary Nichols** came to England when she was three, and has spent most of her life in different parts of East Anglia. She has been a radiographer, school secretary, information officer and industrial editor, as well as a writer. She has three grown-up children, and four grandchildren.

Recent novels by the same author:

THE HONOURABLE EARL
THE INCOMPARABLE COUNTESS
LADY LAVINIA'S MATCH
A LADY OF CONSEQUENCE
THE HEMINGFORD SCANDAL
MARRYING MISS HEMINGFORD
BACHELOR DUKE
AN UNUSUAL BEQUEST

TALK OF THE TON features
characters you may have already met
in BACHELOR DUKE.

TALK OF
THE TON

Mary Nichols

MILLS & BOON®

First published in Great Britain 2006
Large Print edition 2007
Harlequin Mills & Boon Limited,
Eton House, 18-24 Paradise Road, Richmond, Surrey TW9 1SR

© Mary Nichols 2006

ISBN-13: 978 0 263 19386 2
ISBN-10:   0 263 19386 1

Set in Times Roman 15 on 17½ pt.
42-0307-86562

Printed and bound in Great Britain
by Antony Rowe Ltd, Chippenham, Wiltshire

TALK OF
THE TON

Chapter One

The girl, sitting on a rickety chair in the potting shed watching the young man lovingly tend a delicate plant he had been nurturing, wore a pair of breeches tucked into riding boots, a cream-coloured shirt with the sleeves rolled up and a sackcloth apron. Her hair was tucked up beneath a scarf. The clothes were old and a little shabby, but that did not disguise the fact that they were well cut and had once, many years before, been the height of male fashion.

'I wish I could go plant collecting,' she said wistfully, watching his deft fingers. They were blunt and dirty, but she had become so used to that she didn't even notice, any more than she was aware of her incongruous garb and the fact that her own fingernails were far from pristine.

'So you can. The heath is covered in plants, if you look carefully.'

'No, I meant exploring in foreign countries, climbing

the Himalayas or trekking through China or riding a
donkey in Mexico.' Her interest in botany had been
fired when, as a small girl, she had watched Joshua
Pershore, their gardener, working in their garden.
'Plants are like people,' he had told her. 'Look after
them and they will reward you with years of pleasure.'

She had asked him if she could have a patch of
garden all to herself and he had shown her how to
prepare the soil and sow seed and divide plants to
make more. She had watched her garden grow, excitedly noting the first snowdrop, the delicate petals of
roses and the way the bulbs died down each year and
sprang up anew the next spring. And when she discovered that Toby also shared her passion, it forged
a bond between them that sometimes carried them
into the realms of fantasy.

She dreamed of emulating the great plant hunters
like Sir Joseph Banks, who had travelled with Captain
Cook and transformed the Royal gardens at Kew from
a pleasure ground to a great botanic garden with
specimens from all over the world. And there were
others whose exploits and discoveries had fired her
interest, men like Francis Masson, and David Nelson,
who had been both with Captain Cook when he was
murdered by hostile natives and later on the ill-fated
voyage with Captain Bligh when he had been cast
adrift with him in an open boat when the crew

mutinied. That feat had made sure the captain's name went down in history, though David Nelson lost all his specimens.

'You'll have to marry a rich husband and then perhaps he will take you.'

'I'd rather go with you.'

'Then you will have a long wait. It takes a great deal of blunt and that's something I haven't got. I need a rich sponsor who will pay for everything, and where I am going to find one of those I do not know.'

'Then why talk about it?'

'I can dream, can't I?'

'Yes, and so can I.'

He looked closely at her. She was unaware how beautiful she was with hair the colour of a glossy ripe chestnut and brown eyes set in a classically oval face. She had a small straight nose and a determined chin and he loved her. Not that he could ever tell her that; she was far and away above him and he, the son of the estate steward, did not aspire to such dizzy heights, for all the freedom his father was allowed in running the Harley domain. 'Is that all you dream of? Don't you think of things like come-outs and balls and being courted by all the young eligibles in town?'

'Mama is always talking about giving me a Season,' she said. 'I have contrived to delay it until now, but Livvy turned seventeen last month and she says she

will bring us both out together and I suppose I will
have to agree for Livvy's sake. According to Mama,
it is not the thing for the younger sister to marry
before the elder, everyone will think there is something wrong with me.'

'So there is if you are averse to balls and tea parties
and being sought after by all the *beaux* of the *ton*.'

'I want to do something practical, something I'll be
famous for. The woman who discovered a new plant,
hitherto unknown to man.'

'Pigs might fly!'

'That's what you dream of and I know you mean to
try and make it come true.'

'I'm a man.'

There was no answer to that and she stood up and
brushed crumbs of soil from her breeches. 'I must
go. My uncle James is coming on a visit and I have
to change.'

'The Duke of Belfont,' he murmured. 'I should
think he'd have a fit if he could see you now.'

She laughed and hurried out of the building and
along the path that led back to the house.

It was all very well to dress eccentrically in the
confines of the grounds around Beechgrove—breeches
and a shirt were far the most practical attire for gardening—but she knew that it was hardly the apparel for
a nineteen-year-old brought up in polite society. Her

mother had long since given up remonstrating with her, asking only that she never appeared in public thus dressed and certainly not before her uncle, the Duke of Belfont. Uncle James never forgot his rank and took his role as guardian very seriously. To Beth and her sister he was a stern disciplinarian, though Mama said that was only his way and he wanted to do his best for his nieces. And today he was coming to make the arrangements for that dreaded come-out.

'Harri, can that be Elizabeth?' James was standing in the back parlour of Beechgrove, which looked out on the terrace from which steps led to well-manicured lawns and flower beds bright with the yellow of daffodils and the amber of gilly flowers. Beyond that, though it was hidden by a shrubbery, he knew there was a walled kitchen garden and a row of greenhouses and outhouses. It was from that direction the figure on the path had come.

Harriet left the tea tray over which she had been presiding to come and stand beside him. 'Yes, I am afraid it is.'

'Good God!' He watched as Beth strode down the path, head thrown back, arms swinging; if it were not for her feminine curves, he would have taken her for a boy.

'She likes to help in the garden and that is by far

the most practical mode of dress. She is decently covered and can move about without snagging her garments on thorns and suchlike. We should be for ever mending if—'

He turned towards her. 'Are you telling me you *allow* it?'

'Yes, so long as she stays in the garden and we have no guests.'

'Then it is as well I am here. The sooner she is installed at Belfont House and taught how a young lady should dress and behave the better.'

'James, she knows perfectly well how to dress and behave. You are being unkind to her.'

'And how do you suppose a prospective husband would react if he could see her now?'

'But there is no one here, certainly not a prospective husband.'

He sighed and returned to his seat. 'Oh, Harri, why did you not marry again? You would never have had this trouble if there had been a man in the house.'

'I am not having trouble, James. You are making a mountain out of a molehill. And I did not wish to marry again. And as for a man, why would I want one of those, when I have you?'

He laughed suddenly; it lightened his rather stern features and made him look more like the boy she had grown up with, before he had unexpectedly been forced to take on the role of Duke and head of the family. 'And what about Olivia? Is she dressed like the potboy?'

'No. She has gone riding dressed in her green habit.' She smiled. 'Very decorous it is too.'

He accepted a cup of tea from her. 'Then what about bringing them to Belfont House for the Season? You used to come every year before I married Sophie.'

'You needed me to act as your hostess, but, now you have Sophie, you don't.'

'Come as our guests. Sophie will enjoy your company and we can give the girls a Season to remember.'

'Thank you, James. Let's put it to the girls over dinner.'

Put it to the girls, he mused, as if they would be allowed to veto the suggestion. He decided not to comment.

When the two girls appeared at the dining table, they were dressed decorously. Beth's gown was in deep rose-pink silk with a boat-shaped neck, which emphasised her smooth shoulders and long neck. The waistline, in its natural place, was encircled by a wide ribbon. Her hair had been brushed and coiled on top of her head. Livvy was in a blue gown that almost exactly mirrored the colour of her eyes. It was trimmed with quantities of matching lace. They curtsied to their uncle. 'Good evening, Uncle,' they said together.

He bowed slightly. 'Elizabeth. Olivia.'

'Oh, we are in for a scolding,' Livvy said, as they took their places at the table and the maids moved forward to serve them. 'His Grace is being formal.'

In spite of himself, James laughed. 'Not at all, but you are both young ladies now and must be treated as such.'

'Does that mean we are to be given more freedom?' Beth asked.

'What can you mean, more freedom?' he queried. 'You are not confined, are you? You may come and go within reason. I go so far as to say you are allowed far more licence that most young ladies in your position.'

Beth realised that he had seen her coming back to the house, in spite of the care she had taken to come in by the kitchen door and take the back stairs to her room. It probably meant her mother had been scolded about it and she was sorry for that. How she hated the unnatural manners of society, which dictated how she should behave. If she had been a boy… She smiled to herself; she would be Sir Something-or-other Harley, baronet and master of Beechgrove.

It was a large solid house, built a century before in rich red brick. She loved it, she loved everything about it, its nooks and crannies, the huge kitchens, the gleaming windows, the mix of old and new furniture, the surrounding gardens, particularly the gardens, which people came from miles to see and admire. Beth had jokingly suggested they ought to charge them for the privilege, but her mother had been horrified at the very idea. It was their duty to be hospitable, she said.

'You are smiling,' her uncle commented, while her mother picked at the fish on her plate. 'Will you share the joke with us?'

'I was thinking what it must be like to be a boy.'

It was the wrong thing to say because it reminded him of what he had seen. 'Elizabeth, you are not a boy, you are a young lady, and wearing male clothes will not make you one. Where did you get them from?'

'I found them in the attic. I believe they belonged to Papa before he went into the army. He must have been quite slender then, for they fit me well enough.'

That was what she reminded him of when he had seen her in the garden: her long-dead father. She had the same proud walk; had Harriet noticed it too? Was that why she had allowed it, to bring back a little of the husband she had lost or perhaps conjure up the son she had never had but had always longed for? 'I think it is time you had a Season and learned what is expected of you,' he said. 'You, too, Livvy. Naturally, I shall sponsor you both.'

'Oh, that means every impoverished bachelor in

town will be all over us,' Beth said. 'The famous Harley girls, nieces to the Duke of Belfont, on the marriage mart, the objects of every rake, gambler and spotty young shaver who fancies his chances. It will be hateful.'

'You must have a very poor opinion of me if you think I will allow that to happen,' he said. 'You will be protected from the undesirable—'

'And from anyone in the least bit interesting too.'

'Not at all. Credit me with a little compassion.'

'Beth, please don't be difficult,' Harriet said.

'I am sorry, Mama, but you know how I feel about the false way husbands are chosen. I want to be in love with the man I marry. Who he is, and how rich he is, is unimportant.'

'You will not be forced into marriage, Beth,' James said gently. 'The idea is simply to introduce you to society and to allow you to choose for yourself. Your mother married for love, I married for love—I do not see why you should not do so too.'

'Within reason,' she added, suddenly thinking of Toby. He was so easy with her, but then they had known each other since they were tiny children, had as good as grown up together, and the difference in their status was unimportant.

'Within reason,' James concurred, as if he could guess her thoughts.

'I should like to be married,' Livvy put in. 'He must be handsome, of course, and not too old, but rich enough to have extensive stables. Horses must be his passion.'

James laughed. 'Then we shall have to see if we can suit you. But there is no hurry, you are still very young.'

'And Beth must be accommodated first.'

'That would be best,' their mother put in.

'Then I do hope you are not going to be difficult, Beth,' Livvy said, turning to her sister. 'I do not want to let my perfect partner slip through my fingers because you are prevaricating.'

Beth longed to suggest that they should go without her and leave her to her gardening and her dreams of becoming a famous botanist, but she knew that would upset her mother, so she said nothing. They spent some time discussing the arrangements, when they would travel and whom they would take. Jeannette, her mother's maid, would accompany them, of course, and Miss Andover, known as Nan, who had been the girls' governess but had agreed to take over the role of maid to the girls. They no longer needed a teacher and she had decided it was better than being pensioned off. Their coachman would drive them and Edward Grimble, the young groom, would ride Livvy's mare, Zephyr. She positively refused to go without her horse and her mama would not let her ride her all the way to London herself.

'What about you?' James asked Beth. 'Do you wish to have your mount brought to town?'

Beth wished she could suggest Toby rode her horse to London, then at least she would have some sensible company, someone to talk to. They might even go to Kew Gardens together, but she knew it was too much to ask. He would not leave his work in the garden; nature could not wait on her whims. 'I will be quite content with a hired hack, Uncle, thank you,' she said. Wealthy as he was, and however extensive the stables at Dersingham Park, his country seat, he did not keep many horses in London.

'Then shall we say ten days from now? You will be there right at the beginning of the season.'

'And shall we be invited to the coronation?' Livvy asked.

'Oh, Livvy, surely you do not want to attend that,' Beth put in. 'All that dressing up in the heat of the summer and standing about for hours and hours and for what?'

'To see the King and Queen crowned, of course.'

'If her Majesty is allowed anywhere near the ceremony,' Beth added. She held no brief for the Royal family, what with the King's numerous affairs and his efforts to discredit his wife so that he could divorce her and not have her acknowledged as Queen. He had failed in that and Caroline was still the Queen, though

King George refused to have anything to do with her and she lived in a separate establishment. Now the question was, would she be crowned with him?

'You will be going, Uncle James, won't you?' Livvy queried.

'I shall have no choice, not only because every aristocrat in the land will be expected to attend, but I am on his Majesty's staff and involved in the arrangements.' It was why he had been obliged to leave his country estate earlier than usual to take up residence in London.

'In that case, why take on the extra responsibility of bringing us out?' Beth asked.

'That, my dear Beth, will be a pleasure and a privilege.'

Beth felt she was being propelled willy-nilly into something she knew was going to be a disaster. She would have to pretend to enjoy herself or her mother would be hurt and her uncle annoyed, yet it was not in her nature to be anything but honest; pretending would come hard. And she would be leaving Beechgrove just when everything was coming into growth, all the plants and seedlings being planted out, and the rare specimens that Toby had been nurturing would be showing their worth.

'But, dearest, they will all still be here at the end of the Season,' her mother said when she tried to explain how she felt. Harriet had come to her daughter's room to say goodnight as she did every night and was sitting on the bed beside Beth. It was a precious time when they talked companionably together and problems were ironed out. 'It is not as if you are going away for ever. Even if you find a husband, you will still come home to be married from here.'

'I cannot imagine finding a husband among the fops who lounge about town ogling the young ladies being paraded like cattle at market.'

'They are not all like that. I met your papa during my come-out Season and he was certainly not a fop. He was handsome and intelligent and not at all affected.'

'You were lucky.'

'Who is not to say you will not be lucky too? And if you meet no one to your liking, then there is no harm done. You will be out and that will make it easier for you to go out and about when you spend another Season in town.'

'Yes, Mama.'

'Tomorrow, we shall go into Sudbury and have Madame Bonchance make up travelling clothes for us. The rest of our shopping can wait until we arrive. The Duke has offered to pay our bills. Is that not kind of him?'

'Why? We are not poor relations, are we?'

'No, not exactly poor, dearest, but nothing like as

rich as your uncle. Not rich at all, if truth be told. I have never bothered you with things like that before, but now I must confess that the money your dear father left us has been sadly depleted by the needs of the estate and his investments have not performed as well as they might. We need to be frugal.'

'Does that mean we have no dowries?'

'Oh, nothing as bad as that. James will provide your dowries, that has always been understood.'

'Would it not be better to forgo the come-out and let me earn a living?'

'Good heavens, no! Whatever made you think that? It would not look well at all, especially for your uncle. He would not have it said he was too close to look after his sister's children.' She paused suddenly, a small frown creasing her brow. 'Has Toby been filling your head with nonsense about working for a living?'

'No, not at all, Toby's not like that. He has always behaved properly. But, Mama, he has to work, so does his father and all the servants and they seem content enough.'

'I doubt it. And it is not the same thing at all. They were born to it, they know that is their lot in life, but you never were. I am beginning to wish I had said nothing to you...'

Beth flung her arms about her mother. 'Oh,

Mama, we have always been able to talk to each other and I would hate it if you felt you could not tell me things.'

Harriet kissed her daughter's brow. 'Then let us be thankful for what we have. And, Beth, there is no need to say anything to Livvy…'

'No, of course not. Our secret.'

Her mother left and Beth blew out the candle, but she did not fall asleep immediately. She could not stop thinking about her mother's confession and wondering how much of a difference it would make to her life. Would she have to accept an offer of marriage simply because it came from a rich man who could maintain Beechgrove in the old way? And if she did not, did it mean that some of the servants would have to be let go? Mama had not replaced the last chambermaid who had left to be married. Would Toby have to go? Her private dream, the one in which she offered to finance his plant-hunting trip on condition he took her with him, was no more than that: a pipe dream. It made her want to cry, not only for herself but for Toby too. Would a rich husband serve the same purpose? She thumped her pillow angrily. The time had not yet come when she would stoop to that.

The Duke, after riding round the estate with Mr Kendall, left about midday and in the afternoon the girls accompanied their mother to the dressmaker in Sudbury, their nearest town, and bespoke travelling gowns and accessories for their journey to London, which they were promised would be ready in good time.

It was the following day before Beth was able to escape to the potting shed where she expected to find Toby at work. He was nowhere to be seen.

She was about to turn back to the house, but changed her mind. She had come to talk to Toby about the latest developments in her life and she did not want to go back without unburdening herself to him. She set off for Orchard House, where he lived with his father on the edge of the estate.

'Is Toby here?' she asked when Mr Kendall answered the door himself. He was a well-educated man who had been estate manager since before her father died, and Beth knew her mother set great store by him, trusting him implicitly. In his turn, he worked assiduously to keep the wheels of Beechgrove turning. Beth had assumed it was an easy task, but, since her mother's revelation, she knew he must be finding it increasingly difficult. Poor Toby would never set off on his travels unless a miracle happened. She was as sad for him as she was for herself having to go through the charade of choosing a husband.

'No, Miss Elizabeth, he's gone.'

It was then she noticed the bleakness in his grey eyes and the downturned mouth. What had happened? 'What do you mean, gone?' she asked.

'Left. Gone on his travels. To Calcutta.' It was obviously not something that pleased the man who faced her.

'But how could he? The day before yesterday he was saying he did not know how he was ever going to manage it. What has happened?'

'Miss Elizabeth, I think you should go home.'

'I will when you have told me what this is all about. How can he have packed up and gone at a moment's notice? There are any number of things waiting to be done in the garden and glasshouse, he surely would not have left them to someone else.'

'He has. Pershore's lad has been given instructions.'

'I don't believe it. He wouldn't go like that, certainly not without saying goodbye to me. And his instruction would have been to me. He would trust me to follow them implicitly.'

'It's all for the best,' he said wearily.

It was then that enlightenment dawned. Toby had been banished; it was not his choice. 'Who sent him away?' she demanded. 'And why?'

'Go home, Miss Elizabeth, please. It is not fitting you should be here. Put your questions to your mama.'

What did her mother know of it? A little seed of suspicion began to grow in her mind. 'I will. Thank you, Mr Kendall.'

* * *

She could hardly wait to see her mother and dashed up to her boudoir and flung open the door. Her mother looked up from the letter she was writing to confront a daughter whose dark eyes blazed angrily. 'Beth, what is the matter?'

'Toby has gone.'

'Yes, I know. He has always wanted to travel to find new plants and the opportunity arose—'

'Very suddenly it seems,' Beth interrupted her. 'So suddenly he was not even allowed to say goodbye to me.'

'It was for the best.'

'That's what Mr Kendall said. I want to know what he meant.'

'Sit down, Beth, and calm yourself.'

Beth took a deep breath and sank on to a stool close to her mother's chair. 'I am calm.'

Harriet smiled. Calm her daughter certainly was not, but she was waiting for an answer and deserved one. 'You know Toby has always said he wanted to go plant hunting?'

'Of course I do, I was the one who told you that.'

'Well, he has been given the opportunity to go and it was too good to miss.'

'But, Mama, he's gone without me.'

'Of course he has. You did not seriously think you would be allowed to go with him, did you?'

Beth stared at her. 'He's been sent away from me, hasn't he? I wondered what you meant when you asked me if he had been filling my head with ideas about working for a living. You were afraid I might... What exactly did you think I might do, Mama? Elope with him?'

'No, of course not,' Harriet answered so swiftly that Beth knew that she had unwittingly hit the nail on the head. 'But you must admit you have been seeing a lot of him and I believe it is because of him you are so against having a come-out...'

'That has nothing to do with Toby.'

'Nevertheless, a little time apart might be beneficial...'

'And what did Toby say?'

'He understood.'

'The traitor!'

Harriet smiled. 'No, he was being sensible.'

'Why didn't he say goodbye to me? Did you forbid him to?'

'No, that was his decision. No doubt he will write frequently to his father and Mr Kendall will give us all his news.'

Beth's thoughts suddenly took a sharp turn. 'But where did the money come from? After what you said...'

'Beth...'

'Uncle James! The Duke of Belfont is rich enough to buy people.' She laughed harshly, a sound that made her mother wince. 'It was all so unnecessary. I did not need separating from Toby. There was nothing untoward going on, or likely to. I have known him since I was a tiny child and he is like a brother to me. Did you not understand that?'

Harriett sighed, knowing that she had been wrong to confide her unease to James. Her brother had done what he thought was best, but they had made a real mull of it between them. 'I'm sorry, Beth, truly sorry, but you must realise—'

'Oh, I realise, Mama. I realise I am to have no say in how I live my life at all.' And with that she fled to her own room, where she flung herself down on her bed and sobbed.

If she could not make her mother understand, who could she talk to? There was only one other person and that was Toby. But Toby had gone, left her without a word. Why had he been so easily persuaded? Oh, she knew that he had always wanted to go plant hunting and the temptation to accept whatever it was he had been offered must have been very great and she could hardly blame him for it. But why go without explaining himself to her or even saying goodbye? That was what hurt most, the abruptness of it. Uncle James must have been very persuasive. Had he given Toby to understand she knew about the offer beforehand? Did Toby think she did not care?

If it had been done openly, she could have been part of the planning, the deciding what luggage and equipment to take, the boxes and barrels for keeping plants in, the beeswax and special paper to preserve the seeds and prevent them going mouldy in the dampness of the ship's hold on the journey home. They would have talked about the ship he would sail on, the area he would explore, the kind of plants he hoped to find, the journal he would keep and the reports he would send regularly to her. And he would have told her exactly what to do to look after the plants he had left behind. She would have waved him goodbye with a cheerful heart if that had been the case.

How far had he got? He wouldn't have sailed yet because it would be necessary to stop off in London and equip himself and book a berth on a ship—no doubt an East Indiaman, which regularly made the journey back and forth between England and India. Could she catch him before he sailed, just to speak to him, to tell him that, if he had been banished, she had had no prior knowledge of it, to ask for instructions and say goodbye? She imagined his face lighting up at the sight of her. He would take her hand and lead her on board to show her his quarters and the equipment he had brought with him, and when the ship sailed she would return to the quay and watch until the vessel was out of sight.

The more she thought about it, the more possible it seemed. All she had to do was find out the name of the ship, take the stage to London and hire a cab to take her to the docks and there he would be! She knew she could not go with him, but it would be some compensation to be there when he set out and reassure him that she did not condone what her mother and uncle had done. Her tears dried on her cheeks. She scrambled to her feet and hurried down to the drawing room, where she found the newspaper she had seen her uncle reading after dinner two nights before.

She sat down and quickly scanned it for the shipping news. And there it was. The *Princess Charlotte* had arrived at the East India docks with a cargo of tea, spices and ornamental objects, and was due to depart again as soon as it had taken export goods, passengers and stores on board. The East India Company prided itself on its fast turnaround. But supposing, when she got there, Toby wasn't sailing on the *Princess Charlotte*? What then? It would be a wild goose chase and she would have to turn round and come home. But what an adventure!

She sat, staring at the newsprint until the words danced in front of her eyes. *Princess Charlotte* sailing on the afternoon of the following day—dare she go? What would her mother say? But it wasn't as if she was running away or anything like that, she was simply going to see a friend off on a journey, and then she would be back, almost before she was missed. Ought she to take a companion? But who? Miss Andover would treat her like a naughty child and report her to her mother, and none of the servants would agree to go with her for fear of losing their place. It was go alone or not at all.

She folded the paper and replaced it where she found it on the fender where it would undoubtedly be used for lighting the fire next morning, and hurried back to her room where she fetched out her purse and counted out the money she had. Her uncle had given each of the girls five guineas in order to buy fripperies before their trip to London and Beth had not spent hers. She also had the better part of a quarter's pin money, which her mother had put into her hand at the end of March. It ought to be enough for the coach fare and a little to eat. She would not need an overnight stay because she would be coming straight back; coaches to and from Bury St Edmunds and Norwich called at Sudbury all the time. She smiled suddenly, wondering what her uncle would say when he knew his generosity had inadvertently made her journey possible.

* * *

How she managed to behave normally at dinner—which was taken at five o'clock, that being a compromise between town and country hours—she did not know. Afterwards she sat in the drawing room with her mother and Livvy, who was full of what she intended to do and see in London, most of which involved riding in the park, visiting Tattersalls to see the horses and going to the races and what young men they might meet. If anything could make Beth decide to go ahead with her plan, that was it. Once they arrived at Belfont House, there would be no more adventures. As soon as she could, she excused herself, saying she was tired and went up to her room. An early night was called for if she was to be up betimes.

It was a long time before she fell asleep, her mind was whirring with what she meant to do. If it had not been for her uncle sending Toby away in that high-handed fashion and that dreaded Season in London, which she looked upon as the end to all her freedom, she would never have contemplated it. It made her feel a little better about what she was doing, but only a little.

It was the dawn chorus just outside her window that woke her and she silently thanked the birds or she might have overslept and missed the coach. She sat at her escritoire to write a note to her mother, which she left on her pillow, and then dressed quickly in her father's breeches and a clean shirt. There was also a full-skirted coat with huge flap pockets, years out of date, but she didn't care about that—it would be safer to travel as a young man. The ensemble was completed with riding boots and a tricorne hat. She fastened her long hair up with combs and pulled the hat down over it. She put her purse containing her money in her coat pocket and opened her bedroom door.

There was no one about. She crept downstairs, aware of every creak of the treads, and the rattling of utensils coming from the kitchen where the scullery maid was beginning her day's tasks. Carefully she withdrew the bolts on the front door, let herself out and sped down the drive.

It was only a short walk into Sudbury and Beth's only concern was that no one should see her and recognise her, but, as it was not yet fully light, she thought her disguise would pass muster. She had never been in an inn before, had never travelled on a public coach, not even with an escort, never mind alone, and she was nervous. Pulling herself together and pretending nonchalance, she approached the ticket office and asked for a seat on the next coach to London. It was hardly in her hand when the coach arrived in a flurry of tooting horns, sweating horses and scurrying ostlers. The horses were changed, those passengers who had left their seats for refreshment and those starting their journey in Sudbury were called to their places and they were on their way.

It was only as they left the town behind, that Beth, squashed between a fat lady with a live chicken in a basket on her lap and a countryman in a shovel hat who had not washed in a year, began to appreciate the enormity of what she had done. It had seemed easy enough when she had been in her room at home, nursing a grievance against her mother and uncle, not to mention Toby himself; all she had to do was get on a coach and she would be conveyed to London. But now she was on her way, she was beset by doubts mixed with a good helping of guilt. Had her mother missed her? Had she understood the letter she left behind? Would she be very angry? Would she send someone after her? There would be no reason for that, she decided, considering she had made it clear in her letter that she would be back the following morning.

The other passengers were giving her some strange looks and she shrank back in her seat, wishing she could stop the coach and get off. Would the coachman let her off or would he say that she must go on to the next scheduled stop? She pretended to look out of the window at the hedgerows flashing past and chided herself for her lack of spirit. What was so frightening about travelling by stage coach? People did it all the time.

They rattled on, stopping now and again to change the horses and to put down and pick up new passengers, and just under seven hours after they set out, she was climbing down in the yard of the Spread Eagle in Piccadilly. She was hungry and considered going into the inn and ordering food, but nervousness overcame her again and she decided she could wait until she saw Toby. They would eat together while they talked.

'Where do I go for a cab?' she asked an ostler, who was carrying tack across the cobbles.

'There's a row of them in the street. Take your pick,' he said, without stopping. She was inclined to be annoyed by his lack of courtesy, but then remembered she was supposed to be a boy and a young one too, considering her chin was as smooth as silk. She thanked him and went in search of a cab.

Half an hour later she was being deposited at the entrance to the East India docks. The smell of the river dominated everything and beyond the buildings that lined the dock, she could see the tall masts of ships lying at anchor. She walked forward slowly, unsure of herself. The quay was busy; dockers, sailors, passengers, luggage and mountains of stores vied for the available space. One ship was being unloaded, but another was almost ready for departure, judging by the seamen scurrying about on deck. The name on its side was *Princess Charlotte*. The gangplank had not yet been raised and she hurried to the foot of it, wondering if she dared climb aboard.

She became aware of a group of sailors watching her as she hesitated.

'Running away to sea?' one of them asked her suddenly.

'No. I'm meeting a friend—' She stopped suddenly because they were laughing.

'Meeting a friend, eh?' said the man, moving towards her, making her step back in alarm. 'Now would that friend be going or coming?'

'Going. On the *Princess Charlotte*.'

'Then watch out you don't get carried away alonga him. Pretty little boy like you would be welcome...'

She cringed away from him, frightened by their raucous laugh. If only Toby would come. She wondered whether to cut and run, but decided that would make matters worse and stood her ground.

Andrew Melhurst was directing the loading of his luggage from the customs shed on to a large flat wagon. It was extraordinary how much one accumulated in seven years of living abroad. He had pared it down to necessities before leaving, but there was still enough to fill the wagon. It had been dumped on the quay when the ship was unloaded, as if the shipping company, having conveyed it thus far, wanted nothing more to do with it. Too concerned about his grandfather's health to bother with it right away, he had paid to have it stored in the customs shed and gone home, intending to send others back to fetch it for him.

He had been relieved to discover that old Lord Melhurst had rallied while he had been on the high seas and so he had decided it was safe to return with a couple of estate workers and hire a wagon to oversee the moving of his possessions himself. Besides the usual things like clothes and personal possessions, there were antiquities and stuffed animals and carefully wrapped seeds he had collected in the mountains of the Himalayas, which he hoped to propagate. He had also brought one or two plants, carefully packed in special containers, which he had taken home with him. Leaving them on the docks to be handled by hired help who would not understand the need for care would not have been a good idea.

He noticed the young lad standing at the foot of the gangplank facing a group of seamen because he looked so nervous. A new cabin boy, he surmised, judging by his slight figure and smooth cheeks. Too smooth, he decided, for the rough and tumble of life at sea. Had he been forced into it by an impatient parent in order to make a man of him, or was he running away to sea and thinking better of it? His clothes were very loose fitting and years out of date, but they had once been of fine quality. He was from a good family then, fallen on hard times perhaps. The seamen were obviously intending to have some sport with him and he was looking decidedly nervous.

He strolled over to them. 'Let the young shaver be.' It was said quietly, but with such authority he was instantly obeyed. 'Go about your business.'

The men strolled away laughing, and the boy turned towards him. 'Thank you, sir.' The voice was high-pitched, not yet broken. 'Am I too late to go on board?'

'Not while the gangplank is still in place, though you need to be quick. You will probably get a roasting for being late.'

'Roasting?' she said, remembering to deepen her voice. 'You mistake me, sir. I wish to speak to someone on board before the ship sails.'

'Oh, I see.' He looked closely at the oval face, the troubled brown eyes fringed by long silky lashes, the slight heaving of the bosom as he looked upwards. By God! It was not a he but a she and a very beautiful one. How could he have ever imagined that figure belonged to a cabin boy? Running after a lover, was she? Was the lover intent on escaping?

'Is it permissible to go up there?' She nodded in the direction of the deck.

'I wouldn't risk it if I were you,' he said, thinking about the crew who, like the sailors she had already encountered, would undoubtedly have some fun with her, not to mention the humiliation of discovering her lover did not want her. 'Tell me the name of the party and I will go and bring him to you. There might yet be time.'

'Oh, would you?' The smile she gave him was all woman. 'His name is Toby Kendall. He is sailing as a passenger.'

He sprinted up the gangplank and had a word with the sailor who stood at the top, ready to give the signal for it to be hauled away. Beth watched him disappear. She kept her eyes glued to the rail, expecting to see Toby come running. Nothing happened. The activity on deck reached a crescendo as seamen swarmed up the rigging and spread themselves along the spars and someone ran to the last mooring rope, ready to cast off. Now she began to wonder if the man who had gone on her errand would be trapped on board and carried off to sea. Her heart was in her mouth.

She saw a movement, but it was not Toby running to greet her, but the man returning. Did that mean Toby was not on board? Had he boarded some other ship? Had he not gone at all? She was beginning to feel a thorough ninny.

'Was he not there?' she asked as the man rejoined her. Too late she forgot to lower the tone of her voice.

'Oh, he is on board, Miss Harley, but he declined to come out to you.'

'I don't believe you!' In her agitation she had not even noticed he had addressed her by name. 'He wouldn't refuse to see me.'

'I am not in the habit of lying, Miss Harley.'

The emphasis he put on her name made her realise Toby had given her away. 'You know who I am?'

'Indeed I do.' Behind him he heard the shouted commands, was aware that dockers were freeing the mooring rope and pulling the gangplank free. 'The question is, what am I to do with you?' The crack of sails being let down almost drowned his words.

'What do you mean, do with me?' The sails were filling and the ship was beginning to move. Sailors were scrambling down from aloft and, almost hidden behind a stanchion, she saw a familiar face. 'Toby!' she shouted, waving like mad.

He waved back. He was saying something, but she could not make out what it was. It was then she realised the predicament she was in. Toby had refused to see her, she was miles and miles from home, alone with a man who knew she was a girl. And he had said, 'What am I to do with you?' She had been nervous before, but now she was truly frightened. She looked about her. On one side was the river, murky and full of flotsam, on the other the warehouses, customs shed and chandlers that lined the docks. Dockers and seamen hurried back and forth, men driving lumbering carts, shabby women, ill-clothed barefoot children, a few better-dressed gentlemen, but not a single well-dressed lady. Certainly no cabs.

He must have realised she was considering flight, because he took her arm. 'You had better come with me.' And, though she resisted, he propelled her towards a carriage that stood a little way off, calling to the man by his wagon, 'Simmonds, I'll leave you to finish loading that and I'll see you at home in due course.'

'Let me go!' Beth shouted, struggling with him so that her hat fell off and her long dark hair cascaded around her shoulders, making those around grin with amusement. Still holding her, he picked the hat up and crammed it back on her head.

'Come on, I haven't got time to argue.' And with that he bundled her into the coach and climbed in behind her. 'Back to town, Jerry, as fast as you like,' he commanded his coachman.

Chapter Two

'What are you going to do with me?' she asked, trying to push her unruly hair under the hat again as the carriage moved off. It was a luxurious vehicle, its seats padded in red velvet. The man who occupied the opposite seat was fashionably dressed in a well-cut tail coat of green kerseymere and coffee-coloured pantaloons tucked into polished Hessians. His cravat was tied in a simple knot. He was handsome too, fair haired and bronzed from living in a climate warmer than that of England. It seemed to emphasise the blueness of his eyes, which were looking at her with something akin to amusement. She wondered how old he was; nothing like as old as her Uncle James, who must be forty, or as young as Toby, who was only a year older than she was. Twenty-seven or eight perhaps.

'Oh, do not fret, I have no designs on your person,' he said.

'Then let me go.'

'That, I think, would be considered unchivalrous.'

'No more unchivalrous than holding a lady against her wishes.'

'If the lady has no idea of the danger she is in, then a gentleman has no choice.' He laughed suddenly. 'Whatever made you think you could pass yourself off as a boy? A more feminine figure I have yet to meet.' His eyes roamed appreciatively over her coat and breeches as he spoke. The only slightly masculine thing about her was her cut-down fingernails and the brownish stain along the cuticles. He was intrigued by them. 'It is a good thing I intervened when I did.'

She remembered the sailors and shuddered. On the other hand, just because this man was well dressed, did it mean he was to be trusted? 'I have already thanked you for that. If you really are a gentleman, then you would convey me to the nearest coaching inn where I might take a stage back home.'

'Can't do that, I am afraid.' The last thing he wanted was to act the unwilling escort to a spoiled young miss not long out of the schoolroom. He liked his women mature and experienced, so that they both knew where they stood. They could enjoy each other without the complication of broken hearts and dreams of weddings. It was how he had survived since leaving England seven years before. Silently he cursed young Kendall for landing him with this one. He had been at the wrong place at the wrong time. Half an hour's difference and he would have come and gone, or she would have gone on board and spoken to Kendall herself. The young man would have had to leave the ship to look after her. Now here he was acting the knight errant and the young man she had pursued was sailing away.

'I beg you to look after her,' he had said. 'Take her to her uncle, the Duke of Belfont, and try to smooth her way, for I fear his Grace will be very angry.' An irresponsible stripling, a self-willed young madam and an angry Duke—what had he done to deserve being saddled with their problems?

He turned a little in his seat so that he could see her properly. She had taken off that monstrous hat and was trying unsuccessfully to put her hair up with combs. It was beautiful hair, thick and dark and gleaming with good health. Her eyes, beneath winged brows, were a deep amber and her mouth was full and generous with a chin that was jutting proudly. Considering her dishevelled state and the strange garb she wore, that was quite a feat.

'Shall we start again?' he queried. He had a lop-sided kind of smile, she noticed, which made her want to smile back, but she was determined not to do so. It would make him think she approved of his high-handed abduction of her. 'Let me introduce myself.

My name is Andrew Melhurst. I have lately returned to England after some years abroad.'

Oh, so he was a nabob, a nobody grown rich in the sub-continent and come home to flaunt his wealth. The chests and boxes she had seen being loaded on to the wagon, the sumptuous coach and the expensive diamond that glittered in his cravat, bore that out. 'Mr Kendall told you my name, but what else did he tell you?'

'Very little, Miss Harley, there was no time. But he did make it clear he had not asked you to come and he would deem it a favour if I would see you safely home.'

'You think I ran away to go with him, don't you?'

'It matters little what I think. Perhaps you should be more concerned by what the rest of the world thinks. If this little escapade becomes known, you would find your reputation in tatters. Mine too, I fear.'

'Oh.' She knew she had made a dreadful mess of everything. What had made her think her disguise was good enough to deceive? Oh, Toby was always laughing and saying she was more boy than girl and her mother had said how startled she had been when she first saw her in her father's breeches, but that was not enough to pass muster with the man who sat opposite her, regarding her with his bright intelligent eyes. And not only him, the passengers in the coach from Sudbury had looked at her strangely and she was sure those rough sailors had realised she was not a boy. She was lucky to have come this far without being molested and the prospect of returning home in the same way was more than a little frightening. The fact that this stranger had seen fit to point it out to her did not help. 'It is your own fault, you did not need to intervene at all.'

'You know, you are right, I wonder why I did.'

'Because Toby asked you to, I suppose.'

'There is that, but I am not accustomed to doing the bidding of strangers, so it must be that I am a gentleman and gentlemen do not leave ladies in dangerous predicaments when it is their power to help. Now, what about my suggestion that we start again in a more civilised fashion? I know your name, I know you are the niece of the Duke of Belfont, but nothing more.' He smiled suddenly and, in spite of herself, she found herself breathing a sigh of relief and smiling back. 'Suppose you tell me why you set out on this adventure. I cannot believe you meant to worry your family to death.'

'No, I did not. And I was not running away or trying to elope or anything foolish like that. I simply wanted to say goodbye to Toby, to find out—' She stopped suddenly, knowing her reasons would sound foolish.

'To find out what?'

'Oh, it is too complicated…'

'We have plenty of time. I am not letting you out of this coach until we reach Belfont House.'

'Oh, you are never taking me to Uncle James, he will be furious.'

'With good cause, I imagine. But where else should I take you? Is that not your home?'

'No. I live with my mother and sister just outside Sudbury.'

'Sudbury! How did you get from there to here?'

'By stagecoach and cab, how else?'

She was not lacking in courage, he decided. 'I think you had better tell me everything from the beginning.'

She sighed. 'I suppose I had or you will dump me on his Grace's doorstep and leave me to his wrath.'

He did not bother to tell her he would not 'dump' her anywhere, but as for taking her as far as Sudbury, he hadn't bargained on doing that, even though it was not far out of his way. 'Go on,' he said quietly.

So she told him everything: her love of botany, instilled in her by Joshua, and Toby who had been her friend and playmate since childhood, her longing to go plant hunting, to have adventures, though after today she was not so sure she was as intrepid as she had thought she was. And the unfeeling way that Toby had been sent away, simply because her uncle wanted to stop her dreaming and turn her into a conventional débutante.

He smiled. 'I do not think you will ever be that,' he

said, doing his best not to laugh. He looked at her, wondering if she was too proud to laugh at herself, and was relieved when her efforts to remain stern failed and a broad smile creased her face and showed him perfect white teeth. In a moment they were both laughing aloud.

'It is not funny,' she said, fishing for a handkerchief in her coat pocket to dab her streaming eyes.

'Then why are you laughing?'

'I do not know. To stop myself crying, perhaps.'

'Do you want to cry?'

'I think I was very near to it.'

'Oh, how thankful I am that you desisted. I cannot abide weeping women.'

Suddenly embarrassed, she turned from him and looked out of the window. It was beginning to grow dusk and she could not see more than dark buildings lining the road and the light shining from some of their windows. This part of the great metropolis had no street lighting. Once again she became aware of her predicament. She did not like being beholden to him, but there was no doubt that, if she had been left on the docks, she would have had to make her way back to town through these unlit streets. 'Much as I would like to deny it, I am in your hands, so what do you propose to do with me?'

'Take you to your uncle, the Duke.'

'Oh, no! He will give me a roasting.'

'And do you not think you deserve it?'

'Perhaps.'

'There is no perhaps about it. But I cannot take you all the way to Sudbury. That would mean being in each other's company throughout the night and even you must agree that would not be the thing. It would only need someone to see you, someone to ask questions about your absence from home, someone to recognise the Melhurst carriage, for the tattlers to start work on your reputation and my good name.'

'You could put me on a coach.'

'I have told you no.' His answer was almost snapped. He would be every sort of bounder if he did that. His conscience would not allow it.

'Supposing I insist?'

'Insist away. I shall not allow you to leave this vehicle until we are safely at Belfont House.'

She fell silent, thinking of her uncle. He had been cross enough when he had seen her in her male clothes in the garden at home—he would be furious knowing she had ventured abroad thus dressed. 'If it must be Belfont House,' she said, 'could you contrive to speak to my Aunt Sophie and not the Duke? She will help me, I know. I have heard she was once a little unconventional herself, before she married my uncle, that is.'

'Because I do not think I should like to see you

roasted, I will endeavour to do as you ask, but I make no promises and, if her Grace should deem it necessary to send for the Duke, I shall have nothing to say on the matter. After all, I do not know whether you make a habit of disappearing dressed as a male and if your family are out of patience with you.'

'I don't. I have never done it before.' She paused and added softly, 'Thank you, sir.'

They spent the remainder of the short journey talking about travel, about where he had been and the sights he had seen, the heat and smells of India. When she asked about plant hunting, he told her that it was far from a stroll in the garden; it needed meticulous planning and provisioning, with hired guides and porters and, if one was sensible, a medical man because bites, scratches, falls and bad food were commonplace. And that did not take into account the voyage, which might be beset by storms or being becalmed. If he thought that might put her off the idea, he was wrong, but she did admit that if she travelled it would have to be in a properly conducted party with a knowledgeable escort. 'Though how that can be arranged I do not know,' she said. 'Toby said I should marry a rich man—' She stopped suddenly, realising what she had said.

'That would indeed be the solution,' he said, noting

her discomfort, but pretending he did not. 'All the more reason to go ahead with your come-out, don't you think?'

She sighed, knowing he was right, but determined that her dreams of travel would not influence her choice of husband. If there was a choice, of course. She might be considered too much of a hoyden to attract the sort of man who inhabited the drawing rooms of the *ton*. That was why she was so fond of Toby; he took her as she was.

It was completely dark when the carriage drew to a halt outside a large mansion in South Audley Street, but here there were street lights and lanterns alight at each side of the imposing front door. 'Stay out of sight,' he commanded her. 'While I see how the land lies.'

He jumped down and strode to the door and knocked. The duty footman must have heard the carriage because the door was opened almost immediately. 'I wish to speak to the Duchess,' Andrew said. 'On a matter of some importance.'

The footman looked him up and down, as if wondering if he ought to admit a lone caller so late at night. 'Your name, sir?'

'Melhurst. Mr Andrew Melhurst.'

'I will see if her Grace is at home, Mr Melhurst, but

without an appointment…' He allowed his voice to fade to nothing.

'It is of the utmost importance.'

The man ushered him in, then turned and slowly and deliberately climbed the cantilevered staircase with its ornate cast-iron balustrade to the first floor, while Andrew stood and fumed. He hoped Miss Harley would not take it into her head to leave the carriage. The house was one of a row and she could be been seen by neighbours if they should happen to glance out of a window. And there were people in the street going about their business. He had no idea how well known she was in the neighbourhood.

A few minutes later, the servant returned. 'Please follow me, Mr Melhurst.'

The Duchess received him in a first-floor drawing room of elegant proportions. He bowed, surprised to see how young she was, twenty-seven or eight at the most, he decided. 'Mr Melhurst, has something happened to the Duke?' she asked, her voice betraying her anxiety. 'Do tell me quickly, for I cannot bear the suspense.'

'No, your Grace, I have never met the Duke. It is concerning your niece, Miss Harley.'

Her obvious relief was followed by concern. 'Beth? If you have come to make an offer for her, Mr Melhurst, then I suggest you apply to the Duke in the morning. It is late—'

'You mistake me, your Grace. I have not come to offer for her. I have her in my carriage outside this house. She has, I regret to say, fallen into a bumble-bath, from which I am endeavouring to rescue her. She needs a safe haven—'

'She has never run away from home. Oh, dear, the foolish girl…'

'She assures me that was not her intention.'

'Why did you leave her outside? Fetch her in at once.'

'She is anxious not to encounter the Duke, but I collect he is from home.'

'Yes, but that is not to say he will not be told.'

He bowed. 'That, your Grace, is for you to decide. I am merely bringing her home. Could I ask for a cloak? It would not be sensible for her to be seen entering the house as she is.'

'Mr Melhurst, you alarm me. What is the matter with her?'

'Nothing, but she is dressed as a young man.'

To his surprise she started to laugh. 'Oh, dear, I know she likes to do that at home in her garden and very fetching she looks too, but if you are bringing her home you must have found her somewhere else. Unless she inveigled you into her mischief?'

'I am relieved you do not think it was the other way about, your Grace. And she did not inveigle me. On the contrary, she fought to get away. I could not allow that. The docks are hardly the place for well brought-up young ladies, especially at night.'

'Did you say *docks*, Mr Melhurst?'

'Yes, the East India docks. That was where I found her, looking for a young man called Toby Kendall.'

'Oh, now I begin to see. The Duke financed Mr Kendall's ambition to become a plant hunter. Surely she did not think she could go too? Oh, the foolish, foolish girl. But we must not leave her sitting outside. Please wait here, while I fetch her.'

Before he could find a suitable reply to tell her he would leave as soon as Miss Harley was safely indoors, she had sailed from the room in a froth of silk and lace. He paced the room, looking at the ornaments and pictures. The pictures were mostly by modern artists like Turner, Girtin, Constable and Lawrence, though there was a Gainsborough, which he assumed was of an earlier Duke and his family. A couple of classical vases on a shelf he recognised as Wedgwood. Miss Harley definitely came from a well-breeched family. She was undoubtedly spoiled, though if he were honest he would have to admit that she had a lively mind and an articulate way of expressing herself. In the short ride from the docks he had been more entertained than he had been for some time.

He heard the front door shut and voices in the hall,

and then the Duchess, smiling broadly, put her head round the door. 'I am going to take Miss Harley upstairs and hand her over to my maid. Please don't go away. I haven't thanked you properly.' And, for a second time, she disappeared before he could politely take his leave.

Sophie conducted Beth up to the second floor and into her small private boudoir, where her maid appeared from an adjoining room. 'Rose, we must find my niece something to wear.' She pulled off the burnous in which Beth was shrouded, which evinced a gasp of shock from the servant and made Sophie smile, though Beth was far from smiling. Sitting alone in the coach, waiting for Mr Melhurst to come back, she had had time to think and thinking had not made her feel any easier about her little adventure. It was not so much an adventure as an escapade of the sort that schoolboys indulged in and if she got away with no more than a scolding she would count herself fortunate.

While the maid bustled about opening cupboard doors and searching for clothes, Sophie sat Beth down. 'Now, tell me what possessed you to run away from home like that? Did you not think of your poor Mama, and Livvy, worrying about you? And not only your safety, which would certainly worry them, but the scandal. What do you suppose it would do to James if the King ever heard of it?'

'I was not running away,' Beth said. 'I simply went to say goodbye to Toby; if Uncle James had not sent him away so suddenly that he could not tell me he was going, I never would have done it.' Her eyes filled with tears. 'I wish I had not. I did not see Toby. He told Mr Melhurst he did not want to see me, though I only have Mr Melhurst's word for that…'

'Surely you are not suggesting Mr Melhurst would tell you an untruth? Goodness, Beth, he did not have to take you up and bring you home, he was not obliged to do anything for you. But he did, no matter the inconvenience to himself.'

'I know and I am thankful. I told him so, but he did not have to be so insufferably top-lofty about it…' She paused as Rose came towards her bearing a green silk gown trimmed with pale green lace and cream-coloured ribbon.

'I think this will fit you, Miss Harley.'

'Very suitable,' Sophie said. 'Now, change quickly before anyone else sees you.'

'What are you going to tell Uncle James?'

Sophie looked at her with her head on one side, smiling a little. 'What should you like me to tell him?'

'I wish he need not know I am here. Then, perhaps tomorrow, you can arrange for someone to escort me home. I will keep out of sight, I promise. No one need know I have ever been here.' She was stripping off the sadly crumpled suit as she spoke.

'And your punishment?'

'Anything but a jobation from Uncle James. I will be the dutiful niece and daughter for the whole Season, I promise.'

Sophie laughed. 'I should not make promises you cannot keep, Beth.' She watched as Rose helped her into the dress. 'Goodness, I have left Mr Melhurst all alone. I must go down and thank him and offer him refreshment. Come down when you are ready and let him see you are really a lady, and thank him yourself for taking such good care of you.'

Beth did not want to face him again, she would die with mortification. Perhaps if she dawdled over her *toilette* he would tire of waiting and take his leave, no doubt glad to be rid of her.

Andrew was examining a portrait of the Duchess by Frances Corringham, an artist he did not know, which he found particularly pleasing for its delicate attention to detail, when he heard the door open behind him. Assuming it was the Duchess returning, he turned to find himself facing a small boy in a nightshirt. His feet were bare and his hair was tousled, as if he had just woken.

'Hello,' the young one said. 'Who are you?'

'My name is Andrew Melhurst. And whom do I have the honour of addressing?'

'I am Viscount James Dersingham. The Duke of Belfont is my father.' It was said proudly but not, Andrew noted, arrogantly. 'I am six.'

Andrew, to humour him, gave him an elaborate bow. 'At your service, my lord.'

Jamie giggled. 'You may call me Jamie, if you like.'

'Thank you. Does your mama know you are out of bed?'

'I could not sleep. I heard the door knocker and voices. I came to see who had called.'

'And now you have satisfied your curiosity, do you not think you should return to your bed?'

Jamie ignored that suggestion. 'Why are you here? It is the middle of the night.'

'Not quite,' Andrew said, glancing at the ornate clock on the mantelpiece which told him it was half past nine.

'Where is my mama?'

'Yes, where is she?' a masculine voice enquired.

Andrew turned to confront a gentleman in impeccable evening attire who could only be the Duke of Belfont. Before he could do more than bow, young Jamie had flung himself at his father, who picked him up. 'Jamie, why are you not in bed?'

'I heard the door knocker and cousin Beth's voice,

so I came to see her. Why is she dressed in those funny clothes, Papa?'

'I think you must be mistaken, son, she is not arriving until next week. I told you that, did I not?'

'Yes, but she must have come early.'

James strode to the door and called the footman who hovered in the hall. 'Take Master Jamie to his nurse, Foster. Tell her to put him back to bed.' As soon as the boy had been led away James turned to Andrew, who had been listening in acute discomfort. 'Now, sir, who are you and what are you doing here?'

'My name is Andrew Melhurst, my lord Duke, lately back from India. I arrived on the *Princess Charlotte*…' He paused, wondering how to go on.

'Melhurst,' the Duke put in. 'Relation to Baron Melhurst of Heathlands near Newmarket, are you?'

'Yes, his grandson.'

'I know him. He was a friend of my father's. How is he?'

'He has been ill, which was why I returned to England, but he is recovering.' He paused. 'I met a young man on board, a Mr Toby Kendall.'

'Ah, I begin to see. He was going as you were coming.'

'Exactly.'

'And you have a commission from him to me.'

'Yes, your Grace.'

'What did the young bounder want? I have dealt very generously with him and cannot think what else he may require…'

Andrew was nonplussed. 'Your Grace,' he began and then stopped, before taking a breath and continuing, 'He desired me to thank you.'

James laughed. 'Be blowed to that for a tale. Come on, man, the truth, if you please.' He stopped and then added, 'What was my son saying about his cousin Beth being here? Is Miss Harley here?'

'Oh, James, do not blame Mr Melhurst. He has been the epitome of good sense and discretion.'

James swung round at the sound of his wife's voice. 'My dear, I was not blaming him—how could I when I have no idea what I have to blame him for? But, now you are here, perhaps you will put the poor man out of his unease and explain what has happened.'

Sophie went to her husband and took his hand. 'Sit down, James, and you too, Mr Melhurst, we cannot converse properly if everyone is standing. I have ordered refreshments. Poor Mr Melhurst has been too busy on our behalf to eat.'

'Sophie, do not prevaricate,' he admonished, though he did as she suggested and sat down beside her, motioning to Andrew to take a chair opposite them. 'Tell me what has happened.'

'It's Beth…'

'So she is here?'

'Yes, but do not interrupt, or I shall lose the thread of what I am saying.'

'Go on.' It was said quietly, but Andrew could tell that the Duke was not used to being thwarted and would have the truth. He wished devoutly that he could excuse himself and half-rose, but her Grace, seeing this, waved him down again. Perhaps she needed moral support, though she seemed perfectly at ease with her husband.

'James, you sent that boy off on his travels without telling Beth and—'

'That was the whole point, to separate them, you know that. Their association was becoming unhealthy.'

'Fustian! They are friends, more like brother and sister, and she wanted to be part of his adventures—'

'Good God! She did not think she could go too, did she?'

'No, of course not. She wanted to be part of the planning, to say goodbye to him and see him off. She was afraid he might think she had connived at sending him away so abruptly and she wished to reassure him...'

'So, what did she do?'

She took a deep breath. 'She dressed as a boy and took the stage to London and a cab to the docks.'

'Harriet would never so far forget herself as to allow that—' He stopped speaking suddenly. 'Oh, I see, Harriet did not know. So, what was Miss Andover doing?'

'She didn't know of it either. Beth travelled alone.'

'Good God!' he said again. He turned to Andrew. 'And how came you to be involved, sir?'

'I saw her endeavouring to board the ship, your Grace, and undertook to acquaint Mr Kendall of her presence. He told me he thought she had followed him in order to share his adventure and of course he knew that was not to be thought of and asked me to bring her here.'

'You knew she was not a boy?'

'Almost immediately.' He smiled at the memory. 'She looked very fetching, but I do not think anyone could be deceived.'

At that point two servants arrived with trays, one bearing an urn and all the accoutrements for making tea and the other some plates laden with cakes and pastries, which were set down on a table beside the Duchess. The conversation was halted as she set about offering their guest food and drink. She took a cup of tea for herself, but the Duke declined.

James watched Andrew dealing politely with his wife and wished it could have been anyone but Andrew Melhurst who had found Beth. The man had left England after a scandal of some sort, though he could not remember the details, but if past follies were attached to this present situation, he feared for Beth's reputation.

'Were you seen?' he asked.

Andrew, in the middle of biting into a delicious honey-filled pastry, gave him a sharp look. The Duke was only echoing what he himself had said to Miss Harley, but it was one thing to acknowledge the problem to himself and mention it to her, quite another when someone else pointed it out to him as if it had all been his fault. 'The docks were very busy, your Grace, I have no idea who saw us. I hope no one of importance…'

'And when you arrived here?'

'Oh, James, do not quiz the poor man like that,' Sophie said. 'He has done his best to do the right thing and bring Beth to us. He left her in the carriage and I went out with a cloak to fetch her in. No one saw us.'

James, who had been prepared to dislike the man, found himself revising his earlier opinion. A less scrupulous man might have taken advantage of the situation. 'Then I must thank you, sir, for your discretion. If her reputation was to be sullied by this adventure, I fear she would find it difficult to take her place in society and make her curtsy. As for finding a husband…' He stopped, realising he had been thinking aloud and such problems were nothing to do with the man who faced him. 'I am sorry, it is not your fault you have been unwittingly caught up in our problems.'

'If Miss Harley's good name is brought into question, then I will do the honourable thing, your Grace.' Whatever made him say that? Andrew asked himself. The idea of marrying the lady had never crossed his mind until the words came out of his mouth.

James smiled. No doubt he would. The niece of one of England's foremost Dukes would be quite a catch for the grandson of a mere baron. 'I do not think that will be necessary,' he said quite sharply and then relented. 'I mean…you have managed to bring her here with the minimum of fuss and we can find a way of accounting for her arrival ahead of her mother and sister. All will be well, I am sure.'

'But we do, indeed, thank you,' the Duchess put in, smiling. 'I had expected Beth to come down and thank you herself…'

'She has thanked me already,' Andrew said. 'I would not wish to put her to the blush by having to repeat it. I did only what any gentleman worthy of the name would do.' He put his cup down and rose to bring the interview to an end. He felt uncomfortable, as if he were being quizzed as a potential suitor, when all he had wanted to do was hand over the hoyden and take his leave.

The Duchess rose too. 'Mr Melhurst, are you, by chance, on your way to your grandfather's house? I collect it is near Newmarket.'

'Yes, your Grace.'

She smiled. 'And no doubt hoped to be halfway there by now.'

Andrew bowed to acknowledge the truth of this. 'It is of no consequence,' he said politely.

'I hesitate to ask another favour of you,' she began, making her husband look sharply at her, eyebrows raised in enquiry. 'But I know my sister-in-law will be beside herself with worry. Would you, could you, call at Beechgrove on your way and set her mind at rest? I know it is an imposition—if it is inconvenient, please say so.'

'It will be my pleasure, your Grace.' He endeavoured to sound cheerful about it. It was not so much that it would mean taking a small detour, but that he would still be embroiled in the doings of Miss Elizabeth Harley and at the beck and call of the Duke and Duchess of Belfont. Were they so pessimistic about finding the chit a husband they had to drag one in off the street? He felt as though he were being used and he did not like the feeling at all.

'Please tell Lady Harley that we will keep Beth here with us,' the Duchess went on. 'But it would be advisable if she were to bring forward her own arrival in London so that it may look as though they all arrived together.'

'I will do that, your Grace,' he said and took his

leave before she could suggest any other errands for him to do.

He passed out of the room and on to the gallery. He paused outside the door, thankful to have escaped, and made for the top of the stairs to the ground floor. A movement, a sound—he was not afterwards sure which it was—made him look up. Above him, at the head of the stairs, stood a vision in green, one hand on the balustrade, one slippered foot poised above the top step, ready to descend. This was no hoyden dressed in male attire, no untidy miss with dark hair tumbling down beneath an over-large tricorne hat, this was a woman of poise and breathtaking loveliness. The gown swirled about her legs, its tightly fitted bodice revealing a figure no less than perfect. Her hair had been twisted up into coils that emphasised a pale and slender neck. She was staring down at him, as if uncertain whether to descend.

He smiled and bowed. 'Miss Harley, your obedient.'

'Mr Melhurst.' Her foot went back beside the other one. She did not want to go down to him, did not want the humiliation of having to express her gratitude all over again. It would not have been so bad if he had not been so insufferably arrogant. But she could not turn away. His eyes, appraising her, held her mesmerised.

A servant came along the corridor and disappeared into the room he had just left and in a flash she had fled and he was left staring at nothing. Smiling, he descended to the ground floor where the footman who had admitted him rose from his chair to open the front door for him.

He continued to smile as he was driven away. He had been wrong to think of Miss Harley as a chit, only lately out of the schoolroom; it was that strange garb which had made her seem so young. In that exquisite dress she looked poised and mature enough to be already out. There was no need for the Duke and Duchess to drag suitors in from the street, they must be flocking round her. His amused condescension had taken a strange and disturbing turn. He found himself wishing he was not heading for Newmarket.

'Sophie, whatever were you thinking of, asking Mr Melhurst to go to Beechgrove?' James asked. 'I could have sent a courier with a note. We are indebted to him enough as it is.'

'Oh, he did not mind.'

'Whether he minded or not, is not the point. Why did you do it?'

'He is a very fine gentleman, don't you think? And aware of the delicacy of the situation. And servants talk…'

'Not ours, or they would not be in my employ.'

She ignored that. 'And he did offer.'

'To go to Beechgrove? I did not hear him say so, until you asked him.'

'Not to go to Beechgrove, I did not mean that. I heard you talking to him before I came in. He said he would do the honourable thing.'

'You did not take that seriously, surely?'

'Why not? He is handsome and wealthy, judging by the equipage he arrived in, and your father knew his grandfather, so he must be of some consequence.'

'What is that to the point? We know nothing about him. I seem to remember some scandal which made it necessary for him to leave the country.'

'Pooh, to that. You forget my papa had to do the same thing and you did not hold that against me.'

He laughed. 'That was not your fault.'

'And whatever it is may not have been Mr Melhurst's fault. You should not judge him before you know the truth, James.'

He laughed suddenly. 'And supposing Beth is not compliant. She is a true Dersingham and a more stubborn one I have yet to meet. She will not be driven.'

'Oh, James, credit me with a little more sense than that. I am merely making it possible for the acquaintanceship to blossom. Harriet is bound to be grateful and will invite him to call again.'

'On the other hand, the gentleman might consider Beth too much of a hoyden for his taste and decline.'

'He has seen the worst of her and now we must show him the best. I do not consider Beth a hoyden, she is intelligent and spirited and very beautiful when she is properly dressed.'

'And is she properly dressed now?'

'I believe so. I left her with Rose who has found one of my gowns for her.'

'Then send for her.'

'You are not going to give her a jobation, are you, James? She knows how bad she has been and is full of remorse. Scolding her will not make her more compliant—it might even drive her to be more outrageous.'

'I cannot ignore what she has done.'

'No, but be gentle with her, James. If it had not been for you sending Toby away as if he had caused some dreadful scandal, she would not have felt misused.'

'I was endeavouring to prevent a scandal.'

'Beth is not in love with Mr Kendall, James, there was nothing improper in their relationship. She finds him interesting because of his love and knowledge of botany, a passion she shares. You should talk to her about it, you might be surprised at how much she knows on the subject.'

'You are telling me I have made a mull of it.'

She laughed lightly. 'I would not dare to criticise the great Duke of Belfont, known for his wisdom and good sense. Why, even the King listens to your advice.'

He smiled at her flummery and turned as the door opened and Beth made her way into the room and curtsied before him, bending her head very low so that he could only see the shining top of her coiffure.

'Sit down, Beth,' he commanded. 'I am glad to see you safely here.'

She sat and waited.

'You must be hungry,' Sophie said, ringing the hand bell at her side.

'A little.' She was more than a little hungry—she had not eaten since the evening before and she was ravenous. It was why she had taken her courage in her hands and come down. Even then she had paused outside the door before entering and it was how she came to hear all their conversation. She was disappointed in her aunt. Not only had she seen fit to tell the Duke everything, she seemed to be determined to marry her off to Mr Melhurst and that was something she would never consider, even though he appeared to have offered. Surely one short ride in an enclosed coach had not compromised her reputation to such an extent?

She did not even like him, he was pompous with her while he toadied to her uncle when he had promised to try and keep the Duke out of it. And what was that about a scandal and having to live abroad? Did that mean he had done something terrible? Had he wrecked some other lady's reputation? Had he cheated at cards? Had he killed someone in a duel? She would not put any of those past him. Did he suppose she had a vast dowry? If Mr Andrew Melhurst thought he would be marrying a wealthy heiress, he was very mistaken; her uncle was generous, but not so as to make her wealthy. Besides, even if Mr Melhurst was the soul of virtue, she would never agree; he was the symbol of her mortification. She refused to listen to the tiny voice of reason that was telling her she was being unjust.

A servant arrived in answer to the Duchess's summons. 'Tell Didoner we are ready for supper now,' she instructed him.

Beth would rather have had something in her room, and had opened her mouth to say so, but then she saw her aunt slowly shaking her head and realised she was going to have to endure a meal with the Duke, who would either ignore her as if she were not there or subject her to a roasting all the way through the meal. She was not sure which would be worse.

In the event, he did neither. Didoner, their French chef, was a perfectionist and the meals he produced were always first class, whether they were for the Duke and Duchess alone, or a vast company, and Beth did hers justice. There was turbot and shrimps, game and ham, not to mention dishes of vegetables, each cooked in a different way. There was fruit and puddings and tartlets and a light bubbly wine.

'Now,' said the Duke when they had all be served and the servants had withdrawn to wait outside the door until summoned. 'I am led to believe that it is your love of growing things that has led to this contretemps.'

'No, my lord, the contretemps was caused by Mr Kendall being summarily sent away.'

'Beth!' Sophie exclaimed, anxious that her niece's forthright tongue would not shatter her husband's good mood. No one, except perhaps the King, spoke to James in that fashion.

'I am sorry,' she said. 'But if only you had told me…'

'I am not in the habit of consulting those over whom I hold sway when I have a decision to make. Your mama was concerned about your continuing friendship with Mr Kendall and asked my advice.'

'Surely Toby told you there was nothing to be concerned about. We both knew he would leave one day, but not until he was ready. He had plants in the glass house he was tending, and others he was experimenting with out of doors to see if they would survive in our climate. And there were plans to make, proper plans with equipment to buy, an itinerary and goals to decide. I was going to be part of that.'

'Not go with him?'

She smiled suddenly. 'I knew that would never be

allowed, but if the time ever comes when I am independent I should like to go on an expedition, properly
escorted, of course. I should like to study exotic plants
in their own habitat, collect specimens and seeds to
bring back. That is how you obtained those wonderful
shrubs you have in your own garden and conservatory,
is it not? Someone had to bring them to this country.'

'Yes, but not a woman.' His severe look softened.
'It appears that I have misjudged you, my dear, but
are plants all you think of? Surely you sometimes
dream of a husband and children? You are very good
with Jamie and he adores you.' He laughed suddenly.
'Though he is to blame for telling me you had arrived.
He heard your voice and left his bed to greet you.'

'It was Jamie?'

'Yes. Did you hope I would not discover your
presence in my house?'

'No,' Sophie put in quickly, before Beth could
confirm that. 'But we hoped to defer it until the
morning. I was not expecting you back until late.'

'The King decided he would visit Lady Conyngham
and no longer needed me. I think he realises I disap-
prove of his affairs especially since he came to the
throne. In any event, it enabled me to look forward to
an evening at home with you, my dear. I was never
so put out as when I saw a strange man in my drawing
room, chatting gaily to my son as if he belonged here.'

'He is the sort to make himself at home any-where,' Beth put in. 'A more self-opinionated man, I have yet to meet.'

'Not self-opinionated,' her aunt said. 'Self-assured would be more accurate and perhaps he has had to be, travelling the world as he has.'

'You travelled all over the place and it did not make you arrogant,' Beth said, referring to the fact that Sophie had been dragged all over the continent with her parents before they both died in exile and she came back to England to throw herself on the mercy of her mother's cousin, who just happened to fall in love with her and marry her.

'Let us leave the subject of Mr Melhurst's charac-ter,' James said, spearing a piece of succulent ham on his fork. 'It is getting us nowhere. The important thing is what is to be done.'

Beth was about to tell him that if he thought he could marry her off willy-nilly, he was way off the mark, but thought better of it and remained silent.

'We have sent for your mama,' the Duchess told her. 'If she is able to come at once, she should be here the day after tomorrow, or perhaps Friday. Until she arrives, you must stay indoors. It must look as though you all arrived together.'

'Very well,' Beth agreed, though the prospect of spending three days confined to the house was not one she relished. She had always been one for the outdoors, walking, riding and gardening, none of which would be easy in South Audley Street. 'But the servants know I am here…'

'They know better than to gossip, certainly not outside these four walls,' her uncle told her.

But they bargained without the strange way the *ton* had of finding things out and passing them on, adding their own embellishments for good measure.

Chapter Three

As Andrew's carriage turned into the driveway of Beechgrove, he leaned forward for a view of the house. It was a solid mansion, square in shape, made of warm red brick. Its gleaming windows reflected the morning sun, which slanted across pristine gardens. The lawns were well manicured, the flower beds without a weed and the shrubs and trees were tastefully arranged to show off their shape and colours. Some, he noted, came from lands across the sea, but seemed to be thriving. He supposed it was Miss Harley's influence and then, remembering her soiled fingernails, smiled to himself and decided she was not above doing some of the work herself.

He had found himself thinking of her throughout the long night, wondering what her uncle had said to her and what punishment he had inflicted. He supposed she deserved some punishment for putting herself in jeopardy and worrying her family, but she had been impetuous rather than wicked. Her uncle, in his opinion, had not handled the situation well. He wondered what her mother was like and how he would be received. If the Duke was anything to go by, she would be proud. Her daughter wasn't proud though. Miss Harley was a scapegrace, self-willed, oblivious to the niceties of convention, but not top lofty. And that extraordinary disguise! He almost laughed aloud. Had she really imagined she looked like a boy?

And what had possessed him to offer for her? He had been in her company less than an hour and in that time they had fought and argued and finally conversed, but only about botany and travel, which was hardly enough of an acquaintanceship on which to base an offer of marriage. He must have been mad. Thank goodness the Duke had not taken him seriously. Or perhaps he had, but had decided he did not meet his exacting standards as a husband for his niece.

But that vision at the top of the stairs had unsettled him. She had looked so feminine, so lovely, she had taken his breath away. He could not get her out of his head. Whenever he tried to turn his mind to other subjects, she was there, plaguing him for the most part, giving him her opinion of whatever it was he contemplated doing, whether it was deciding to change horses at a particular inn or what to order to eat, or whether he should transplant his botanical specimens in good garden loam or mix it with clay and manure. How did he know what her opinion would be? he asked himself and the only answer he could find was that he just knew. It was uncanny.

He heard galloping hooves and, glancing across the park, he saw a young lady riding hell for leather for the six-barred gate that divided the park from the drive. She cleared it magnificently, but it was not her fearless riding that made him gasp in shock but the girl herself. In the moment when she had launched herself and her mount at the gate, he thought it was Beth who had somehow transported herself from London to Sudbury ahead of him. Reason told him it was not possible and when the young lady reined in to turn towards him he realised it was not Beth, but someone extraordinarily like her. Her sister, he decided, as she trotted towards the carriage, which his driver had sensibly brought to a halt.

'Good morning,' she called to him. 'You are an early caller, I am not sure Mama will be ready to receive you.'

He put his head out of the door and smiled. Although very like her sister, she was younger by a couple of years, her hair was lighter, her eyes grey, and she still had the adolescent bloom of the schoolgirl about her, but she was confident and not at all shy. Now, why did that not surprise him? 'Miss Olivia Harley, I presume?'

'Yes, how did you know?'

'You are very like your sister.'

'You have seen her?' she asked eagerly. 'You know where she is?'

'Yes, she is safe with your uncle at Belfont House.'

'Oh, thank the good Lord. Our mother was sure she would come back yesterday because she left a note to say she would be and she sent Mr Kendall, our steward, to Sudbury to meet all the coaches, but when Beth did not come, she was almost out of her mind. She will be greatly relieved by your news.' She did not wait for a reply, but added. 'Follow me to the house, if you please, and you may tell Mama yourself.'

She set off up the drive at a decorous trot and dismounted at the side of the house, handing her horse over to a groom. Andrew's carriage pulled up at the front door where he alighted and she conducted him into a wide hall that smelled pleasantly of spring flowers and beeswax.

'Mama! Mama!' she shouted, mounting the stairs two at a time, grabbing the skirt of her habit in both hands and revealing trim breeches tucked into riding boots. 'Beth is safe!'

Andrew smiled. She and her sister made a pair when it came to hoydenish behaviour. Was that how they had been brought up? Was their mother the same?

He was disabused of that idea when Lady Harley appeared at the top of the stairs. She was in an undress robe of blue silk, her hair loosely tied by a ribbon, but there was no mistaking the aristocrat, even though she was anxious about her daughter.

'Livvy, do you have to shout?' she queried. 'And if Beth is home, where is she? Hiding from me, I shouldn't wonder, considering the torment she has put me through.' She stopped suddenly when she saw Andrew looking up at her from the hall. 'Oh. Who are you?'

She started to descend as he made his bow. 'Andrew Melhurst, my lady. I have come from Belfont House. You daughter is safe with her uncle, the Duke.'

She had reached ground level and came towards him, smiling. 'Thank goodness for that, though he is the last person I would expect her to apply to.'

He smiled. 'She did not exactly apply to him, my lady. I am afraid I gave her no choice.'

'Oh, dear, you are confusing me. I did not sleep last night and my brain must be a little fuddled. Do come into the drawing room and I will order refreshment and then you may tell me the whole. And do not keep anything back.' She was leading the way into a large airy room that looked out on to the garden at the back, which was a riot of spring flowers. Livvy, so consumed by curiosity she ignored the fact that she was wearing riding boots and her habit was dragging on the carpet, followed them. 'You see, I know my daughter very well and I know how headstrong she can be. Do sit down.' She waved him to a sofa and he folded his long frame into it. 'Livvy, don't stand there gaping like a fish out of water, go and change. And before you do, please tell Mrs Jobson to bring coffee and cakes. Or would you rather have breakfast, Mr Melhurst? I can easily arrange it.'

'Thank you, but I had breakfast at an inn in Sudbury before I came.'

'Have you come straight from Belfont House?'

'Yes, my lady. The Duke was most anxious you should be relieved of your anxiety, as was Miss Harley,' he added, though why he should try to mitigate what she had done, he did not know.

'And no doubt you have driven through the night. Oh, how grateful I am, but you must be fatigued—'

'Not at all my lady. I was able to doze in my coach and I am accustomed to going without sleep. Think no more of it.'

A servant arrived with refreshments; though it was evident Lady Harley was anxious to have news of her daughter, politeness dictated that she must wait until he had been given refreshment. They were shortly joined by Livvy, now in a light silk dress the colour of the daffodils that bloomed so freely in the garden. She sat down next to her mother and leaned forward, agog to hear all about Beth's adventures.

'Mr Melhurst, please tell us everything,' Harriet

began. 'I was about to send Mr Kendall to London to tell my brother what had happened and enlist his help in tracking her down. But it seems he knows already.' She paused. 'But you said you gave her no choice…'

'No, my lady. I returned from India three—' he stopped to correct himself '—no, four days ago now and met your daughter on the quayside. She was dressed somewhat…' he paused '…unusually.'

'I discovered that when I searched her room to find out what she was wearing.'

'No doubt she thought it would give her a certain protection if people thought she was a young lad, but as a disguise it was lamentable.'

She managed a chuckle. 'I realise that. But she was not entirely unfeeling. She left me a letter telling me what she meant to do, and, though I know she is confident and self-possessed, she has naturally never travelled alone and I feared for her.'

'She has plenty of spirit, my lady, but when I spoke to Mr Kendall, he asked me to take her to her uncle.'

'Mr Toby Kendall, I collect you mean. He is the son of my steward.'

'Yes. He was most anxious about her, but the ship was about to sail and he was worried that if he left it to take her home, the Duke would be angry that he had not fulfilled his part of their bargain. And it would also compromise her reputation…'

'He did not think it would be compromised by handing her over to you?' she asked with a gentle smile.

'I had a closed coach nearby, my lady, and could convey her without her being seen.'

'Then I thank you.'

'What did Uncle James say?' Livvy asked. 'I bet he was furious with Beth.'

'Concerned, I should say,' he said wryly. He turned back to Lady Harley. 'He suggested that as your daughter was already in London, you should bring forward your visit and arrange to go to Belfont House as soon as possible. I believe he intends to keep Miss Harley indoors until you arrive.'

Livvy giggled. 'He would have to, considering she has no luggage with her. He could hardly let her out dressed in Papa's old clothes.'

'Do not be foolish, Livvy,' her mother chided her. 'Your Aunt Sophie will have found something for her to wear. But I can see it would be easier if everyone thought we had arrived in London together. I think I can be ready by the day after tomorrow…' She paused. 'Mr Melhurst, you are welcome to stay and rest before returning.'

'Oh, I am not returning, my lady, I am on my way home to Newmarket.'

'Newmarket!' Livvy exclaimed. 'Do you, by chance, have any connection with horse racing?'

He smiled at the way her eyes lit up in much the same way as her sister's had when talking about botany. 'My grandfather, Lord Melhurst, has extensive stables and is well known in racing circles.'

'Oh, I have heard of the Melhurst stud,' she said. 'There is Melhurst Sunburst and Melhurst Moonshine, both prime goers, and Pegasus, who is top of the trees over the jumps. Do you ride in the races, Mr Melhurst?'

'I have been out of the country, Miss Olivia, but I sometimes did before I left seven years ago.'

'Oh, how I should like to do that.'

He laughed. 'Ride in a horse race, Miss Olivia?'

'Yes, why not? I am a first-class rider…'

'I do not doubt it, but there is more to it than being able to ride well and it would never be allowed.'

'Of course not, Livvy,' her mother put in. 'What nonsense you talk sometimes.'

'I do not see why a woman could not be as good as a man. She would be lighter, for a start.'

'But would she be able to keep her seat if she was barged?' Andrew put in. 'It does go on, you know, and ladies' saddles were never designed—'

'Not side saddle, Mr Melhurst, that would put her at a disadvantage from the start. No, it would have to be astride—'

'I think you have said enough on the subject,

Livvy,' her mother said. 'Mr Melhurst will think the whole Harley family is eccentric.'

'Not at all.' He smiled. 'But if you and your daughters were to find yourselves in the Newmarket area, I would be very pleased to show you round the stables at Heathlands.'

'Oh, would you?' Livvy enthused. 'Then we must contrive to find ourselves in the area very soon.'

He was only being polite, he told himself, he did not, for a moment, think they would take him up on his offer, but then he realised that he was hoping they would, especially if Miss Harley was also of the party. He could see her in his mind's eye, dressed conventionally, strolling with him along the gravel paths, admiring, not the horses, but the gardens. He had sent many unusual plants back to England from his travels in the Himalayas and the Far East, and, though a good many had died in transit or could not survive in the English climate, some had thrived. He would enjoy talking to her about them and finding out just how knowledgeable she was, exchanging plants perhaps.

'I collect you are going to London for the Season, Miss Harley.'

'So we are. But the Season ends in July…'

'And by then you may have found other interests.'

She laughed. It was a light musical sound, lighter

than her sister's deep chuckle. 'You mean I might have found a husband?'

He bowed to confirm this.

'I am more likely to find one to suit me at Newmarket than in London, Mr Melhurst. Horses are my passion and my husband must share it.'

'Poor man,' Lady Harley said. 'To have to compete with a horse must be the ultimate humiliation. Now I think we have detained Mr Melhurst long enough.' She rose to her feet and Andrew quickly stood up and bowed over the hand she offered. 'I cannot tell you how grateful I am that you brought us good news,' she said. 'Please visit us again.' She smiled. 'We shall be in London for the Season, but you will be welcome after that. Or are you, perhaps, going up to town yourself? You could call on us at Belfont House.'

'I had no plans to return, my lady, but I thank you.'

He took his leave and was conducted to the door by a footman. He could hear the young lady's voice as he went. 'Mama, I would much rather go to Newmarket than London…'

He climbed back into his coach and settled himself in the corner to sleep the three hours it would take to convey him home to Heathlands. Tomorrow he would send his groom to take the hired horses back to Sudbury where he had last changed them and then go on and fetch his own horses from his first stop. It was not what he had planned. Before he met Miss Harley he had intended to drive leisurely behind the wagon with frequent stops and would not have needed to change horses. The extra expense of post chaise did not trouble him, but he was surprised that the Duke had not suggested compensating him. On the other hand, it had been the Duchess who had asked him to come to Sudbury and she would not have given it a thought. Money was of no consequence to her.

He wondered how well off Lady Harley was. What he had seen of the house and particularly the garden had been delightful, but he could not help noticing the frayed carpets, faded curtains and scuffed paintwork, things that would undoubtedly have been remedied if she had had the blunt to do it. He guessed they were reliant on the Duke to help support them. In that case his Grace would have the last word when it came to approving husbands for his nieces. He smiled to himself; he doubted if he would fit the bill. He was the heir to a baronetcy, but even if a baron was considered elevated enough, his past would catch up with him. There was bound to be someone on the London scene who remembered Lady Katherine Haysborough, as she was then, and would not be averse to reminding everyone.

He had made himself look no end of a fool over her. She had been married at the time and spoiling for an affair and he, enjoying his first Season in London after finishing at university, had been flattered and blind to the fact that she was using him. She professed to love him, had appeared at the same functions he did and, though he made every effort to be discreet, she had made no secret of her interest, until it had come to the ears of her husband who threatened publicly to call him out. The whole thing looked set to blow up into a scandal of monumental proportions and his grandfather had called him over the coals for it.

'You silly young fool,' he had said, his normally placid countenance red with anger. 'She's years older than you are and has had so many lovers you need more than your ten fingers to count them. Do you want to be one in a long line, all discarded when her husband threatens to divorce her? She doesn't want a divorce; she simply wants the expensive presents her lovers give her to add to those her husband gives her when they are reconciled...'

'I do not believe that. She has been ill used and—'

'It is you who are ill used, my boy, believe me. And not only you, but me too. My success as a breeder of racehorses depends on the good will I have built up over the years. I am respected and trusted by those who have dealings with me and I will not have you undermining that with unsavoury scandal. If you must take a mistress, for goodness' sake take one of your own age and be more discreet.'

The next time he had seen Kitty was at a ball and he had watched as she flirted outrageously with every man present, laughing at his discomfort. He had decided his grandfather was right; she was certainly not worth fighting a duel over and he had taken himself off to India, not so much for his own sake but his grandfather's. He had become very wealthy in the process, besides older and wiser. Lord Haysborough had subsequently died and the not-so-grieving widow had married his cousin, Edward Melhurst, son of his father's younger brother. He had been about to return home at the time, but decided to stay away because his arrival so soon after the new marriage might have revived the scandal and he did not want the family name sullied. It was only his grandfather's failing health that had brought him home in the end.

And what a strange arrival: Grandfather better, though not back to his previous robust health, Teddy and Kitty living close by and toadying to the old man, and meeting the extraordinary Miss Elizabeth Harley. He began comparing her with Kitty and then stopped when he realised the absurdity of doing that. There was no point at which they were comparable. 'Chalk and cheese,' he murmured, drifting into sleep.

As he dozed he dreamed he was hacking his way through a tropical jungle surrounded by exotic plants with colourful flowers the size of saucers, but instead of stopping to admire and classify them, he was pressing on, trying to find a way through dense undergrowth towards the woman's voice that called to him with more and more urgency. He knew she was near at hand, knew she needed him, but he could not quite reach her. He glimpsed a flash of green silk and a huge black hat, but the more he hacked away at the undergrowth the more out of reach she seemed. And, behind him, he could hear the thundering of hooves, which was impossible given the nature of the terrain.

He woke up with a start as the carriage turned into the gates of Heathlands and realised that it had been the change in pace of his own horses which had roused him from his dream. He shook the sleep from him as the coach made its way towards the house. It was a large ivy-covered mansion, set in extensive grounds where thoroughbreds grazed. The stables stretched for a hundred yards on one side of the house and here there were men at work, feeding, grooming, cleaning out the magnificent animals, under the watchful eye of John Tann, his grandfather's master of horse. Until he was out in the heat of the subcontinent, he had not realised how much he loved the place, loved the air of quiet efficiency, the tranquillity, even the pungent stable smell that pervaded almost everything.

Leaving the coach, he bounded up the steps to the front door, which was opened as he reached it. 'How is my grandfather, Littlejohn?' he asked the footman, as he handed over his hat and gloves.

'Better, sir. He is up and dressed. No doubt he will be pleased to see you back again. You will find him in the conservatory.'

Andrew hurried across the spacious hall where, on cold days in winter, a huge log fire burned. Today it was unlit, but the area was warmed by the sun that poured through the long stained-glass window on the half-landing. He went through to a back room that was library, study and office all in one and was cluttered with books, papers, ledgers, trophies, statuettes of horses, a couple of riding whips propped in a corner and bits of coloured silk and brass objects which had been there so long everyone had forgotten their original purpose. Andrew smiled at what appeared to be untidy clutter, knowing that his grandfather knew exactly where everything was and became very irate if anything was moved.

'Who is that?' a voice demanded from the other side of an open door.

'Drew, Grandfather.' He crossed the room in three or four longs strides and entered the conservatory. It was almost a jungle itself, being full of plants that needed the heat and humidity of the glass room, where they grew to gigantic proportions. It was his grandfather's favourite place to sit because, like the plants, he enjoyed the warmth. One side gave a view over rolling meadows, the other faced the stable yard and he could see the men and the horses coming and going.

'You are back, then?' he said from the depths of an armchair. Clad in a burgundy dressing gown, he was thin and frail, only a shadow of the big muscular man he had once been, but his mind was still sharp and very little escaped him. 'Did you get your business done?'

'Yes.' He pulled up a chair to sit close to the old man, so that he could be heard and seen. 'How are you?'

His lordship ignored the question. 'Don't know why you couldn't have left it to Simmonds and Carter. Home half a day and gone again.'

'But I'm back now.'

'For good, I hope.'

'If that is your wish.'

'Of course it is my wish. It is where you belong. You are my heir…'

'It is not something I want to think about for a long time.'

'Gammon! I am old and you will have to take over the reins sooner or later, might as well settle down to it.' He paused. 'But who will take over the reins from you? That it what I keep asking myself. It is time you made a push to find yourself a wife and start a family of your own.'

'There is plenty of time.'

'Not for me, there isn't. Put the past behind you, Drew, and look to the future. The last thing I want is for the offspring of *that* woman to inherit and it will happen if you do not make a move to prevent it.'

'They have children?'

'A son, though I ain't at all sure he's a Melhurst. Seven-month baby, they said, but he was a big 'un if he was. The woman is too old to conceive again. Get married, Drew, do it before I stick my spoon in the wall, then I will die happy.'

'I will do my best, sir.'

'Good. Tonight I think I shall dress for dinner.' He rose stiffly and Andrew hurried to help him. 'Teddy's coming. Can't keep the fellow away. He is probably hoping I will change my mind and name him my heir.'

'Can you?'

'I can. Nothing is entailed.' He accepted his ebony stick from Andrew and made his way slowly through the office to the front of the house. 'But do not worry, my boy, it will not happen. Not if you marry, that is.'

It sounded like an ultimatum to Andrew, which annoyed him. 'And is Kitty coming too?'

'Yes, you do not mind, do you? You are not still mooning over her, are you?'

'I never was.'

The old man chuckled. 'It looked like mooning to

mè. But if you have got over it, I am glad. She was not the one for you.'

'I know,' he said fervently. 'I will marry when I find someone for whom I can have a real affection and who will feel the same towards me.'

Andrew was suddenly confronted with an image of Beth Harley, in a man's breeches and an ancient coat, struggling to get away from him, her face pink with anger. He had offered to marry her out of politeness and because he thought it was expected of him to save a lady's reputation, but the more he thought about it, the more attractive the idea became. Would she have him? The answer to that was almost certainly no. Would the Duke agree? Again he told himself no. His Grace had already told him his chivalrous offer was unnecessary. Being a man about town, his Grace had probably heard of the previous scandal. Not that he thought Beth Harley herself would care about that, being quite prepared to invite gossip herself.

Would his grandfather approve of her? He smiled. Not in that rig, he would not. In the green dress, feet in dainty slippers, hair elegantly coiffured, the niece of a Duke? Yes. But then the breeches were so much a part of her, it was suddenly important that she should be accepted for what she was, not for her antecedents. He stopped his errant thoughts; the whole idea was nothing but a pipe dream. He went upstairs to wash away the dust of travel and change into country clothes. For the moment he would concentrate on transplanting his tiny plantlets into their new surroundings and sow the seeds he had brought home with him. It would soothe him and put him into a calm frame of mind to meet his cousin Edward and Kitty later in the day.

Beth was almost mad with boredom. Being indoors and trying to avoid the servants except Rose and the chambermaid who looked after her room and brought her meals, and, more importantly, not to be seen by her aunt's callers was having a bad effect on her temper but, realising the confinement was justified, she manfully kept it in check.

Only since she had been at Belfont House had she realised how foolish she had been. At Beechgrove, where life was free and easy and she was subjected to the minimum of restriction, it had been easy to imagine the adventure would work and no harm would be done, but the reality had been very different. It could so easily have ended in disaster. If Mr Melhurst had been other than a gentleman of honour; if those sailors had decided to do more than mock her; if there had been an accident on the road and no one knowing who she was or where she belonged… The list was endless and being confined for a couple of days was no more than she deserved.

She waited in her room for the arrival of her mother and sister, drawing pictures of flowers to wile away the time, reading and pacing back and forth from the door to the window, wishing she could be out in the garden. 'No, I am afraid not,' Sophie told her when she asked. 'The garden is overlooked and Mrs Anstruther is the greatest tattler imaginable; if she were to see you from her window, she might ask why you had come ahead of your mama and I do not want to have to lie to her.'

'No, of course you must not lie, I would not ask it of you. How long do you think Mama will be?'

'I cannot say, Beth. Even supposing Mr Melhurst made good time and delivered the message for her to come, I imagine your mama would have arrangements to make, appointments to cancel, packing to do. It might be a few days…'

'A few days! Oh, Aunt Sophie, what a mess I have made of everything, and now I am being punished for it.'

'I am sure they will be here as soon as they can. Harriet will want to assure herself you have come to no harm…'

Beth gave a little chuckle. 'And deliver a roasting, I shouldn't wonder.' She sighed. 'Truly, I did not mean to put everyone to such inconvenience, Aunt.'

'I know.'

The door of the room burst open and Jamie, dressed

in neat breeches and a white frilled shirt, tumbled into the room. 'I knew Cousin Beth was here. Why have you not been to see me, Beth?'

'Jamie, you should not burst into a lady's room like that,' Sophie said. 'It is very impolite. Now, make your bow and go back to Miss Gordon.'

'Oh, Mama, I want to talk to Beth.' He climbed on to her lap. He was too big to nurse, but she loved the weight of him on her knees, the soft hair tickling her chin, the warmth and sweet smell of him. One day, God willing, she would marry and she might have a child like Jamie. A son to love would perhaps be enough to smother her unladylike ambitions.

He noticed the book on the table at her side, discarded in her restlessness. 'What are you reading?'

'It is Mr Sydney Parkinson's account of Sir Joseph Banks's journey with Captain Cook in the *Endeavour*.' Sir Joseph had gone to discover new plants and bring back what he could, and Parkinson was an artist who had travelled with him to record every find. The book was lavishly illustrated with his drawings.

'Is it an adventure?'

'Oh, yes, a very great adventure.'

'Will you read it to me?'

'You must ask your mama if I may.'

'Mama?'

Sophie smiled. 'He knows you are here now, so

you might as well, but do remember, Beth, that he is a small boy and do not fill his head with things only an adult should know.'

Sophie, who was an accomplished author herself, knew as well as Beth did that the account of the great naturalist's expedition included tales of terrifying ordeals of storm and near-shipwreck and of the native women they had encountered and whose company they had enjoyed. On another voyage, so it was said, though it had never been publicly admitted, Sir Joseph had attempted to take a woman on board disguised as a man. Beth wondered if it was that story which had given her the idea to go plant hunting herself. It was an impossible dream, of course, and one she would have to awake from because, from now on, she must behave with the decorum of a débutante having a first Season and do nothing to cause the tiniest whiff of scandal.

'Of course I won't.'

'Then I will leave you together.'

Beth set him on his feet. 'Now, sit down on the little stool by me and we will begin.'

'Cousin Beth,' he said, as she picked up the book and opened it, 'why did Papa say you were not going to come until next week?'

'That was the plan, sweetheart, but I found I needed to come to London ahead of Aunt Harriet and Livvy, so here I am. Your papa was not expecting me.'

'Why?'

'Why what?'

'Why did you need to come to London before the others?'

'I wanted to see someone, someone who was going on a long voyage...'

'Like the man in the story?'

'Sir Joseph Banks. Yes, just like him.'

Reading the account of Sir Joseph's adventures, especially the storms at sea, made Beth wonder how Toby was settling down to his voyage. He would be looking forward to reaching his destination to begin his exploration. Had he given her another thought after handing the responsibility for her safety over to Mr Melhurst? She was reading with only half her attention because thinking of Toby inevitably led to thoughts of Mr Melhurst and the humiliation she had endured at his hands. She could feel her face growing hot even now. What imp of mischief had led her to believe she could sustain the character of a boy? He had seen through her disguise in seconds and found the whole situation highly amusing. Oh, how she disliked him for that!

Determined to put him from her mind, she returned her attention to what she was doing and soon became absorbed in re-reading the book for the benefit of her small cousin. It helped to pass the time until he was fetched away by his governess for nursery tea. When he had gone she continued to read and study the illustrations, losing herself in the entertaining account, which was an invaluable source of reference for botanists and anyone interested in the natural world.

She put the book away when the chambermaid who had been allocated to look after her, brought in a tray containing dishes of food, plates and cutlery. She was followed by Sophie. 'James has gone to dine with the King,' she said. 'So I thought I would keep you company, if that is agreeable to you.'

'Of course it is. I welcome your company. You have no idea how boring it is to be cooped up indoors, even when I am being well looked after.'

Sophie laughed. 'I have, you know. When I was expecting Jamie, I was nearly tearing my hair out with boredom. Why pregnant women have to be hidden away from society, I have no idea. It isn't as if it's a secret, is it? Would it offend you to see a woman walking about looking like one of those balloons they send up from Hyde Park now and again? If she was suitably clad, of course.'

'No, of course not. The common people do it and think nothing of it.'

The maid had laid out the meal on a small table in the window where they could catch the last of the evening sun before it went down behind the rooftops, and then retired, leaving the two ladies to help themselves.

'I'll tell you a secret, shall I?' Sophie continued. 'Jamie is to have a brother or sister.'

'Oh, congratulations! When is it to be?'

'Not until October, but not a word. If it gets out I shall be confined to the house, so the longer I can hide it the better.'

'I expect Uncle James is pleased.'

'Oh, yes. I do hope it is a girl. I should so like a daughter.'

'So long as she is not like me.'

'There is nothing wrong with you, my dear. You have a lively mind and a curiosity about the world that is to be commended.' She laughed suddenly. 'I was just like you before I met the Duke and I thought nothing of thumbing my nose at convention. I went out alone on the day the Duke of Wellington came back from the wars and was nearly trampled to death by the mob. And then I was abducted by some unscrupulous people and James had to risk life and limb to rescue me.'

'Good heavens! I did not know that.'

'Not many people do. It was hushed up. It would never do for the wife of the Duke of Belfont to be considered other than the epitome of proper behaviour. The King would dismiss him on the spot.' She smiled suddenly. 'Not that I sometimes think that wouldn't be a good thing. James is too much at his Majesty's beck and call. It does not matter that he has promised to take me out, or it is Jamie's birthday or I am giving a party to which all our friends have been invited, the King demands his presence and so to the King he goes. It is ten times worse this year with the coronation in July and heads of government coming to town from all round the globe and James having to oversee the arrangements for their accommodation and security.'

'I understand,' Beth said, smiling a little. 'I must not—what is the phrase?—upset the apple cart.'

'In a nutshell. But I know you won't. Now, eat up and we will pass the time planning what we shall do when your mama and Olivia come. Already the capital is becoming busy and there are any number of events being arranged to commemorate the coronation. Balls, routs, picnics, fireworks, balloon ascents and, being the Duchess of Belfont, I have been included in almost every invitation. The question will be what to accept and what to decline. I am looking forward to taking you shopping...'

'Mama will not like us to be extravagant,' Beth said, remembering her mother's homily on the state of their finances.

'There is unnecessary extravagance and there is extravagance that is justified,' Sophie said. 'You are come to London to enjoy a Season, to be seen out and about and to meet…'

'Prospective husbands,' Beth interrupted her.

'I was going to say new friends.'

Beth laughed. 'Whatever you were going to say, I know what you meant.'

'Do you mind so very much? After all, every young lady should marry and having a Season is the tried and tested method. How else are you to meet eligible young men?' She stopped and her eyes twinkled. 'Except by encountering them on London docks.'

'Oh, must you remind me of that? I burn with shame every time I think of it. Toby always used to say I looked like a boy and Mama said I reminded her of Papa when they first met, but they were only funning me. Mr Melhurst was so amused he could hardly keep a straight face and then to have Toby repudiate me was the last straw.'

'Mr Kendall did what he thought was right when he agreed to go. James pointed out that you were becoming too fond of him and it might lead to…difficulties.'

'Naturally I was fond of him. We grew up together, found mischief together, shared secrets. You might as well say Livvy was too fond of him; he was the brother we never had, a kind of prop to lean on, to help us out of scrapes. And then for him to turn from me when I had come so far to see him… I was never so mortified in my life that Mr Melhurst should have a hand in that.'

'Well, I, for one, am glad he was there and, if you are honest, you will admit you were too.'

'Yes, I admit it, but I am glad he has left town. I think if I ever saw him again, I should die of embarrassment.'

She desperately wanted to forget the man, but found she could not. He was in every way memorable. His height and the breadth of his shoulders were above average. His laughing blue eyes and broad smile revealing even white teeth, set against a suntanned complexion, set him apart. His evident wealth and clothes that were obviously the best money could buy and his unmarried status were enough to make every mama with a marriageable daughter drool. Time and again, she found herself picturing him and imagined a very different conversation from the one they had really had, a conversation in which she shone and he listened in rapt attention, deferring to her status as a mature lady. But dreaming did not alter the facts and they were that she had made a fool of herself. She did not need her aunt to admonish her never to let it happen again. She never would. From now on her guard would be up.

Chapter Four

The carriage containing Lady Harley and Olivia arrived the following afternoon and both ladies hurried into the house, leaving the Belfont footmen to help her ladyship's maid and Miss Andover to supervise the bringing in of the luggage. Sophie was in the hall to greet them, and, after kissing them both, she led the way up to her boudoir where Beth waited in some trepidation.

As soon as her mother appeared, she flung herself down into a deep curtsy, bowing her head. 'Oh, Mama, I am so sorry. Please forgive me.'

'Get up, Beth, for goodness' sake, I am not going to beat you.'

Beth rose and her mother stepped forward and kissed her on each cheek. 'You are forgiven. As soon as I have washed and changed out of my travelling clothes, you shall sit down and tell me exactly what happened. I have had Mr Melhurst's account, naturally, but I want to hear it from you. Most of all, I want to know why.'

'You can do that in the dining room over a meal,' Sophie said. 'I am sure you must be hungry.'

'I am ravenous,' Livvy admitted.

'When are you not?' Beth turned to her sister and held out both hands, which Livvy took. 'It is good you see you, Livvy.'

Livvy grinned. 'Not least because it means you are released from your confinement.'

'How did you know about that?'

'Mr Melhurst, of course. He is a handsome gentleman, is he not?'

'Handsome is as handsome does.' Beth was annoyed that Mr Melhurst knew of the Duke's decree and had seen fit to pass it on. Did it amuse him to humiliate her even further?

'Whatever can you mean? Surely you have not taken an aversion to him, when he saved you from being carried off to India?'

'I was never in danger of being carried off to India.'

'Enough!' Harriet said. 'Beth, I have brought a chest of clothes for you and instructed the footmen to take it to your room. I suggest you go there and let Nan help you into one of the gowns and then come down to the dining room as if you had arrived with us. Livvy, go and change too. We must not keep your Aunt Sophie waiting.'

The sisters left together. 'You may not like Mr Melhurst,' Livvy said as they went up the next flight of stairs to the bedrooms. 'But I do. He was most civil when he called at Beechgrove and did you know he is the grandson of Lord Melhurst?'

'No, I did not. Who is Lord Melhurst?'

'Why, he is one of the foremost breeders of race-horses in the country and has a huge stable at Heathlands, just outside Newmarket. I am surprised you have never heard of him.'

'I do not share your passion for horses, Livvy. The only horse trader I know of is Tattersall.'

'Lord Melhurst is not a common *trader*, Beth, how can you say that? He is a baron and a top-of-the-trees breeder. Mr Melhurst invited us to visit and promised to show us round. I intend to make sure Mama accepts. If we ask nicely, he might take us to the races.'

'I thought we were in London to find husbands.'

'Oh, as to that, if Mama likes to think that and Uncle James is prepared to pay, so be it, but I think I would like to be married to Mr Andrew Melhurst…'

'You cannot possibly mean that!' Beth was horrified. 'Why not?'

They had reached Beth's bedroom door and she paused with her hand on the knob. 'He is—' She stopped. What was he? A top-lofty nabob who thought he could kidnap her and force her into his carriage and then laugh because she could not escape. And then to tell her uncle all about her escapade, when she had especially asked him not to do so, made him far from the gentleman he purported to be. He was a rakeshame of the lowest kind and she would be happy if she never saw him again. Why, then, had she felt so flattened by Livvy's pronouncement?

'He is too old for you,' she said lamely. 'And you know nothing of him. Just because his grandfather owns a stable does not mean he is worthy...'

'I shan't know if he is worthy or not unless I encourage him, shall I?'

'You would never be so bold.'

'Why not? You were. You chased after Toby Kendall, which was much worse, considering you wore Papa's clothes and went on a stage coach all alone. I want to hear all about that, not the version you are going to tell Mama, but the real truth.'

'I shall tell Mama the truth and you will have to be satisfied with that. Now, I am going to change. I will see you downstairs in half an hour. You can have Nan, I can dress myself.' And with that she went into her room and shut the door, leaning against it, breathing hard. Her sister had only been in the house a few minutes and she had quarrelled with her and they never quarrelled, except for a little tiff now and again, which amounted to nothing and was soon smoothed over. It was all *that man*'s fault.

She started unbuttoning the borrowed gown she wore, wondering what had happened to her since leaving Beechgrove to make her so snappy. She did not like herself and resolved to try to make amends. Mr Melhurst was certainly not worth a falling out with her sister. Pulling gowns out of the chest, she found a pale blue muslin trimmed with dark blue lace, which fastened at the front, brushed her hair and secured it with ribbon and made her way downstairs, mentally preparing for the ordeal of confessing all.

The meal was a light one because they would be dining later, when Sophie hoped the Duke would join them. A quiet evening at home was envisaged before the hurly burly of social life in the capital began the following day. Sophie began by asking the new arrivals about Beechgrove and what had been happening in the country, but it was not long before Harriet began questioning Beth about why she had taken it into her head to disappear all alone and what exactly had happened.

Beth tried her best to explain how upset she had been to learn that her uncle had sent Toby away on the flimsiest of excuses, and how she did not want Toby to think she had condoned it. She could not write to him because etiquette forbade an unmarried lady to correspond with a man who was not a close relative and he might never know that she had had no part in sending him away.

'I am sure he would never have thought that, Beth,' her mother told her.

'Perhaps not, but I wanted to talk to him about what he planned to do, find out exactly where he would be exploring, so that I could follow it on a map. I wanted to know if I could help by looking after the plants he was leaving behind and preparing the ground for those he would bring back with him…'

'You were not planning to go with him?'

'No, Mama. I should have liked to, but I knew that was not possible.' She smiled suddenly. 'Livvy said I should marry a rich man who would indulge my fancies.'

Harriet returned her daughter's smile. Beth was so like her dead father in looks and like him in her love of adventure that she could not be angry with her for long. 'Then we must see what can be done. But it will be done with the proper regard for the proprieties, you understand?'

'Yes, Mama.'

It was the signal for the conversation to turn towards the social calendar and Beth breathed a sigh of relief.

'Shopping first,' Sophie said. 'You must be kitted out for every occasion. James will arrange for you both to make your curtsy at a reception next week and then you can attend the first ball of the Season at Lady Myers's.'

'We are never going to meet the Queen?' Livvy gasped.

'No, that would not be politic at all, considering the Duke is part of the King's entourage. You will make your curtsy to his Majesty. It will give you a flying start to the Season and ensure you are invited to everything.'

'I should think being nieces to the Duke of Belfont would take care of that,' Beth said.

'So it would, but James is determined to make your come-out memorable. I am instructed to make sure you want for nothing in the way of garments and fripperies; as your mama has excellent taste, you can be sure you will be the best-dressed young ladies in town, no matter how many others arrive. I am confident you will be suited by the end of the Season.' She accompanied this speech with a warm smile.

Beth's heart sank. It was not that she did not like going to balls, or any of the other social events being arranged, but the purpose of it all appalled her. How could she fall in love with anyone, however attractive, in the artificial atmosphere prevailing at these occasions? And even if she did, how could she let the man know how she felt? How would she know how he felt if he could not speak of it before asking her uncle first? The whole thing was fraught with hazards. She had promised to conform, and conform she must, but that did not mean she had to accept any offer. She returned her aunt's smile and all four retired to the drawing room where the tea tray had been taken and where they were presently joined by the Duke, who was amiability itself and made no mention of her prank. Everyone was determined to behave as if it had never happened.

The whole of the next day was reserved for shopping for dresses, habits and accessories and for choosing the materials and patterns for the gowns they would wear for their presentation to the King at Carlton House, which would signal their formal coming out. Everything had to be exactly right—the style, the fit and the material of the dresses—and then accessories had to be chosen and approved by their mother, making it an exhausting business. They were glad to return to Belfont House, with the only evening engagement being a small reception given by the Countess of Bostock at which they did not stay long.

It was not until the following afternoon that they were able to draw breath and accede to Livvy's request to take a carriage ride in the park. She would have liked to go riding, but her mount, being brought in slow stages by the young Pershore, had not yet arrived. Besides, Sophie wanted them all to be seen together to reinforce the notion that the Harley girls had both been brought to London by their mother.

The sun was shining, though it was too early in the year for it to have much warmth. They dressed warmly in carriage dresses and short jackets, braided in a military style. Harriet's was a deep purple with silver frogging, Sophie's, dove grey trimmed with blue, Livvy's, rose pink, and Beth's, cornflower blue. All wore matching shallow-crowned bonnets with deep brims. Sitting in the Belfont carriage, they presented a striking picture of feminine elegance. Andrew Melhurst certainly thought so.

He was riding through the park with Lord Henry Gorsham, whom he had met by chance at Tattersalls that morning. Andrew had known Henry before he went away because he was a keen horseman and an excellent judge of horseflesh and often visited Heathlands. They had talked of horses, that being the subject of most interest to Henry, and then the social calendar. Henry, who had only recently come into his title, had come to London to find a wife, or, as he so crudely put it, 'to look over the fillies to find one to mate with'. They had left Tattersalls together and, as both were staying at Stephen's Hotel in Bond Street, decided to ride there together through Hyde Park.

'What about you?' Henry was saying. 'Are you thinking about entering the matrimonial stakes now you are home again?'

'It is something I will have to consider sooner or later, but it is not my reason for coming to town—' He stopped suddenly when he saw the Belfont carriage and its occupants and was disconcerted to find his heart was beating at twice its usual rate. He was undecided whether to ride forward and greet them or turn away and pretend he had not seen them. He knew perfectly well Miss Harley would prefer the latter. She would not wish to be reminded of her humiliation. On the other hand, he could not refuse to meet Lady Harley, who had been very gracious to him, nor turn away from the delightful Miss Olivia, who had just caught sight of him and was, even then, pointing him out to her mama.

'I say, Melhurst, do you know those pretty little fillies?' Henry asked. 'They seem to be pointing at us.'

'I have a slight acquaintance with them all.'

'Then present me, there's a good fellow.'

Andrew was not at all sure that Henry was the sort of person the Duchess and Lady Harley would favour, having little finesse and referring to everything, including young ladies, in equine terms. However, he could not politely refuse as the carriage was moving towards them and the Duchess was already smiling a greeting. He rode forward and reined in as the carriage stopped abreast of him. 'Ladies, your obedient,' he said, doffing his riding hat to all the occupants in one wide sweep.

'Why, Mr Melhurst,' the Duchess said. 'I did not think to see you again so soon. How do you do?'

'Very well, your Grace.' He paused. 'May I present my friend, Lord Gorsham?'

'Lord Gorsham. How do you do.' She made a slight inclination of the head.

'Her Grace, the Duchess of Belfont, Lady Harley, Miss Harley and Miss Olivia Harley,' Andrew added, completing the introduction.

He swept off his hat. 'Ladies, I am honoured.'

'Are you in town for long, my lord?' the Duchess said.

Beth hardly heard his reply, nor any of polite conversation that was taking place between his lordship and her mother and aunt—she was too uncomfortably aware of Mr Melhurst looking at her with his head on one side and a slight smile playing about his lips, as if trying to gauge her mood. It seemed as if his eyes, so very, very blue, were devouring her like the sea swallowed up the sand on an ebbing tide, drawing it into itself, sucking it up. Like the sand, she was powerless to resist such a force.

He smiled. 'Miss Harley, is all well?' His voice was a low murmur, unheard by the others.

'It is.'

'No uncomfortable repercussions?'

'No.'

'I am glad.'

'What are you doing in London? I collect you were going home to Newmarket.'

'So I did, but I found I needed to come back again.'

'What for?' She knew it was presumptuous of her to have asked the question and his startled look told her he knew it too, but he recovered swiftly and smiled.

'Would you believe the lure of a pretty face was too tempting to resist?'

'Oh, I can believe it,' she said. 'You must point its owner out to me some time.'

He smiled wryly. 'One day perhaps I will.'

They were sparring with each like a couple of pugilists, dancing round each other, feinting blows, but not quite able to deliver them. He was teasing her, she knew, but she could not quite bring herself to give him the ultimate put-down, which would end the bout. If he turned from her now because of her behaviour, she would never see him again and that mattered. It mattered so much it left her breathless and shaken, her face hot with embarrassment. Why was she fated to be put to the blush by this top-lofty man?

'Mr Melhurst.' The Duchess's voice made them drag their attention away from each other and turn to face her. 'I am having a small soirée next Tuesday—would you and Lord Gorsham care to join us? There will be music and conversation, nothing elaborate.'

'Oh, do come,' Livvy put in. 'I want to hear all about the Newmarket races and your horses. The one you are riding is a splendid example. Is he from the Melhurst stables?'

'No, Miss Olivia, I bought him today at Tattersalls. Coming as I have from a long stay abroad, I had no riding horse and I needed one.' He reached forward to pat the stallion's neck. 'His name is Firefly.'

'I should have expected your grandfather to supply you with a mount,' Beth said. 'My sister has told me he has an extensive stable.'

'Except for the carriage horses, most of the Melhurst animals are racehorses, Miss Harley, too finely tuned for day-to-day riding.'

'But sometimes it is a good idea to mix their blood with sturdier animals to produce stayers, is it not?' Livvy queried.

'Indeed, yes, Miss Olivia.'

'Are you going to breed from Firefly?'

'Livvy!' exclaimed her mother. 'That is hardly a subject for polite conversation.'

Henry chuckled. 'Like horses, do you, Miss Olivia?'

'Oh, yes. Riding is my passion.'

'Miss Olivia Harley is a fearless horsewoman, Henry,' Andrew put in. 'A five-barred gate is nothing to her.'

'A filly after my own heart,' Henry said, then, realising his blunder, tried hastily to retract. 'I mean young lady, of course. Forgot myself. Please forgive me.'

'Oh, you are forgiven,' Livvy said, though her mother was looking reproving. 'I do not mind being compared to a horse. Horses are often preferable to humans as companions, don't you think so, Mr Melhurst?'

'Not when the humans are as charming as you are, Miss Olivia.'

'Well said, Drew,' Henry said, with a laugh.

'So, will you come to my aunt's soirée?' Livvy asked.

'It will be my pleasure.' Andrew was addressing the Duchess, who had issued the original invitation, but his eyes were on Beth. 'I shall look forward to it.'

'Lord Gorsham, may I count on you?'

'Indeed, your Grace. I shall be delighted to accept.'

The Duchess gave the order to the coachman to proceed and the two riders bowed and trotted away.

'Nearly sunk myself without trace,' Henry said when they were out of earshot.

Andrew laughed. 'So you did, but fortunately the younger Miss Harley has a keen sense of humour.'

'What about the other? I notice you were in deep conversation with her.'

'Just passing the time of day.'

'How did you meet them?'

'I was introduced by the Duke.' And that, in a roundabout way, was the truth, and all he was going to say on the subject.

'You are a dark horse, my friend. Back in England a week and already you are consorting with the highest in the land.'

'I wouldn't say consorting. I had occasion to visit Belfont House, that is all.'

'And now we are to go to supper there. I'd best look to my wardrobe. Need to be in prime kilter. I will leave you now. A visit to my tailor is called for.' And with that he wheeled away, leaving Andrew to proceed alone.

Did he need to refurbish his wardrobe? he asked himself. His clothes had been made for him by a native tailor in Calcutta, who managed somehow to keep abreast of fashion and who charged a pittance, but perhaps someone as lofty as the Duke of Belfont would detect flaws in his dress: the wrong buttons, the wrongly shaped lapels, pantaloons too wide. He smiled to himself. Why did he think he needed to impress that gentleman? He was not one to toady to anyone, Duke or commoner, and certainly not to young ladies who thought nothing of dressing in male garb at least twenty years out of date. He smiled, re-membering… Like a whirlwind that comes in the eye of a storm, she had taken his breath away. He was not sure he liked the feeling.

Beth's emotions were in turmoil as they continued their ride, bowing this way and that at acquaintances and sometimes stopping to greet a particular friend of the Duchess's. They drew a great deal of attention, which amused Livvy and their mother, but Beth hardly noticed. If she had been asked a week before if the sight of anyone could make her go weak at the knees, she would have laughed in scorn and said, 'No, I am far too level-headed. Unless you mean the Duke, of course, because he can be very intimidating.' But it had not been her uncle who had produced this latest bout of trembling; it had been Mr Melhurst. She was still going over the conversation they had had. It amounted to nothing more than a polite exchange and yet it was charged with volatility, as if the words spoken were a code to something else. Which was nonsense.

Determined to stop thinking about him, she began an animated conversation, prattling on about how splendid the sight of a contingent of horse guards were with their colourful uniforms and glittering accoutrements, and laughing at the sight of a dwarf walking on stilts for the amusement of the crown, anything to take her mind of *that man*.

* * *

After half an hour the Duchess decided that the ride had achieved its purpose and half the *beau monde* must know of the arrival in town of the Harley sisters; and they might as well return home for tea.

It was while they were waiting in the Duchess's cosy sitting room for the tea tray to be brought in that Beth picked up a newspaper the Duke had discarded when he left to go to court that morning and her eye was caught by a notice of a lecture to be given by Mr John Wedgwood at the Horticultural Society on the plants of the tropics and their suitability for growing in the climate of England. That, more than anything, would serve to distract her.

'Are we engaged for anything tomorrow evening, Mama?' she asked.

'No, I do not think so. Why do you ask?'

'I should like to attend this lecture.' She handed the paper to her mother and pointed to the item.

'A lecture!' exclaimed Livvy. 'We are not come to London to educate ourselves.'

'Why not? There is little opportunity for such enlightenment in Sudbury.'

'I do not see why we cannot arrange something,' Harriet said. 'I will ask the Duke.'

'Why must we ask him?'

'Because we will need a suitable escort.'

'You do not expect me to go, do you?' Livvy said. 'I shall be agape the whole evening.'

'You may stay at home if you wish,' her mother told her. 'But I should like to go.'

'I shall be at home,' the Duchess said. 'Livvy and I will be company for each other.'

The Duke was unexpectedly free the following evening and he offered to escort them himself. 'Having funded young Toby Kendall to go plant hunting, I had better try and understand what it is he finds so fascinating about them,' he said. 'I can understand importing plants for their medicinal value and growing tropical fruits to eat, but I am not so sure about ornamental trees and strange flowers. The cost of such endeavour is prodigious.'

'It is the challenge of making them grow in this country,' Beth told him, wondering if he begrudged the money he had evidently given Toby. 'I collect there is a splendid orangery at Dersingham Park.'

He smiled. 'Built by my father. I never give it much thought except when my steward tells me how much it costs to heat it.'

'Yes,' Harriet put in. 'We have had to stop heating the conservatory at Beechgrove for that very reason. Toby does his work in a small glasshouse at the bottom of the kitchen garden.'

Her mother's words reminded Beth of the need to be frugal. They would never be poor because the Duke would take care of them, but it wasn't the same as being independent and able to make her own decisions about what she wanted from life. So, was this her last chance of a Season in London, her last opportunity to find a husband in the accepted way? Did she mind? She minded most for Livvy, who had set her heart on a husband who had money enough to indulge her passion for horses.

Livvy, who had been chattering excitedly about the prospect of entertaining Mr Melhurst and his friend at Belfont House, had said she might like to be married to Mr Melhurst, but she hadn't meant it, had she? She had only met him twice, once at Beechgrove and again today; and having a grandfather who bred racing horses was surely not enough on which to judge a man.

He was insufferably superior, as Beth knew to her cost, and he was not above riding roughshod over people's feelings. Look how he had betrayed her to her uncle when all he had undertaken to do was fetch her Aunt Sophie. Reluctantly she was forced to admit that once the Duke had entered the house and found Mr Melhurst there, he would have been obliged to state his reasons for calling; to do anything else would have compromised her aunt, but if he had driven away as soon as she had left his coach he would not have encountered Jamie or Uncle James and the problem would not have arisen.

She stopped her wandering thoughts suddenly when she realised she was judging him on equally slight grounds. Besides, Mama and certainly the Duke would soon give him a right-about if he were considered unsuitable for Livvy and it was better to put him from her mind. That was easier decided than done, she realised that evening.

They arrived at the lecture hall in good time to find seats near the front and Beth, sitting between her mother and her uncle, spent the waiting time looking about her. The hall was filling up and there was a low murmur of conversation as acquaintances greeted each other and commented on the turn out and the weather and spoke of their own efforts to raise unusual plants, exchanging information and advice. On the platform, there was nothing but a lectern illuminated by a lamp.

A hush descended as the Chairman came out and greeted everyone, thanking them for their attendance and promising any money collected would go towards financing future expeditions. 'I am afraid I have a disappointment for those of you who have been looking forward to hearing Mr Wedgwood speak,' he went on. 'I am sorry to tell you he has been prevented from coming by unforeseen circumstances.' There was a murmur of voices and he held up his hands for silence. 'But we have, at very short notice, persuaded Mr Andrew Melhurst to take his place.'

Beth's gasp was almost audible as he continued, 'Mr Melhurst, as the botanists among you may be aware, is well known as a traveller and collector of plants. His scholarship is unrivalled, especially since the sad demise of Sir Joseph, and he has first-hand experience of collecting botanical specimens hitherto unknown in this country. Mr Andrew Melhurst.' He extended his arm to the side and Andrew, carrying no more than a single sheet of notes, walked on to the stage and took his place at the lectern.

Beth stared in disbelief. Mr Melhurst had never said a word to her about being a botanist, even though he knew of her own interest. Perhaps she should have guessed when he lectured her about the difficulties and hazards that plant hunters were likely to encounter, but she had assumed he was simply trying to discourage her from taking what he considered too bold a step for a lady.

She sat forward to listen intently, ready to criticise and question, but as Andrew began to speak she forgot her antagonism because he was not only knowledgeable but amusing, and the tales of some of his adventures had the audience chuckling aloud. At other times, when he spoke of the dangers, his listeners were impressed by the courage of those who risked so much to gather specimens. The voyage alone was enough to deter most people, but the trek inland was also fraught with hazards: the density of the jungle, the bitter cold of the mountains, the hostility of some of the natives they encountered. He knew his subject and he knew how to hold an audience and at the end he received an enthusiastic ovation. Beth clapped as hard as anyone until she realised he had seen and recognised her and was smiling towards her. Her handclapping slowed and she found the heat rushing into her face.

'How very interesting,' the Duke murmured. 'I had no idea it could be so eventful. I wonder how young Kendall will fare. Does he have sufficient courage and tenacity, do you think?'

'Of course he has,' Beth said. 'He had read a great deal on the subject.'

'Let us go and congratulate Mr Melhurst,' Harriet suggested.

Before Beth could demur, the Duke had agreed and she was obliged to follow as they made their way to the back of the stage where a small crowd had gathered round Andrew, eager to ask him questions. When he saw them he broke away and came towards them.

'My lord Duke, Lady Harley, Miss Harley. I had not realised you would be here.'

'It was Miss Harley's idea,' James said. 'But I wanted to come, being newly introduced to the subject by Mr Kendall.'

'I hope you were not too disappointed to find Mr Wedgwood could not come.' He was addressing the Duke, but his attention was on Beth.

'Not at all. I am sure you made an excellent substitute.'

'Excellent,' Harriet said. 'I did not know you were a botanist. I had thought your interest was in the Melhurst stables.'

'Those too, my lady,' he said smiling.

'A man of many parts,' Beth murmured.

He bowed. 'I hope you found my little talk interesting, Miss Harley, though I collect we have already had some conversation on the subject…'

Again that reminder of her humiliation. Why could he not leave it alone? 'It is a subject that fascinates me and I cannot hear enough of it, Mr Melhurst.' She tried her best to keep her voice level, but she was aware of a slight tremor and a hoarseness that made her want to clear her throat.

'Then might I be permitted to escort you round the Royal Gardens at Kew? I was there today and it is much changed since I left England. It has been transformed into a centre of horticultural scholarship. I am sure you will find it interesting.'

While Beth's desire to learn did battle with her ambiguous feelings towards the teacher, her mother was accepting on behalf of them both. 'Thank you, Mr Melhurst. When should you like to go? It ought to be soon, before the Season is truly underway. Both my daughters are expecting to be much in demand...'

He smiled, his eyes on Beth, trying to discover what she thought of the idea, but she refused to meet his eye. 'I do not doubt that, my lady. Shall we say the day after tomorrow? I will call for you in my carriage at two in the afternoon, if that is convenient.'

Harriet turned to Beth? 'What do you say, Beth? Have you arranged anything for that day?'

'No, Mama.'

'Then, Mr Melhurst, we shall be delighted to accept.'

There were other people anxious to ask him questions and reluctantly he excused himself and went to oblige them.

'He is such a pleasant young man,' Harriet said, as they returned to the Belfont coach. 'You do not know how lucky you were to encounter him on the docks, Beth, and not some unscrupulous rogue. Goodness knows what would have happened to you if you had.'

'Mama, please do not remind me of it. I know what I owe to Mr Melhurst.'

'Then I do not understand why you cannot be more gracious towards him. You hardly said a word.'

James chuckled. 'There is nothing like being obliged to someone to make that someone abhorrent. It is human nature.'

'I never said he was abhorrent, Uncle.'

'I should hope not!' Harriet said, as they took their seats for the journey back to South Audley Street. 'If you do not wish to acknowledge your debt, I have no such reluctance. And surely the fact that he shares your interest in botany is a point in his favour?'

'In his favour? Mama, you are surely not expecting him to pay his addresses to me?'

'He might, given a little encouragement.'

'Only because he thinks he is obliged to do so. I would never accept a man on those terms.'

'Why should he feel obliged to?' James asked.

'You know why. He offered, did he not, when he brought me to Belfont House? I am not sure whether it was my reputation or his own he was trying to save.'

'It is because of his prompt action that neither has been compromised,' her mother put in.

'And I am constantly being reminded of it.' Beth was near to tears, not only because she wholeheartedly regretted the impulse that made her go to the docks in the first place, but because she could not understand why she was so sharp with everyone and so reluctant to admit she found Mr Andrew Melhurst disturbingly attractive. The sight of his handsome face turned her knees to jelly and his blue-eyed gaze rendered her almost speechless. And when she did at last find her tongue, it was to utter a sharp retort that was so unlike her it might have been someone else speaking. 'If you are so sure you want him as a son-in-law, then marry him off to Livvy. She has told me she would like to be his wife. After all, he has all the attributes she requires, good looks, wealth and a stable full of horses.'

'I am persuaded she was bamming you,' her mother said.

'Ah, I see,' the Duke said.

'What do you see?' Harriet asked.

'Oh, nothing,' he said, smiling. 'Just one of my theories.' He paused, but if Beth thought he was about to enlighten them she was disappointed. 'I am afraid I will not be free to go to Kew with you, but I am sure you do not need any other escort than Mr Melhurst.'

'Oh, I think we can manage,' Harriet said.

Andrew, who had come to London as a result of an urgent plea from the secretary of the Horticultural Society to fill in for Mr Wedgwood, had, at the time, no intention of prolonging his stay beyond the couple of days necessary to give his lecture, but once here, he had bought a horse, twice met Miss Harley again, albeit by accident, agreed to go to supper at Belfont

House and offered to conduct Lady Harley and her daughter round Kew Gardens. Never would he have guessed, when he met that strange figure on the docks, that he would become so involved. But involved he was.

He was by no means sure, because Lady Harley was charming and not at all stiff, but he had a feeling of being manipulated. Was he being tried and tested for the role of husband to Miss Harley? He smiled at the lady who had asked him about growing gardenias, though the smile was more for his own foolishness. It was plain enough that Miss Harley herself was against the idea. In spite of her protests to the contrary, she had probably set her heart on Toby Kendall, who was undoubtedly considered ineligible or he would not have been packed off to India.

If the Duke or Lady Harley thought he could be used to disentangle Miss Harley from that attachment, they were in for a disappointment. He would choose his own wife when he was ready and then only if the lady wanted it too. He ought to marry. His grandfather wanted him to marry. As soon as that invitation from the Horticultural Society had come, the old man had told him to stay in town for the Season and find himself a wife. 'Open up the London house,' he had said. 'The servants have been idle long enough.'

'But I came home especially to be with you,

Grandfather,' he had said. 'You grumbled when I left again the other day…'

'Oh, take no note of that, my boy. London is not the other side of the world. You can easily get back if I need you, which I am persuaded I will not. I feel well enough.'

Andrew decided that his grandfather's illness was of the kind that came and went according to his convenience. He was aware of the honour the Horticultural Society was bestowing on him by asking him to speak, so he had returned to London, but as he did not intend to prolong his stay, he had taken a room at a hotel rather than open up Melhurst House. He had intended to call on the Duchess and Lady Harley to pay his respects, no more than that. He had imagined meeting Miss Harley again in the constricted atmosphere of the drawing room, where stilted politeness reigned, but it had not turned out like that and he felt everything was spiralling out of his control. But did he have to compound that by issuing his own invitation and one he knew Miss Harley would find difficult to resist?

The last of his questioners had departed and he took his leave of the officials and made his way to White's club on foot, where he had arranged to meet Henry for a game of whist, musing as he went. If only he had not had that foolish affair with Kitty, he might be married by now and father of a brood of little Melhursts. If only he had not met Miss Harley in such strange circumstances, they might have met in a conventional setting and, in the fullness of time, come to an understanding. If only…

He entered the portals of the club where Henry was already ensconced in a corner, waiting for him. What was the point of such conjecture? It had happened and he could do nothing but let events take their course.

'There you are,' Henry said, pouring him a glass of wine from the bottle at his elbow. 'Thought you'd never come. The gaming room is filling up. We will have to take our chances for seat.'

Gambling was the least of Andrew's concerns. He enjoyed a game of cards as well as the next man, but it was not a passion as it was with some men—and women—he knew; he did not mind whom he played with as long as they did not cheat. He picked up his glass and followed Henry into the card room. The place was packed and a blue haze of tobacco smoke hung over it. There was very little conversation as the players concentrated on the cards, although an occasional grunt or the few words necessary to place a bet or the muttered, 'That's me out,' or 'You'll take my voucher?' broke the silence.

'There,' Henry said, pointing to a table where two

of the occupants had evidently decided they had had enough and were standing up to leave.

Henry and Andrew took their places. It was only as they settled in their seats that Andrew realised that one of the players was his cousin Edward.

'Hallo, Drew,' he said. Six months younger than Andrew, his hair was darker, his eyes were grey rather than blue and his complexion lacked any evidence of time spent out of doors, but there was a family resemblance in the shape of the face and the long straight nose. 'Found yourself a wife yet?'

'Teddy! What are you doing here?'

'Kitty decided she wanted a Season in town, and what Kitty wants, she must have. Besides, I thought it might be amusing to watch how you go about getting yourself a wife.'

'That's my affair…'

'Oh, no doubt of it, coz, wouldn't dream of interfering, but you must hope that the old scandal does not rear its head…'

'Why should it? Lord Haysborough is long dead and you have married Katherine and have a son…'

'True, but it would help, don't you think, if we are seen as one big happy family? You will need to entertain and that means you will want a hostess. At least that is what Kitty says.'

Andrew groaned inwardly. The oily smile on his

cousin's face boded no good at all. He wondered what the man was plotting. If the old scandal was revived so that he became the subject of gossip, it would make him unacceptable in the drawing rooms of the *ton*, especially the drawing room of Belfont House...

'Wake up, Drew,' Henry said, swiftly cutting the cards for Teddy, who was dealing. 'Let's see your blunt on the table.'

Andrew sighed and complied.

Chapter Five

Beth told herself firmly that the only reason she had accepted the invitation to Kew was because of her interest in botany, not in the man. If she told herself that enough times, she might come to believe it. And to reinforce it, she said it to Livvy, who had been green with envy when she heard that the lecture she had so decried had been given by Mr Melhurst and, according to her mother, had been more interesting than she had expected and Mr Melhurst had been very informative and amusing.

'You might have told me he was to be the lecturer,' she said. 'I would have come with you.'

'I did not know; anyway, you have always maintained you have no interest in botany.'

'Ah, but if I want the man to notice me, then I must develop one.'

'It is not a subject you can learn in five minutes.'

'Oh, I don't want to learn it, only to appear interested and eager to learn. Can I help it if I am a bufflehead?'

Beth laughed. 'So you want to come to Kew, do you?'

'Why not?'

And so Livvy was waiting with Beth and her mother when Andrew called the next day. If he was surprised, hc gave no sign of it and welcomed her as one of the party.

They spent over two hours in the gardens and the glass houses where Andrew pointed out some of the plants he had been instrumental in sending to the gardens from India, and others which had been brought from other distant parts of the world, including the *Cattleya labiata*, the mysterious plant that had come to Britain from Argentina as packing material and which had been persuaded to grow and flower. The orchid had attracted enormous attention and other plant hunters had been dispatched to discover more. There were also acacias, sago palms, eucalyptus, as well as cacti and smaller shrubs with strange-shaped leaves.

Beth lost all her antagonism as she fired questions at their guide and he, basking in the glow of her approbation, answered in detail, realising she was more than usually knowledgeable not only of the theory but the practical side of horticulture, which reminded him of her stained fingernails when they first met, though now they were beautifully manicured. He was not sure which side of her he found most intriguing, the hoyden in men's clothes who did not mind getting her hands dirty or the beautiful young lady in the cornflower-blue jaconet gown and becoming bonnet trimmed with silk flowers.

'How came you to be interested in botany?' she asked.

'It was through my father,' he answered. 'He loved to travel to out-of-the-way places and was fascinated by the plants he encountered, particularly the trees; being a good draughtsman, he made detailed drawings and brought them back to England to have them identified. When he learned they were unknown in this country, nothing would serve but he must return and bring back cuttings and seedlings and try to make them grow. Many failed to thrive, but some survived. I was only a bantling at the time, but I used to watch him tending them and from there developed an interest myself. Alas, he died of a snake bite on one of his expeditions and I kept the gardens up in his memory.'

'And your mother?'

'She died when I was very small. I have no memory of her.'

Olivia, anxious not to be left out, asked questions about the plants too, though of the kind that a schoolgirl might ask. He smiled and humoured her and explained why he thought it was important to bring new plants to Kew. 'The wider our knowledge of growing things, the more we can use them for the benefit of mankind,' he told her. 'There are medicines that natives have been using for centuries, and spices and foods we have yet to discover. If we can learn to grow them…'

'Some are purely ornamental, surely?' she asked, looking up at him, smiling winningly. 'The orchid is not a food or a medicine.'

'There is a place for that too,' he said. 'We should not decry beautiful things because they have no practical use.'

'Oh, how clever you are! And how right. Otherwise why do men marry women who have nothing to commend them but their beauty?' Her eyelids fluttered up at him.

He knew she was trying to flirt with him and it would have amused him to respond by saying something complimentary about her beauty, if he had not also been aware of Lady Harley frowning a little and Beth walking a few steps ahead with her nose in the air. The situation was suddenly fraught with embarrassment and he hastily brought the tour to an end and suggested tea at Grillon's in Albemarle Street.

Beth, who had been so animated in the gardens, became very quiet at the hotel and spoke little. Now, when it looked as though her sister was setting her cap at Mr Melhurst and he was responding like a man be-witched, she made the startling discovery that she liked Mr Melhurst after all, that he was all she could hope for in a man: handsome, clever, interesting and chivalrous. She had known all that before, so what had made the difference? She did not know, but wished, with all her heart, she had not been so indifferent to him before. The shaking of her limbs when he looked at her, the terrible feeling of jealousy that beset her when he paid attention to Livvy, all told her she was in love.

It was a startling revelation and she found she could not look at him, could not find a voice to speak and so concentrated on sipping tea and nibbling a small cake for which she had no appetite. Had he noticed? Did it amuse him? To the humiliation of having him rescue her from her own folly was added the embarrassment of falling in love with him and not knowing what to do about it, how to behave, especially as Livvy seemed set on having him for herself. She could not steal him from her sister, even if she knew how to. If only she did not have to see him again, but tomorrow was her aunt's soirée and he would be there.

An invitation from the Duchess of Belfont was much prized and as the house was a large one, she was apt to ask everyone and anyone to whom she took a fancy and so the reception rooms were crammed with ladies and gentlemen, young and old, all talking at once. The men tended to congregate in corners talking about gambling and horse racing, who had taken whom to bed, what the King had said to so and so and speculating on the coronation. 'She's bound to turn up,' one said of his Majesty's estranged wife. 'When all's said and done, she is still the Queen and there's no precedent for denying the crown to a lawful spouse.'

'My money's on the King,' Henry Gorsham put in. He was dressed in a blue tailcoat, white breeches, white stockings and black court pumps. 'He's said he won't have her and his word is law.'

'Ten guineas of mine says she is crowned with him.'

'And fifty says she isn't.'

'Done.' The two men shook hands.

'Did you know Melhurst's grandson is in town?' a third man said suddenly.

'Teddy. What of it?'

'Not Teddy, the other one. Andrew, I think his name is.'

'Is he now? That will put Teddy's nose out of joint. He's been toadying to the old man for years, especially since he became a father.'

'Which is the elder?'

'Drew by a few months.' This was said by Henry. 'He's the son of the old man's elder son and therefore his heir. Edward's father was the younger brother. No doubt Teddy hoped his cousin would stay away for ever.'

'Why did he go in the first place? Have a falling out with his grandfather, did he?'

'Can't say,' Henry said cautiously. 'I think he went plant hunting.'

'Plant hunting! Is that the story being put about?' This from an older man in a waistcoat so tight the buttons threatened to pop and a cravat that threatened to choke him, so stiff and tall it was. On the other hand, his breeches, the colour of honey, looked as though they had been stuffed to give some semblance of thigh muscles. 'I know for a fact there was a scandal.'

'Go on, Bosney, tell us,' urged another. 'I'll wager it was a woman…'

'Course it was. His cousin's wife.'

'Good Lord! The muckworm. And now he's back.' He stopped suddenly because Henry had spotted Drew and was waving to him to join them. Beth, who had heard it all from behind a huge flower arrangement she had helped to create, moved quickly away.

She had not meant to eavesdrop, but had simply been approaching the men with a smile on her face, determined to break the little group up and suggest they disperse and make themselves pleasant to the ladies. She had stopped in her tracks when she heard

Mr Melhurst's name mentioned and dived out of sight, but not out of earshot. Now she was both appalled and intrigued. What had that fat man been going to say about Mr Melhurst? Was it very dreadful? More to the point, was it true? And what did she think and feel about it? She did not know what to think or feel. Her emotions had been confused before, now they were doubly so.

'There you are, Beth,' her sister said, catching sight of her. 'Where have you been?'

Beth pulled herself together. 'Helping to look after Aunt Sophie's guests. There are so many, it is a dreadful crush. And I am not sure they are all gentlemen.'

'Aunt Sophie likes to mix everyone up, I think. Have you seen Mr Melhurst?'

'I believe he is over there, talking to Lord Gorsham.' She nodded in the general direction of the gossiping men.

'Oh, I see him. He is very handsome, isn't he?'

'Is he? I hadn't noticed.' Which was a downright untruth. She had noticed how he stood out from the crowd in his forest-green cutaway evening coat, his pale lemon embroidered waistcoat and skilfully tied cravat, not to mention his long legs encased in trousers strapped under his shoes. How could he be so self-assured if what she had heard was true? Perhaps he thought everyone had forgotten. Or was he counting on his connection with Belfont House to see him through? If that was the case, how fortuitous it had been for him to encounter her on the docks. He had used her! Oh, how confused and angry she felt!

She had barely managed to calm herself when he suddenly appeared before her. 'Miss Harley.' He bowed.

'Mr Melhurst.' A tiny curtsy was all she could manage, sure her knees were about to give way under her.

'There is such a crush, I had not seen you before.' That, too, was an untruth; he had been watching her. She had a smile for everyone, had made sure they were made welcome, stopped to have a little conversation, introduced strangers to each other, and passed on, still smiling. He had seen part of her lemon yellow skirt and one slippered toe peeping from behind the bank of flowers and wondered what she was doing. It looked as if she were eavesdropping on Henry and his companions and he wondered what she had heard. Whatever it was, it had agitated her. In the short time since they met, he had come to know her so well he could tell when she was upset, when relaxed and when she was bubbling over with enthusiasm, and at this moment she seemed deflated, her lovely eyes troubled. Surely her little escapade had not become public knowledge? 'Shall we promenade a little?' He offered her his arm.

'No, sir, I have to find my mother,' she said, and fled.

He stared after her.

'Oh, take no note of my sister, Mr Melhurst,' Livvy said. 'She has been a glum pot ever since we arrived in London. I expect she is missing Toby. I will walk with you.' And she laid her fingers upon his arm and there was nothing he could do but smile and stroll with her round the circumference of the room.

'How glad I am that you found Beth,' she said. 'I shudder to think what might have happened to her if you had not.'

'Glad to be of service,' he said.

'If you had not, we would not have met, would we? And we would not now be talking together as if we had known each other all our lives.'

'Perhaps we would all have become acquainted in different circumstances. I would have come to town and your mama would have brought you both here for the Season; we should perhaps have met at someone's house, if not the Duchess's.'

'True, but you rescuing Beth gave us a flying start, don't you think?'

'Perhaps, but I do not think we should remind her of it, nor speak of it. If it gets about, there might be gossip...'

'Oh, surely not? It was only a scrape, after all.'

'Nevertheless, I think Miss Harley would find it deeply embarrassing.'

'Do you think it will harm her chances of finding a husband?'

'It depends on whom she chooses.'

'I hope it does not, because Mama has said she must be settled before me...'

'Oh, and do you have someone in mind?'

'I might have,' she said airily. 'But I cannot tell you his name.'

'Why not?'

'Because he does not know it himself yet.'

'Then I shall not ask it.'

They continued for a few more paces until they reached Lady Harley when he relinquished Livvy with a bow. If he had been hoping then to find Beth, he was disappointed; she was nowhere to be seen.

Beth was reading more of Mr Parkinson's book to Jamie. Not wishing to come upon any of her aunt's guests and definitely not Mr Andrew Melhurst, she had been hurrying to the tranquillity of her own room when she saw her little cousin. He should have been asleep, but the sounds drifting up the stairs had kept him awake and he had crept out on to the landing to see the ladies and gentlemen arriving. Beth had taken him back to bed and given in to his entreaties that she should read to him. It served to divert her for a little while, but, when he fell asleep, her troubled thoughts returned.

She rose and made her way to her own room, where she sat at her dressing table and stared at herself in the mirror. 'You are a fool, Beth Harley,' she told her reflection. 'Breaking your heart over a man who, if rumour is to be believed, is not worth it. A man who can dangle after his cousin's wife is a rakeshame and you had best forget him.'

Resolutely, she tidied her hair, pinched her cheeks to give them some colour and returned downstairs, only to find Mr Melhurst talking to her mother, who had evidently asked him if he felt the cold, coming as he had from India.

'When I first arrived, I did,' he said, glancing at Beth and noticing her heightened colour, though she appeared perfectly composed. What had caused her flight earlier in the evening he could not imagine. 'Coming up the Channel and into the Thames, I felt the wind keenly, but I soon acclimatised. I am not sure that the plants I brought back with me have settled so easily…'

'I wonder you left them,' Beth said. 'Surely they need looking after?'

'Indeed they do, and I would not have abandoned them to the mercy of the gardeners at Heathlands if I had not been asked to give the lecture at the Horticultural Society. It was an honour I could not refuse.'

'Oh, that was the reason you came back to London,'

she said, unable to resist teasing. 'You told me it was the lure of a pretty face.'

He laughed. 'That too, of course.'

'And will you be going back to Heathlands soon? I imagine you are anxious to see how you plants are faring.'

'I shall have to go soon, but the pretty face is still luring me.'

'Then she must be very pretty to compete with your botanical specimens for your attention.'

'Beth,' her mother interrupted. 'It is unkind of you to tease Mr Melhurst. He does not know you well enough to give you the put-down you deserve.'

'Oh, I think I can hold my own, my lady,' he answered, smiling. 'And perhaps I invited it.'

'Invited what?' Livvy had come to join them from talking to a group of young people to whom her aunt had introduced her.

'A roasting from your sister, Miss Olivia.'

'Oh, what is she roasting you about?'

'The fact that Mr Melhurst returned to London, lured by a pretty face,' Beth answered for him. 'Though he refuses to say who its owner might be.'

'Oh, then we shall have to guess.' Livvy was looking up at him, fluttering her eyelashes and smiling and Beth wondered if it was as obvious to him as it was to her what her sister was up to.

'Livvy, Beth, stop this,' Harriet said. 'Mr Melhurst, I wonder you do not have a disgust of both my daughters. I apologise on their behalf.'

'No apology needed, my lady. If you will excuse me, I see Lord Gorsham beckoning to me. Miss Harley, Miss Olivia.' He bowed and left them, making for the door and the two girls were left to endure a jobation from their mother for their discourtesy.

The success of the evening was the subject of discussion at breakfast the following morning and that inevitably led to a general appraisal of the young men who had been there. 'There was no one to compare with Mr Melhurst,' Livvy said. 'Mr Robert Young is too fat, and though Viscount Rapworth was polite enough, he is too thin. And too young.'

'He is two and twenty,' Sophie said. 'And destined for the army, so I am told.'

Livvy laughed. 'He will make a very poor target for enemy fire. If he stands sideways, he will be almost invisible.'

'What about Lord Gorsham?' Beth asked. 'He seems to know a great deal about horses.'

'No more than Mr Melhurst. And Mr Melhurst is the handsomer.'

'Do you know Mr Melhurst's cousin?' Beth asked her aunt.

'Do you mean Mr Edward Melhurst? I believe he was presented to me once, but I cannot say I know him. Why do you ask?'

'No particular reason. I heard him spoken of last night.'

'By Mr Andrew Melhurst?'

'No. Mr Melhurst has never mentioned his family to me, but I wondered if there was ever any trouble between them?'

'Not that I know of. Why do you ask?'

'I overheard some gossip. It was suggested that was why Mr Melhurst was obliged to leave the country.'

'But I collect that was seven years ago. I was not in the country myself at that time. It is no good asking me.'

'I do not think we should judge a man on gossip, Beth,' her mother said.

'But if it should be true? And if it was very dreadful?'

'Then we should ask him outright,' Livvy said.

'You will do no such thing,' Beth protested. 'He will want to know the source of the story and I would not like him to think I listened to gossip.'

'No, of course not, considering it would seem like the pot calling the kettle black.'

'Girls, that is enough,' Harriet commanded. 'If there is anything we should know, I think Mr Melhurst is gentleman enough to tell us of it himself. And please remember, Livvy, as far as the world is concerned, Beth came to London with us.'

'And does that also mean Mr Melhurst never came to Beechgrove and never invited us to Newmarket?'

'Livvy, you are being foolish. There is no reason why he should not have visited us with a message from the Duke.'

'Good, because I do so want to go to Newmarket to see the Melhurst stables. After all, if I am one day to be mistress of Heathlands…'

'Olivia, wherever did you get that idea?' her mother demanded. 'Surely Mr Melhurst has not made an approach to you?'

'No, Mama, but I am persuaded he will. We were talking last night…'

'When and where?'

'Oh, it was all very proper, we promenaded round the room when Beth ran away.'

'I did not run away. I simply did not care to talk to him any more,' Beth interjected, but no one paid her any heed, being more concerned with what had happened between Mr Andrew Melhurst and Olivia.

'What did you talk about?' Harriet asked her younger daughter.

'He asked me if I had anyone in mind and of course I could not tell him straight out, but I said I might have and he understood I meant him.'

'Livvy!' Beth was appalled. 'How could you be so forward?'

'Isn't that how it's done?' Livvy asked, affecting innocence. 'Words are spoken that mean something else, it's a kind of code to let the man know you would not be averse to receiving his offer. How else is he to know?'

'Oh, dear,' Harriet said, though Sophie was finding it difficult not to laugh. 'I do hope the poor man does not think he is under an obligation…'

'Then that would be two obligations he has and he cannot answer both,' Beth said sharply.

'What do you mean?' Livvy demanded.

'Why, he has already told Uncle James he would offer for me, being an honourable man, or so he likes us to think.'

Livvy turned to the Duchess. 'Aunt Sophie, is this true?'

'Yes, but I believe it was said in the heat of the moment. The Duke appreciated the offer, but declined, saying it was not necessary.'

'Which was a great relief,' Beth said.

'You could do worse,' Harriet said.

'I would not dream of accepting him simply to appease his conscience,' she said. 'He is too top-lofty by far, continually reminding me of how we met when he knows perfectly well we are all trying to pretend it did not happen.'

'At least he has seen the worst of you,' Sophie put in. 'There can be no unpleasant surprises, which often happens when a young man offers for someone he has not had the opportunity to get to know well.'

'A man would be a fool to offer for anyone he did not know through and through,' Beth said. 'And the same applies to a woman. She should not take a man simply because he is handsome and has deep pockets. It is the character of the man that matters.' She stopped suddenly. How well did she know Mr Melhurst? Not very well if he could flirt so openly with her sister after asking her to walk with him. She was suddenly reminded of Toby. They had grown up together and she had always thought she knew him, but that was obviously not the case because she would never have foreseen that he would go off without saying goodbye to her and then hand her over to a complete stranger as if washing his hands of her.

'True,' her mother agreed, 'but we need not concern ourselves with it for the moment. The Season is only just begun and who knows what might have transpired by the end of it?'

Their court gowns arrived the following morning and they congregated in the Duchess's boudoir to try them on. Because they were not yet out, both gowns were white and of a simple style with waists where they should be and modest necklines, but that did not mean they were simple. The bodices were heavily encrusted with shining beads and embroidered with swirls of silver thread. The skirts were full and round over half a dozen petticoats, which in themselves were works of art. The sleeves were tight to the elbow and then flared out in a froth of silvery lace. The only difference between the two was the colour of the ribbon that encompassed their waists and were looped through the hem of the skirt to reveal the topmost petticoat. Beth's was lime green, Livvy's pink.

'Oh, they are beautiful,' Harriet said. 'Sophie, you have made my daughters into duchesses.'

'Not quite that,' Sophie said. 'Bachelor dukes are few and far between, but the girls will undoubtedly attract the attention of the highest in the land.'

'Ugh! Not the King!' Beth exclaimed. 'I could not bear to be noticed by him.'

'He could hardly fail to notice you,' Harriet said. 'You will be making your curtsy to him.'

'I did not mean that and you know it.'

'He only likes grandmothers,' Livvy said. 'We shall be quite safe.'

'He might not even speak to you,' her mother said. 'You will line up with all the others and curtsy as you pass him. That's all there is to it. The King is not seen so much in public these days and will retire as soon as the line has passed him.'

'And for that you have bought all this finery?' Beth queried. 'It is an unwarranted extravagance.'

'I did not buy it,' Harriet said. 'You are indebted to your uncle and he will not have you outdone by anyone. And the gowns can be adapted for balls afterwards.'

Miss Andover was required to dress their hair and help them into silk stockings and satin shoes and hand them reticules and fans, so that they could practise walking up and down and making a full curtsy.

'I shall be thankful when it is all over,' Beth said.

'Yes, and then we shall be out,' Livvy added. 'We can go to balls and routs and wear colours and flirt with the eligibles and break their hearts.'

'I hope you will do no such thing, Olivia,' their mother said.

'All except one,' Livvy added, grinning mischievously at Beth. 'And you know who he is.'

No one answered her because the Duke came in at that point and added his compliments to their mother's. 'I shall be the envy of everyone,' he said.

'Will there be many there?' Beth asked.

'No, not many, not by the King's standards—a hundred, perhaps a few more. He becomes tired very easily these days and the preparations for the coronation are particularly fatiguing, so he is curtailing his public appearances and saving his strength for that day. It will be a prodigious occasion.'

'And will the Queen be there?'

'His Majesty has said not. We are making no arrangements for her attendance.'

'I feel sorry for her,' Beth said. 'How terrible it must be to be trapped in a loveless marriage. I would rather remain unwed.'

'Then I wish you would fall desperately in love,' Livvy said. 'Otherwise you will not be married before me.'

Beth did not deign to answer, but turned to ask Miss Andover to help her out of her gown. She thought Livvy was being particularly tiresome, but her sister did not know about the strange feelings that beset her whenever the subject of marriage was mentioned, the sudden vision of a tall fair man with amused blue eyes which came before her and prevented her from seeing properly. It was all because of that encounter on the docks and the way he had compounded her embarrassment. If only she could put the clock back!

She had a little respite from her troubled thoughts when the Duke took them to Carlton House. The King was very, very fat, and weighed down by clothes and jewels, but he was gracious and, contrary to her mother's predictions, he did speak to them. 'London is indeed fortunate to have such beauties to grace the social calendar,' he said, stepping forward and taking Beth's hand to raise her from her curtsy. 'We shall hope to see more of you in the coming days.' Then it was Livvy's turn and he said much the same thing to her. And before they had time to draw breath, their uncle was ushering them into another room where refreshments were being served. An hour later they were on their way home.

'That went very well,' James said. 'Everyone will have noted that His Majesty spoke to you both.'

'I expect it was because you are on his staff,' Beth said.

'Perhaps,' he admitted.

'He was more agreeable that I expected,' Livvy said. 'We shall be in great demand, now, don't you think?'

'We would have be anyway,' Beth said. 'Everyone will try to use us to solicit Uncle James. They think he will get them an invitation to the coronation.'

'If they do, they will be disappointed,' James said. 'I work by strict rules, which is why the King trusts me.'

It seemed Beth's predictions were to prove correct when the next morning the callers started to arrive. Those who had been at the Duchess's soirée used it as an excuse to come and thank their hostess and offer invitations of their own. Those who had not been there, but had heard of the great honour the King had bestowed on the Harley sisters, came out of curiosity and to make themselves known so that they might be included in future invitations. A large proportion of them were young men, all hoping to be noticed and vying with each other to escort the young ladies to this or that function: a carriage ride in the park, a picnic, the theatre or a concert. Beth and Livvy were hard put to know which to accept, and usually deferred the decision to their mother.

One who came was Mrs Edward Melhurst, arriving on the arm of her husband. She was several years older than he was, though the make-up she wore was intended to make her look younger. She was statuesque and wearing a hat from which three great pink feathers emerged. It was so tall she had to duck to get through the door.

'My dear Duchess,' she greeted Sophie in a voice that carried across the room to where Beth was talking to the roly-poly Lady Myers, an old friend of the Duchess's. 'I simply had to come and let you know we were come to town. I was sure you could not have known or you would surely have asked us to call. After all, we have been acquainted these many years...'

'Oh, to be sure,' Sophie said, having no notion at all who the woman was. 'How do you do?'

'Oh, I am very well and so is Mr Melhurst.' She indicated her husband, who bowed to the Duchess. 'But we are both fatigued from looking after his lordship and thought a little time in town might be just the thing to revive us…'

'His lordship?'

'Why, Lord Melhurst. Did Cousin Andrew not tell you we have taken on the task of seeing to Grandfather's affairs? He has become increasingly feeble minded and, with Drew out of the country, he has needed us and very grateful he is too. He has loaned us the house in Mount Street so that we might entertain a little. On Andrew's behalf, of course, with him being a bachelor and having no hostess. One happy family we are and we shall all be delighted if you and Lady Harley and her charming daughters would honour us by accepting an invitation to an evening of music next Friday week.' She stopped for want of breath, just long enough for Sophie to reply.

'I am not sure if we are free that evening.'

'Then I shall change the date. Drew would be so disappointed if you could not come. He has told us how condescending you have been towards him and I know he would like to repay your hospitality.'

'In that case, I shall consult Lady Harley and let you know if we are free,' Sophie said. 'Please do take some refreshment before you leave.'

It was a pointed dismissal which would have made

a lesser person quail, but not Kitty. 'Thank you, your Grace, I shall await your reply.' And with that she almost dragged her husband across the room and out of the door, almost knocking off her hat in the process.

Sophie crossed the room to Harriet and the girls, who had heard every word as everyone else had. 'Well, what do you make of that?' she asked.

'I do not know. Do you think Mr Melhurst sent her?'

'I have no idea, but it seems to give the lie to the gossip about the cousins having a falling out. Or, if they did, it must have been mended.'

'Shall we go to her musical evening?'

'Why not? I am curious, aren't you?'

They would have been even more curious if they had heard the exchange between Andrew and Kitty on the doorstep. He was about to lift the knocker when the door opened and Teddy and Kitty emerged.

'What are you doing here?' he demanded.

'Why should I not call on the Duchess?' Kitty asked. 'We are known to her and, being in town, it is only politeness.'

'And what did you talk about?'

'Oh, this and that. I issued an invitation on your behalf.'

'On my behalf? You had no right to do that. Teddy, I wonder you allowed it.'

'Oh, Kitty will have her way.' His cousin shrugged.

'And it can do no harm. It is only for a musical evening at Mount Street on Friday week.'

'The house is shut up. I have been staying in a hotel.'

'Then we will open it up,' Kitty said. 'Grandfather told you to do so, didn't he? And you will surely wish to return the Duchess's hospitality.'

'And what did she say?'

'She will come.'

He was becoming angrier by the minute. 'How can I organise a musical evening?'

'Oh, you do not need to. I shall do it all for you.'

'I wish you had asked me.'

'Why? You are too slow to take advantage of opportunities when they arise. Fate sent you to Belfont House and you should seize the chance…'

'To do what?'

'You cannot be blind to the possibilities, Cousin. Being an associate of a Duke and one so much in Royal favour will open any number of doors, not only for you—'

'I am not a toadeater.' He paused, suddenly aware of the significance of something she had said. 'What do you mean, fate sent me to Belfont House?'

'What else can you call it but fate? To meet a young lady on the docks, quite by chance, only the day after arriving back in England, cannot be called anything else but fate, especially when that young lady is a member of an illustrious family and is there alone quite unbeknown to her relations.'

'How did you learn about that?'

'Simmonds told us. He was there on the docks, loading your luggage, if you recall, and he heard every word. As soon as he got back to Heathlands, he asked your coachman what had transpired.'

'And how did Simmonds come to be talking to you about my affairs?' he demanded angrily. 'I'll have his head for it.'

'Simmonds is a loyal servant to your grandfather. He was concerned that you were about to fall into a bumblebath and the old man's health will not stand any more upsets.'

'And you think…' He looked up when he heard a discreet cough and realised the footman was still holding the door open for him and had probably heard every word. 'I have changed my mind,' he told him, and seizing his tormentors by the arms, propelled them away from the door towards the carriage in which they had arrived.

'Oh, Andrew, do not be such a glum pot,' she said, as he almost pushed her into her seat. 'We did it for you.'

He did not believe that for a moment, but if the invitation had been issued and accepted, there was nothing he could do about it without making a cake of himself. He stood to one side while Teddy climbed in, then shut the carriage door. 'You may come to Mount Street tomorrow morning,' he said coldly. 'We will discuss this then.' He stood back and watched the carriage out of sight.

He wondered whether to go back to the house to find out exactly what had been said, but that would look very strange and so he turned away and strode off down the road. If Melhurst House was to be opened, there was much to do. The few staff who kept the place secure would have to be augmented, the dust covers taken off all the furniture, the rooms aired and supplies of food got in. Ensuring everything was as it should be to entertain a Duchess would keep him busy for the next few days, just when he was hoping to see more of Miss Harley.

Somehow, he had to find a way through the wall she had built up around herself. He guessed it was defensive, though why she felt she needed to defend herself from him he did not know. Until he had breached those defences, he would get nowhere with her. And it had become important that he did. He supposed he had known all along that she was the woman with whom he wanted to share the rest of his life. She was so special, so out of the ordinary, so exactly the kind of wife he wanted, it was as if everything that had gone on before: his immature adventures with the demi-reps on the edge of society, his self-imposed exile, his work as a botanist and his return to England had all been leading to his meeting with her. Kitty had been right about that, even if her motives were questionable. He smiled a little to himself. He would go along with her outrageous plans so long as they suited him. Anything to further his acquaintance with Miss Elizabeth Harley, because, and he admitted this to himself for the first time, he had fallen in love with her.

The Duchess's callers left at last and after nuncheon, taken in a small dining room on the ground floor, Beth decided to walk in the gardens of St James's Park with Jamie and his governess, which she enjoyed because Jamie was such a delight with his enthusiastic chatter. They were just returning to the house when they met Andrew, striding purposefully in the direction of Mount Street, having paid off his hotel and arranged for his luggage to be transported to Melhurst House. That he had deliberately walked out of his way on the chance he might encounter her, he would not for a moment have admitted to anyone.

'Good afternoon, Miss Harley. He doffed his hat, then smiled at Jamie. 'My lord Viscount. How are you?'

Jamie giggled. 'I remember you. You came to see Mama. I said you could call me Jamie.'

'So you did.'

Miss Gordon took the boy's hand and led him into the house, leaving Andrew facing Beth. 'Are you enjoying your stay in London, Miss Harley?' he asked, wishing she would smile. He knew she could smile, could tease and laugh, but now she seemed almost grim. He wondered what he had done, apart from trying to rescue her from a bumblebath.

'Oh, yes, there is so much to do and see.'

'More gardens?'

He was on safer ground there and this time she did smile. 'Jamie and I have been taking a stroll through St James's. The garden is well kept, but not significant.'

'True. I doubt exotic specimens would last very long there.'

'No, but we should not forget our more humble native plants.'

'Oh, indeed not, some of them are very beautiful.' He was looking into her face and smiling, and she found herself growing uncomfortably warm.

'I must go in.'

'Yes. Good afternoon, Miss Harley. I shall hope to see you at Mount Street on Friday week.'

'We are all looking forward to it, Mr Melhurst.'

He replaced his hat and strode off down the road, leaving her to enter the house. He evidently knew nothing of the gossip or he surely would not have behaved so openly. It might not be true, of course, but how long would it be before he heard it and what would he do about it?

The days passed with more shopping and making calls and more young men dancing attendance, and in that time they did not set eyes on Mr Melhurst, which Beth's head told her was a mercy, but her heart conveyed something very different.

Olivia's horse had arrived at the mews and she was impatient to be out riding. Lord Gorsham, had asked if he might be permitted to ride with her and, as it was necessary for her to be chaperoned, he had offered to provide Beth with a hack in order to fulfil that role. 'It will save his Grace the trouble,' he said. 'Glad to do it.'

'Oh, do say yes,' Livvy had begged her. 'I cannot wait to be on horseback. It will do you good too, you have been looking a little downpin these last few days.'

'I am perfectly well and I should enjoy a ride if his lordship would be so good as to find me a mount.'

And so it had been arranged and on Friday morning Grimble brought Zephyr to the door just as Henry arrived on his own mount, leading another for Beth, a quiet mare called Lady. The girls were in new riding habits, Livvy's was dark blue and Beth's forest green. Both wore fetching hats with tall crowns and brims trimmed with sweeping feathers. He sprang down, described each an elegant bow accompanied by a wordy compliment, which made them smile, then helped them to mount and all three set off at a decorous walk to Hyde Park.

They had not been on The Ride long when they met Andrew, trotting towards them on Firefly. He halted and swept off his hat. 'Ladies, your obedient. Good morning, Gorsham.'

'Where've you been this last week?' Henry demanded. 'Haven't seen hide nor hair of you.'

'Had things to do.' He was speaking to Henry, but looking at Beth. She looked pale and her amber eyes had lost some of their brilliance. Perhaps town life did not suit her or had the gossip about her being alone on the docks already spread? He would not put it past his cousin's wife to make sure it did. What he had ever found attractive in the woman he could not now remember. She and Teddy had arrived at Melhurst House the morning after the Duchess's soirée, accompanied by a second carriage bearing a load of boxes, bags and trunks, intending to move in.

'Must remain united, so Grandfather says,' Teddy told him. 'And hotels are damned expensive, don't you know. And they don't suit little Georgie.' This was a reference to their six-year-old son whom they had brought with them. Why the child could not have been left at home with his nurse, Drew did not know. In no time at all they had made themselves at home and begun the business of preparing for the musical evening, ordering food, wine, flowers and musicians, all to be charged to Andrew, of course. They had produced an invitation list that covered several pages of Kitty's close scrawl. Half of them he had never heard of, but Teddy assured him they were all top-of-the-trees *ton*, and as he had been out of the country he could not argue with him. Now everything was ready and he had come out for a ride to clear his head and escape from Kitty's chatter.

'I hope you are not too busy to join us,' Livvy said. 'Poor Lord Gorsham has been obliged to entertain us both. Do make a fourth.'

'I shall be delighted,' he said. 'If Miss Harley is agreeable.' This was addressed to Beth.

'Please do, sir,' she said, forcing herself to sound neutral and bending forward to pat Lady's the neck to hide the shaking of her hands.

He turned his horse about and somehow contrived to ride beside her, leaving Livvy to ride beside Henry. 'Are you well, Miss Harley?' he asked.

'Very well, Mr Melhurst.'

They rode on in silence for a minute and when it seemed she had no more to say, he said. 'I see Miss Olivia has brought her mount to London. It is an exceptional mare for one so young.'

'Yes, Uncle James bought Zephyr for Livvy when she outgrew her last pony. She is excessively fond of riding.'

'And you are not?'

'I enjoy it well enough, but it is not a passion with me as it is with my sister.'

'No, yours is for botany. How did your interest begin?'

'Watching the gardener at Beechgrove and helping him with his tasks and then I found that Toby—Mr Kendall—had been keenly interested in botany ever since he read Sydney Parkinson's account of Sir Joseph Banks's journey with Captain Cook to the Antipodes. It was given to him as a present by one of the masters at his school and he lent it to me and that fired my interest. My uncle also has a copy in the library at Belfont House and I am reading parts of it to Jamie…'

'Surely he is a little young for that?'

'Naturally he does not understand all the Latin names, but then neither do I, not all of them, but he is thrilled by the adventures and the dangers the explorers overcame and he likes the pictures.'

'I collect that is something you wish you could do yourself. Go exploring, I mean.'

'I know that is not possible.' She spoke sharply because she was suddenly back on the East India docks, being waved at by a departing Toby, reminding her of her mortification. 'I would be laughed to scorn if I attempted it and I doubt if any sea captain would agree to carry me.'

'He would if you were accompanied by a husband.'

She twisted in the saddle to look at him. He was riding smoothly, his head half-turned towards her, apparently completely unperturbed, unaware of the hammering of her heart. 'Have you been talking to Livvy?'

'On what subject?'

She felt the colour flood her face. He knew perfectly well what she had meant, but he was trying to make her speak of it, to talk about her marriage prospects. It was very uncivil of him. 'About me.'

'I have had some conversation with your sister, Miss Harley, as you know, but it is not my nature to talk about a lady behind her back. That smacks of gossip.'

'And you, of course, would know all about that.' She had not meant to say that; it had simply popped out of her mouth of its own accord and she immediately regretted it. His expression darkened and she could tell by the rigid jutting of his jaw that he was annoyed.

'Oh, I see,' he said. 'You have heard.'

'I am sorry, I should not have said that. Please forgive me. I had no right…'

'Miss Harley, I give you the right. Your good opinion of me is important to me. If anything has been said to sully that, then I should like to know of it.'

'Nothing has been said to alter my opinion of you,

sir. It is as it was. I was referring to the possibility that my actions might have caused talk.' Now, instead of him reminding her of her humiliation, she was doing it herself. It was as if she were castigating herself for being so foolish as to fall in love with someone to whom she owed a huge debt. Somehow it doubled it.

'If they had, I would certainly wish to do something about it…'

He was, she realised, speaking of that strange offer to her uncle, as if such an offer would ever be taken seriously by her. 'I should not like you to think that you felt yourself under any obligation to me,' she said.

'Nothing is further from my thoughts, Miss Harley.'

They had reached the end of the Ride and neither had spoken to Olivia or Henry who had been following them, having their own conversation. Beth was not sure that it was quite proper and wondered who was supposed to be chaperoning whom. They turned to go back the way they had come, which meant that Henry and Livvy were now a little ahead of them.

'Oh, I am bored with this walking,' Livvy cried out suddenly. 'It is no exercise for Zephyr at all.' And with that she set her mare at the railings and was over them and pounding the grass towards a copse of trees, near the great lake.

'Livvy!' Beth called, but her sister took no notice.

'My God! She has a prodigious seat,' Henry exclaimed. 'I'm after her.' The words were hardly out of his mouth before he was leaping the rails and following at full gallop.

Andrew looked at Beth, who had halted and was staring after her sister in perplexity. She showed no sign of wanting to follow and he could hardly leave her. They watched helplessly as Henry caught up with Livvy and the pair of them raced towards the trees. Livvy's hat had come off and her hair was streaming out behind her. Even at that distance they could hear her laughing. And what was worse, several other riders had stopped to watch and comment. 'Go to it, little lady,' a voice called and Beth turned to see Viscount Rapworth and two of his friends watching in laughing admiration. She wished the ground would swallow her.

'Come,' Andrew he said gently. To go after them would make matters worse, but they could not sit there gazing after them, which would draw attention to themselves. 'Let us ride towards the Stanhope Gate. They will be sure to join us there.'

They began to walk their horses slowly towards the gate, both conscious of the stares of other riders and the people on the carriage way who looked with disapproval on the unchaperoned young lady. She could imagine their whispers. 'Is that not one of the Harley sisters, niece to the Duke of Belfont? How disgraceful. Wait until the Duke hears of it.' And he would hear of it, she was sure.

'It was not your fault,' he told her, guessing her thoughts. 'You were not to know your sister would be so foolish.'

'That makes two of us,' she said, with a dismal attempt at humour. 'The Harley sisters will become notorious for eccentric behaviour.'

'Oh, come, it is not as bad as that,' he said. 'It was youthful high spirits on the part of your sister, nothing more.'

'Are properly brought-up young ladies allowed youthful high spirits?'

'Naturally they are. She will be forgiven.'

'Will I?' It was a heartfelt plea, though why she should ask it of him she did not know. 'Will I ever live it down?'

'What are you blaming yourself for? You cannot be responsible for your sister's actions.'

'But I should be. She is younger than I and I should set a good example. Instead, I—' She stopped. Her own indiscretion was going to haunt her to her grave.

'How so? No one knows of your little adventure except close family and me, and you may rest assured I shall say nothing.' Even as he spoke he remembered Katherine. She knew and he could think of no one more dangerous.

'But we are riding unaccompanied now and the whole world is looking on.'

'There is a cure for that, my dear.' He paused, drew breath and went on before his courage could desert him. 'Marry me.'

She was so startled she tugged too hard on the reins and her mare objected by prancing about and flinging her head up. Bringing Lady under control occupied several seconds, which seemed like hours to Andrew. When the horse was brought to a standstill, Beth turned towards him, her face pink with anger. 'Is that your idea of a jest, Mr Melhurst?' she demanded and then she began to laugh. It was a cracked humourless sound that startled him into reaching out to touch her arm. She shrugged him off and began walking her horse forward, careful not to go faster, which she would have liked to do. There had already been enough for the gabble grinders to get their teeth into without adding to it by being seen fleeing from her escort.

He followed half a head behind, not speaking, not trying to explain himself. He knew he had made a sad business of what should have been a loving proposal and he had cooked his goose.

A few minutes later, Livvy and Henry joined them. Livvy was flushed and excited and Lord Gorsham was grinning. No one spoke as all four rode back to South Audley Street.

Chapter Six

Beth would have given almost anything not to have to go to Melhurst House that evening, but could think of no excuse that would satisfy her mother or her sister, who was determined to go. She had gone to Livvy's room when they went up to change out of their habits after their return and had taken her to task over what she had done. 'I doubt we will live it down,' she said. 'And what will Uncle James say when he hears of it?'

'You surely do not mean to tell him?'

'No, I shall not tell him, but there are any number of other people who will. The ride and carriageway were packed with witnesses. Whatever were you thinking of?'

'I was bored and Zephyr needed the exercise.'

'Did you not give a thought to the consequences? Lord Gorsham chasing after you and me left alone with Mr Melhurst…'

'Yes, I am sorry about that. I thought it would be Mr Melhurst who came after me…'

'And that would have made it right, would it?'

'It might have made him realise his true feelings if he thought I might be in danger.'

'You were never in any physical danger,' Beth said grimly. 'It was your reputation as a chaste young lady that was at stake and you compromised me as well as yourself…'

'You are quite capable of doing that to yourself, Beth. I did not dress up in Papa's old clothes and climb aboard a stagecoach and make a fool of myself at the docks.'

'Livvy, that is unkind. I bitterly regret what I did and I am thankful that no one knows of it.'

'Oh, but they do. It is the talk of the town. Lord Gorsham told me.'

'Oh, no!' She was horrified. 'Mr Melhurst promised me he would never speak of it.'

'Well, someone has. Oh, do not look so downpin, Lord Gorsham said it was of no consequence, we are so rich and so well connected that no one will think a thing of it.'

'Uncle James will. He will be furious, especially after the trouble he went to, to have us received by the King. It might even cost him his position at court.'

'Fustian! You don't really believe that, do you?'

'It could. Even if it does not, all our invitations will

be rescinded. No one will call and the Duchess's friends will cut us dead. What will you give for your chances of finding a suitable husband then?'

'No worse than they are now. Mr Melhurst knows us for what we are and I intend to turn it to my advantage.'

'Livvy, I beg you not to. I fear for you.'

'I can look after myself.'

'Promise me you will never do anything like that again.'

'Of course I won't. You can't use the same ruse twice over. It becomes too obvious. Now, go and change or we shall be late.'

'I would rather not go.'

'What! And have your worst fears confirmed? No, Beth, you must go and give the lie to the tattlers.'

It was unfortunate that Olivia was right. Beth could do nothing but dress decorously and behave like the well brought-up young lady she was supposed to be— the well brought-up young lady she truly was. As for that ridiculous suggestion of Mr Melhurst's, she would pretend it had never been uttered. But, oh, how she wished he had truly meant it and meant it for the right reasons! She would never agree to marry him in order to prevent scandal even if her sister was evidently prepared to do so.

She dressed in a soft apricot silk. Two wide bands at the hem were trimmed with ruched satin ribbon and there was more ruching on the three-quarter-length sleeves. The boat-shaped neck was filled with lace and fastened with a tiny posy of silk flowers. She refused to let Miss Andover thread ribbons and pearls through her hair, saying it was too ostentatious for the occasion. Slipping her feet into satin pumps, she picked up her beaded reticule and went downstairs to join the Duchess, her mother and Livvy.

The road outside Melhurst House was crammed with vehicles and Beth's heart sank. This was no ordinary evening of music; half the *beau monde* was already here. It was several minutes before their carriage arrived at the front door and they were able to make their way into the house. It was not a particularly large dwelling and the crowd of guests made it seem smaller. At the top of the stairs they were announced by a footman in outdated livery and made their way into the salon, where Mrs Melhurst came forward to greet them.

She had eschewed the hat with feathers for a turban of cerise satin on which a diamond clip sparkled. Her dress, of the same material, was wide skirted and covered with colourful embroidery. 'Duchess, how pleased I am that you have honoured us,' she said. 'And Lady Harley and her famous daughters. Welcome. Welcome.'

'What do you think she meant by famous?' Beth whispered to Livvy as they made their way into the room.

'Nothing. She is a gusher and is basking in the glow of being known to Aunt Sophie.'

'I hope you are right.'

'Ladies, you are come.' Andrew had seen them arrive and detached himself from the group he had been talking to in order to pay his respects. 'I am honoured.' He executed an elegant leg to encompass them all. 'Will you take a glass of wine before the proceedings begin? Or perhaps ratafia?' He clicked his fingers at a waiter.

'Wine, please,' Livvy said, earning a reproving look from her mother, which she ignored.

The Duchess chose to drink a glass of wine, and Lady Harley and Beth followed suit. Beth was not a wine drinker and would normally have chosen ratafia or a cordial, but she needed something to give her a lift. The sight of Mr Melhurst in his black superfine evening coat and white ruffled shirt had seriously disturbed her all over again. He was looking at her now, his head on one side, his blue eyes taking in every detail of her dress and demeanour. She lifted her head and put her chin up to gaze straight back at him, her expression so haughty, he immediately looked away and began a conversation with her mother about the weather.

Beth turned from him and, espying Lord Gorsham

talking to Lady Myers, strolled over to join them, anything to get away from *that man*. 'Beth, you are in looks tonight,' her ladyship said. 'That peachy colour suits you.'

'Thank you, my lady.'

'You have not forgotten my ball, have you? Sophie tells me it is to be your first after your come-out, so we must make it memorable.'

'I had not forgot,' she said. 'That is, if you still want us to come.'

'Why should I not?' She looked puzzled. 'Oh, I collect you are talking about that incident in the park this afternoon—think nothing of it. I do not.'

'You are very kind, my lady, but it is obvious, from the speed with which the story has circulated, that others are not so sanguine.'

'It always amazes me how quickly these things get about and are exaggerated,' Lord Gorsham put in. 'I shall certainly squash any rumours I hear.'

'Then you did not have a hand in spreading them?'

'Great heavens, no! I am not such a muckworm. I hold you and your delightful sister in high esteem…'

'Then why did you gallop after Livvy and compound her folly?'

'Couldn't let her go off alone, could I? She might have been thrown or ducked in the lake. Fine sort of friend I'd be to let that happen.'

'You are making a mountain out of a molehill, my dear,' her ladyship said, putting her hand on Beth's arm. 'Olivia is young and full of energy, people understand that.' She smiled suddenly. 'From what I have heard, most who saw her admired her prowess.'

'Well, why wouldn't they?' demanded Henry. 'Never saw a filly with a better seat, nor as much bottom. Girl after my own heart, she is.'

Beth managed a smile. Perhaps she was making too much of it, especially as she was not without fault herself. Mr Melhurst's answer to her concerns was to suggest marrying her, something she would not contemplate, unless he came to her on bended knee and told her he loved her. And pigs might fly before that top-lofty man did that. Would marriage to Livvy be Lord Gorsham's solution too? And if it was, what would her sister make of it? She had set her heart on Andrew Melhurst. Oh, what a dreadful muddle it all was!

A gong sounded and their hostess announced that the musicians were ready in the next room and asked everyone to take their places.

The room had been laid out with rows of chairs facing a small dais, which had been erected at the end on which a quartet of musicians were poised to begin. It was evidently going to be a professional recital and not, as Livvy had supposed, musical items provided by the family and guests. Beth, taking her place on one of the chairs, was glad of that. She could listen to the music and relax and no one would notice that she was preoccupied.

All went well until the interval when the musicians left the dais to be offered refreshments in an adjoining room and the audience was left to amuse itself for half an hour. Beth, who had somehow become detached from the rest of her family, found herself listening to the conversation of two people behind her, a man and a woman.

'I only came out of curiosity.' Although the woman was whispering it was a whisper that carried as well as if she had been speaking in a normal voice. 'To think they're living under the same roof. It makes you wonder…'

'Gammon! She married his cousin.'

'Only because he abandoned her. Any gentleman worth the name is supposed to take care of a mistress he no longer needs, not turn his back on her.'

'He hasn't turned his back on her, has he? She is living here with her husband.'

'Do you think Teddy knew of the affair when he married her?'

'Everyone knew. Why d'you think the young pup left the country?'

'He's not a pup now.' This was followed by a

giggle. 'Fine dog he is and single too. If I were a few years younger…'

The man chuckled. 'I heard Lord Melhurst has ordered him to find a wife. The old man don't like Teddy above half. My money's on one of the Harley chits.'

'You never mean the Duke of Belfont's nieces? His Grace would never countenance it. He'd expect them to fly higher than that.'

'We shall see. Ten guineas says I am right.'

'Drew can't marry them both.'

'I know that. I'm backing the elder. I heard he has already compromised her, driving her about in his carriage and riding in the park without a chaperon.'

'Is that so?' The woman laughed. 'I would not for the world leave town this Season, even if there was no coronation.'

Beth could take no more. She stood up and, without turning to face the speakers, pushed her way along the row and out into the aisle. Here she paused, wondering where her mother and sister were. She must tell them what she had heard and they must return to Beechgrove as soon as possible. Let the gossiping woman enjoy her Season in town without the titillation of watching her and her sister being made laughing stocks.

She caught sight of Livvy at the back of the hall surrounded by young dandies, including Viscount

Rapworth. Her sister was loving the attention. Afraid of yet another indiscretion, Beth made her way over to them.

'Oh, Beth, I am having such fun. All these gallant gentlemen want to take me riding.'

'I'll warrant they do,' Beth said, trying to disguise her agitation and smile at them. 'And what have you said?'

'I have said I must ask Mama, of course. And I insist on you coming too.'

'Oh, do, Miss Harley,' they chorused.

'As my sister has told you, we shall have to consult our mother. We have a great many engagements. Now, if you will excuse us, I believe the musicians are returning.' She took her sister's arm and almost dragged her away.

'Beth you are hurting me. What have I done wrong now?'

'Nothing.' She released her grip. 'I have just heard people talking about us. It was dreadful.'

'They do say eavesdroppers never hear good of themselves.'

'I was not eavesdropping. They were sitting behind me and talking very loud. We have to find Mama and go home.'

'We can't. What will everyone think if we disappear halfway through the evening? Besides, I want to ask Mama about going riding with Viscount Rapworth.'

'I thought you were set on Mr Melhurst.'

'It won't hurt him to have a little competition.'

'Livvy!'

'Well, we cannot go now, the orchestra is tuning up again and we must go to our seats. And stop clucking round me like an old hen, Beth. I can look after myself.' And with that she flounced into the nearest chair, depriving the young gentleman who had been sitting there during the first half of the entertainment.

Beth did not want to go back to her seat and risk being recognised and so she left the room quietly and returned to the salon where a handful of people who could not find seats in the music room were chatting quietly. She found a seat behind a potted palm that at any other time would have interested her as a botanical specimen, but which she hardly noticed, except to decide it would make a useful screen.

The music, relayed as it was through a wall, soothed her, and she was set about reviewing her situation and that of her sister. She could see nothing for it but to put everything before her mother and leave her to decide what to do. She would not tell her of Mr Melhurst's strange proposal because he had not truly meant it and she certainly did not mean to accept even if he had. Ordered to marry, was he? And people making wagers? And abandoning his mistress. And what was worse, compromising her. How had that got about?

'Miss Harley, does the music not please you?'

She turned to find Andrew standing beside her, smiling down at her, and all her hard-won composure left her. If he thought smiling like that would melt her heart, he was wrong, very, very wrong. She would never marry him, not to save her own reputation and certainly not to save his. 'It is very fine, but I have the headache.'

'I am sorry for that, Miss Harley. Would you like to rest somewhere? I am sure Mrs Melhurst will find you a quiet room upstairs. Shall I ask her?'

'No!' It was blurted out in an overloud whisper that betrayed her agitation. 'No, thank you, sir,' she repeated more normally. 'I shall be better directly.'

He pulled up a chair and sat beside her. 'Miss Harley, if I could relieve your unease, I would willingly do so. Tell me how.'

'Then go away.'

He stood up. 'Very well. I will inflict myself upon you no longer. Good evening, Miss Harley.' He bowed stiffly and strode away.

He did not see the one bright tear that squeezed itself over her eyelashes and ran down her cheek, nor the wild scrabbling into her reticule to find her scrap of handkerchief. He might have felt somewhat better if he had.

It was not until the following morning that Beth was able to relay to her mother the conversation she had overheard. 'Mama, we cannot let it go on,' she said. 'Our names are being linked with his.'

She had not gone down to breakfast, pleading a headache that was now a fact. Her head was pounding from lying awake all night, and her mother had come to her room to console her and offer a tisane. Instead she had been confronted by a tearful daughter and such a tale of such woe it was not difficult to divine the real reason behind it. Beth was in love with Mr Melhurst and being torn apart by conflicting emotions.

'There will always be gossipmongers, Beth,' she said, taking her hand. 'And they are skilful at making something of nothing. Do you truly think Mr Melhurst is such a rakeshame?'

'I do not know what to think. I am so confused. And it is all my fault.'

'How can it be your fault?'

'If I had not been so determined to see Toby off, I would never have met him and he would not have come here, nor to Beechgrove, and Livvy would not be setting her cap at him and people would not be talking about us…'

Harriet smiled. 'Which do you think is worse, people talking or the fact that you think Livvy is enamoured of him?'

'I do not know. Both. She will have her heart broken.'

'Oh, dearest, I do not think so. Livvy's heart is very

robust, you know. Now, dry your eyes and I will ask James to endeavour to get to the bottom of the rumours. He will know what to do.'

'Oh, you will never tell Uncle James…'

'I think I must, but I will talk to your Aunt Sophie first. And I might have a word or two with Livvy.'

'Oh, please do not scold her. She does not understand.'

'Then she must be made to understand. I know very well she finds town life restricting, but she must remember she is a member of an illustrious family and must behave accordingly.' She stopped to smile at her daughter and take her face in her hands. 'As you must. And that means being above gossip and holding your head up. You can do that, can't you?'

Beth nodded and Harriet bent forward and kissed her brow. 'Now wash away those tears and come downstairs. We are all going on a picnic this afternoon to Hampstead.'

'All?'

'Yes, your uncle and aunt, Jamie and Miss Gordon and we three. No one else. It will put the roses back in your cheeks, you see.'

The picnic had been Sophie's idea. Jamie, like the rest of the family, liked to be outdoors and there was little to do except go for carriage rides with his governess or walks in the gardens with anyone he could persuade to go with him. He should have been left at Dersingham Park, but Sophie could not bear to be parted from him and, as she was obliged to be in town until after the coronation, had brought him with her. Today was to be his treat.

The little outing required two coaches, the Belfont chaise and Lady Harley's coach, not only for the passengers but in order to take the picnic and a maidservant who travelled on the box beside the Duke's driver. They left at noon and arrived a little over an hour later. As soon as the coaches came to a stop, Jamie was out and demanding to go for a walk.

The maidservant, the Harley coachman and his lordship's driver were left to look after the carriages and unload the picnic things while everyone else strolled over the heath with Jamie chattering excitedly. It was so good to be in the fresh air, away from the bustle of London, and Beth slowly began to relax.

There were wild flowers growing on the wayside and Jamie set about picking a little posy of them. 'What are they called, Cousin Beth?' he asked.

'You know these two, surely?' she asked, pointing. 'That is a buttercup and that is a daisy.'

'Yes. And this one is a harebell and that a speedwell. Here is vetch and this is shepherd's purse.'

'Were they brought here by the plant hunters?'

'No, they have always been here. But many of the flowers in your garden and glasshouse at home were brought by men like Sir Joseph Banks, flowers like delphinium, gladioli, amaryllis, clematis and red-hot pokers.'

'And did they have adventures like Sir Joseph did?'

'Yes, they did.'

'I think I should like to go plant hunting when I am old enough,' he said solemnly. 'Then I can have adventures too.'

James laughed. 'Oh, not another one.'

He was in a good mood, Beth noticed, so if her mother had said anything to him of the rumours he was not unduly troubled by them.

They were not the only ones enjoying the fresh air. The sunny weather and the fact that it was a Saturday had brought the crowds out. They wandered about, played ball games, had races and enjoyed the impromptu entertainment of jugglers, acrobats and musicians who went round with a hat afterwards. Returning to the carriages, they found the picnic had been laid out in the shade of a spreading oak.

Having eaten their fill, they sat back to relax, the ladies using parasols to keep the sun from their faces. They were all indolently thinking of nothing of any consequence, when a misdirected ball came flying over and landed on the grass a few feet away. Jamie, who was fidgeting at the inactivity of the adults, jumped up to pick it up.

Its owner was a lad about the same age as Jamie and the two boys stood and stared at each other for a moment, then Jamie handed the missile back. 'Georgie, say thank you to Master James,' a familiar voice called out.

All the adults were suddenly roused from their torpor. Mrs Melhurst was tripping over the grass towards them. 'What a happy coincidence!' she called out. 'We were only saying a few moments ago, what a shame it was that George has no other little boy to play with. And here you are.'

Beth's euphoria vanished to be replaced by alarm. She found it hard to believe it was coincidence, but how could it be anything else? No one had said anything about a picnic before that morning, though she supposed her aunt had planned it earlier in order to make sure her husband would be free. She did not like Mrs Melhurst and it had nothing to do with the rumours she had heard about her and Mr Andrew Melhurst, or so she told herself. The Duke, who had not been present at Sophie's soirée and had not met the lady, was looking puzzled.

Before the Duchess could present her, Mr Melhurst, Mr Edward Melhurst and Lord Gorsham hove into sight. Mr Edward was dressed in country clothes of nankeen jacket, supple leather breeches and knee-high boots, but the other two were in riding coats and breeches. 'My lord Duke,' Andrew said with a slight bow. 'May I present my cousin, Mr Edward Melhurst, and his wife. I believe you are acquainted with Lord Gorsham.'

Beth, her heart in her mouth, waited for her uncle's reaction, but all he did was stand up and bow politely. 'Mrs Melhurst, your obedient. Mr Melhurst. My lord.'

'This is George,' Kitty said. 'Make your bow to the Duke, Georgie.' The child did as he was told. 'Will you permit your son to play ball with Georgie, your Grace?' she went on. 'It is a lonely time for a child in London in the Season. I expect Master James finds it so.'

The Duke was too much the gentleman to rebuff her. 'For a few minutes, so long as they do not go out of sight.'

'Naturally not, your Grace. I cannot bear to be apart from George, which is why I brought him to London. No doubt the Duchess understands that, being a mother too.'

Sophie managed a polite smile.

'Why don't we all play ball?' Livvy said, jumping up. 'Come on, Beth, join in. I am sure Mr Melhurst can think of a suitable game.' She fluttered her eyelids at him.

Beth looked at her mother in supplication. Her

mother looked at Sophie, who looked at the Duke. 'Why not?' he said. 'If we could improvise a bat and some wickets, we could play cricket.'

'No need to improvise, I've got the very thing,' Teddy said and disappeared in the direction of his carriage, which was parked close by, and came back with a half-size bat and a couple of wickets, obviously intended for a child.

Beth was shocked. Her mother could not have said anything to her uncle about the gossip or he would have made an excuse to leave, pressing duties which meant he had to carry his family off; it would have been easy enough. Now she would have to pretend to enjoy a game of cricket with Andrew Melhurst.

It was not a proper game; the ladies could not run in their long skirts and the game had to be adapted to take account of two small children and the fact that they were too few to make up teams. It was everyone against the person batting. It involved Beth standing to field any hit young George might make from the Duke's gentle bowling. He was not so gentle when the other gentlemen were taking their turn to bat, much to the squealed enjoyment of the boys. They squealed even more when Beth, who had been stationed in the outfield, managed to catch Andrew out.

'Oh, well caught, Beth,' Livvy called. 'Your turn to bat now.'

Beth walked to the crease and Andrew handed over the bat. Briefly their hands touched and he looked into her face, but she could not divine his thoughts from his expression. It was blank. She knew why that was; she had told him to go away and remembered his reply. 'I will inflict myself upon you no longer.' She had asked for that riposte and wished her own words unsaid.

'Well caught,' he said quietly before taking his place as a fielder.

Beth faced her uncle's bowling. It was deadly accurate and she was so shaken up by her encounter with Mr Melhurst she could not concentrate and was soon bowled out. Livvy took her turn at the crease and swung the little bat enthusiastically, though she missed the ball more times than she connected, laughing every time. In the end she was caught by Andrew. 'Oh, that is ungallant of you, sir,' she called to him.

'Then you may try for your revenge,' he said. 'Try bowling me out.'

'You know I never could.'

'You do not know what you can do until you try.'

She tried without success and then Jamie had a go at bowling and Andrew allowed himself to be caught by the Duke.

George was clamouring to bowl and he was faced by his father, who allowed his enthusiasm to get the better of him and thrashed at the ball, sending it high into the air. Livvy, trying to catch it, was dazzled by the sun and it slipped through her fingers and caught her temple. She went down like a stone.

Everyone began running towards her at once, but Andrew, who had been fielding quite close to her, reached her first, followed closely by Henry. They both dropped to their knees beside her, but it was Andrew who put his arm under her shoulders and lifted her head. 'She's out for the count,' Henry said. 'And look at that lump on her brow. It is already turning colour.'

'Find some water,' Andrew said, pulling off his kerchief, intending to dip it in water to bathe her forehead. Livvy began to moan quietly. 'Lie still, Miss Olivia,' he added. 'You are quite safe.'

Her eyes fluttered open and her hand lifted and fell, clutching at Andrew's handkerchief. She muttered something that sounded suspiciously like 'Drew'. It was then that Beth, who knew her sister better than anyone, realised she was faking. If she had been stunned, it had only been momentary and she was enjoying all the attention, especially from the gentlemen. Mr Melhurst was looking concerned, Henry anguished and Teddy remorseful. As for Jamie, he was in floods of tears and Beth stooped to comfort him, telling him she was sure his Cousin Livvy would be better soon.

'I'll carry her back to our carriage,' James said, bending down to lift Olivia. 'The sooner we get her home and into bed the better. I'll get my physician to take a look at her.'

'Pray to God she has no more than a headache,' Henry said.

Livvy, realising she was being carried away, decided it was time she took a part in the proceedings. 'Where am I? What happened?'

'That idiot—' Henry indicated Teddy with a jerk of his head '—lashed at the ball and knocked you out. I never saw anything so careless in my life.'

'I am most terribly sorry,' Teddy said, following in the Duke's wake and leading a procession of all the others. 'I would not for the world have hurt the young lady. Do please forgive me.'

Livvy smiled wanly. 'Accidents happen. I am sure you did not mean it.'

'I am mortified,' Kitty put in. 'We were having such a happy time and it had to end like this. I do not know what to say.'

'Then say nothing,' Andrew advised her.

James put Livvy on the seat of his own carriage and arranged a cushion behind her head. There was no water, but he took the handkerchief from Livvy and poured a little leftover wine on it to dab her forehead. She took it from him and held it there.

'If there is nothing more I can do, your Grace,' Andrew said, 'we will take our leave.'

'Nothing, thank you.' To his son's governess he said, 'Miss Gibson, you and Jamie ride with Lady Harley and Miss Beth. Miss Livvy will be more comfortable in our coach.'

Kitty still hovered. 'Your Grace,' she said addressing Sophie, 'I am struck low by what has happened. Permit me to call tomorrow to discover how the invalid is.'

Sophie, who liked the woman even less than Beth, nodded without speaking, before climbing in beside Livvy and taking her hand. Satisfied, the lady followed her husband and Andrew to the Melhurst carriage. Andrew saw them safely in, then mounted his own horse and rode back to town beside a thoughtful Henry.

He was glad of his friend's silence. He was furious with Kitty. The whole episode, except for the accident that befell Miss Olivia, had been orchestrated and she had made it look as though he had had a hand in it. When Kitty had said she was contemplating a family outing to Hampstead, he had agreed to go too because he wanted to give Firefly a good gallop; he had not yet tested the stallion's mettle for any distance. Henry, on being told, had made himself one of the party, riding beside him while his cousin's family went by coach. Andrew had been surprised to see the Duke and his family also enjoying an outing. After the set-down Miss Harley had given him, it was the last thing he had wanted. It made it seem as though he had gone there deliberately to push himself forward.

As Beth travelled with her mother and Jamie, she had no opportunity to speak to Livvy before they reached home and even then she was prevented because Livvy was put straight to bed and the physician sent for. He confirmed that Livvy was not seriously hurt. She had a bump on her head, which would give her a headache for a day or two, but nothing worse. He administered a dose of something to help her sleep and departed.

The Duke was obliged to dine at Carlton House, leaving the ladies to spend the evening without him, a not unusual state of affairs. 'I suppose we shall have that odious Mrs Melhurst on the step betimes,' Harriet said. 'I cannot think why James did not give her the cut direct when she approached us this afternoon. I suppose he did not want to be uncivil to Mr Andrew Melhurst.'

'Why should he consider Mr Melhurst?' Beth wanted to know. 'He can have no consideration for our sensibilities to allow that woman to intrude on our family party. Unless he thinks we shall soon be related. Livvy is as determined as ever to catch him and I cannot think he will resist. After all, to be connected to the Dersinghams would be a feather in his cap and might even silence the gossips, especially if Mrs Melhurst is received at Belfont House. I wonder Uncle James has not realised it.'

'Yes, I wondered that,' Harriet said to Sophie. 'I collect you cannot have passed on what Beth overheard.'

'Indeed I did,' she said. 'But he is not disposed to act on it. He says gossip that is seven years old is not worth considering. It only resurfaced because of Mr Melhurst's return to this country and will die down soon enough.'

'I do hope he is right. But what about the linking of our names with his? I cannot like it.'

'I do not think he does either, but, short of cutting the man, there is nothing we can do about it and James says if we do cut him we shall descend to the level of the tattlers.'

'What about me?' Beth asked. 'I do not care to have people saying Mr Melhurst has compromised me and taking wagers on him marrying me. I cannot think how it got about, unless he told someone himself.'

'Oh, I cannot believe that,' Sophie said. 'He assured us that he would say nothing. And what has he to gain by it, except more calumny? I am sure he does not wish for that.'

'What did James make of Mrs Melhurst?' Harriet asked.

Sophie chuckled. 'He is too much the gentleman to say, but I cannot think she would spread rumours when it is obvious she is trying to gain an entrée into the *ton* through us. I am used to people pushing themselves forward, but she does it too brown.'

'What shall we do, then?'

'James says we must rise above it, but if the rumours continue then we must take into account the good name of the family and James's position at court and take action.'

'What action?'

'I do not know. I should not like to punish Mr Melhurst for someone else's mischief.'

'You do not think he is to blame?'

'No, I hardly think he would spread gossip about himself, do you?'

'Perhaps he has not heard it. He is surely too much the gentleman to inflict himself upon us if he had.'

None of this served to ease Beth's troubled spirit and she excused herself, saying she wanted to write up some botanical notes she had made on reading Mr Parkinson's book. 'It is a pity Sir Joseph did not publish his journal,' she told them, as if her hurried departure needed explaining. 'Especially as other people on the expedition have told their own stories. Now he has died I wonder if it will ever be in the public domain.'

She went up to her room and sat herself at her escritoire, pulling a sheet of paper towards her and picking up a pen, but that was as far as she got. Her mind began to wander and, try as she might, she could not bring it back to the task in hand.

She was jealous of her sister, that she was obliged to admit, and she was also angry with her. How could she play-act like that? It was not like the little sister she had known and loved all her life. They had always been so close, but now they were divided and divided over a man. Was Livvy truly in love with him or was she in love with the idea of being mistress of Heathlands and being among all those horses? They would not be hers, of course, but, married to Andrew Melhurst, she would have free run of the stables. Was she prepared to overlook the gossip for that end?

Beth put her arms on the desk and laid her head upon them, weighed down by misery. She asked herself over and over again if she could stand by and see her sister married to the man she loved? The answer had to be yes. She only hoped it was what he wanted too. It would certainly silence the gossips who were linking her own name to his. Getting wearily to her feet, she undressed without waiting for Miss Andover to help her, and climbed into bed.

She shut her eyes, but the images still flickered before her and would not go away. Andrew Melhurst giving those horrible sailors the right about. Andrew Melhurst talking easily to her in his coach; riding in the park; giving a brilliant lecture; turning sharply from her when she told him to go away, almost as if she had struck him. Andrew Melhurst laughing with her sister and Livvy's pale face as she collapsed on the grass of Hampstead Heath and the look of concern in his face when he knelt to put his arm about her. That, as far as Beth was concerned, was the last straw.

She could not afterwards tell exactly when she finally fell asleep, but she was woken by Miss Andover pulling back her curtains and letting the sunshine stream in. 'It is a lovely day, Miss Elizabeth,' she said. 'And Miss Olivia is remarkably cheerful considering what happened yesterday. She is having breakfast in her room, but is talking of getting dressed as soon as she has eaten it.'

Beth washed, put on a dressing gown and hurried along the corridor to her sister's room. Livvy was sitting up in bed with a flimsy wrap about her shoulders, tucking into a boiled egg. 'How are you, Livvy?'

'I have a bump on my head. It's sore, but not enough to keep me in bed. After all, it is a battle honour and I must display it.'

'Oh, Livvy,' Beth said, surveying her sister's face. The bump had subsided a little, but the bruise had come out and the side of her face round the eye had turned purple. 'You are incorrigible. But I wish it had not happened as it did. You know what everyone is saying about Mr Melhurst.'

'I am surprised at you believing tittle-tattle, Beth. You, more than anyone, must know that Mr Melhurst is an honourable and chivalrous man. Far from compromising you, he saved you.'

'Are you never going to let me forget?'

'No, but, my dearest Beth, do not feel badly about it. If it had not been for you, I would never have met him.'

'Do you love him? Truly love him, I mean.'

'How do I know?' she asked dismissively. 'How does anyone know?'

'I think if you do not know, then you cannot be in love. I am persuaded that everyone knows when they are in love and there is no gainsaying it.'

'And you would know, I suppose.'

'What do you mean?'

'Well, you are in love with Toby.'

'Whoever told you that?'

'No one, but if you are not, why did you go chasing after him, hoping he would take you to India with him?'

'I never did. You are mistaken. I went to see him off.'

'So you say now, but no one believes you. And the worst of it was, he repudiated you and left you stranded to be picked up by Mr Melhurst.'

Beth's heart sank. It was so very nearly the truth, except she was not in love Toby and she did not believe he would have left her stranded. As for the rest...would she never live it down? 'You know Mama is very troubled about the gossip...'

'Oh, that,' she said dismissively. 'If you come from a prominent family, then you must expect people to talk about you. It will blow over, especially when Mr Melhurst offers for me. Act as if you did not care.'

That would be difficult because she did care, she cared very much, not only for herself but for her mother and the Duke and Duchess, and Livvy, who was being very silly but whom she loved and did not want to see hurt. As she was hurting. She forced a smile. 'Yes, you are right, the Harley sisters against the world, that's the way of it, and the Harley sisters are strong enough to win. I am going back to my room to dress. We will go down together.'

Chapter Seven

'**Y**ou knew the Duke would be taking his family to Hampstead yesterday, didn't you?' Andrew said. He had come down to breakfast to find Kitty already at the table in a flimsy robe that did little to hide her voluptuous figure. Once it might have inflamed him, but now he was repulsed.

'How can I have known?' she demanded, spreading butter thickly on a piece of toast. 'I am not privy to what goes on in his Grace's household. I wanted to give Georgie an airing, there is nothing wrong with that, is there?'

He sat down at the other end of the table and poured himself a cup of coffee from the pot the servant had placed at his elbow. 'You are up to something.'

She smiled. 'Now, what can you mean by that?'

'Toadying to the Duke. You know he has great influence at court and I suppose you are hoping he will use that influence to grant Teddy favours.'

'He might.' She paused and smiled knowingly. 'So long as you do not sink the boat by inviting gossip.'

He gave a mirthless laugh. 'And you do not, I suppose?'

'If you are referring to what happened seven years ago, it is very unkind of you. If you had sat tight instead of fleeing the country, it would have blown over all the sooner. You knew perfectly well William would not have fought a duel with you.'

'I did not flee the country, I left to make my way in the world, which I have done. It was, you may recall, you who turned your back on me.'

'I knew you would obey your grandfather and I wasn't going to wait to be humiliated. But that doesn't mean I had an easy time of it. William was being particularly difficult and many of my acquaintances cut me. I didn't know you were so popular, Drew, even though there were some who called you a coward.'

'Did they now?' he asked with interest. 'Is it too late to prove I am not?'

'Don't be a gudgeon. No one believed it, knowing how expert you are with a rapier and a first-class shot too.' Her laugh was a tinkle she had spent hours in front of the mirror perfecting, though why she continued to practise it on him, he did not know. 'Your grandfather put it about that you left to spare William the embarrassment…'

'I am much obliged to him.'

'I would have died of mortification if it had not been for Teddy. He came to my rescue.'

'Then I am glad of it. But I do not see what that has to do with what happened yesterday.'

'It is unfortunate that Miss Olivia sustained an injury, but I am persuaded it did not amount to much. At any rate, it will give me a reason for calling at Belfont House this morning.'

'A note would suffice.'

'No, it would not. I must be seen to be a close friend of the Duchess.'

'You think that will silence the gossip?'

'If there is any gossip, you have brought it upon yourself, Drew, no sooner back on home soil than you are picking up that Harley girl dressed as a boy.' She laughed. 'Picking up boys, dear, dear!'

'You have an evil mind,' he said, controlling his temper with an effort. 'Miss Harley did not look anything like a boy. I was not deceived.'

'Then your folly was compounded. Don't you know you are expected to marry a chit you have compromised?'

'She has not been compromised.' Not for a moment would he admit that he had offered and been rejected. That first offer had been made out of chivalry, but since then he had come to realise that part of his brain and certainly his heart, unrecognised by him at the time, had known what he really wanted. And then he had bungled it. 'And I cannot see what it has to do with you.'

'I am trying to protect the good name of the family.'

'Teddy, you mean?'

'And Georgie and Lord Melhurst. When you went away, he was brought very low. Fortunately Teddy was at hand, but if there should be a new scandal…'

He suddenly realised where the conversation was leading. If he was discredited all over again, then Lord Melhurst would leave the estate to Edward, or so she hoped. 'I am sure his lordship is suitably grateful,' he said coldly.

'Naturally he is, and now his rakeshame elder grandson has returned and thinks he can spoil everything.'

'Ah, but if that grandson should fall victim to scandal for a second time, then he will be banished again, is that what you are thinking?'

'Not at all. You quite misunderstand. I have no wish to see you banished. All I want to do is forget the past and make everyone else forget it too.'

He laughed mirthlessly. 'Then we are agreed on that point at least.'

'Yes, we have to show the world that we are a united, happy family and how well in with the people who matter. If the Duke likes us, who knows what doors it might open?'

He burst into laughter. 'Oh, my dear Kitty, you are incorrigible. What are you hoping for, an earldom for Teddy?'

'You may laugh, but the Duke is very influential, and it is not beyond the bounds of possibility, especially if you are married to one of his nieces. I am indifferent as to which.' Angered by his hilarity, she stood up. 'I am going up to change and then I am going to call at Belfont House to enquire after the invalid and perhaps take her some chicken broth.'

She had hardly left the room when Teddy strolled in. He was in a dressing gown and Turkish slippers. 'Morning, Drew,' he said, going over to the sideboard to inspect the breakfast dishes. Having helped himself to scrambled eggs, he brought his plate to the table and sat down. 'You are up betimes.'

'I have become used to rising early. In the heat of India the best time of the day is early morning. What is Kitty up to? She seems to think she can prise an earldom for you through the Duke of Belfont.'

Teddy laughed. 'Oh, take no note of her, I don't. It makes for an easier life to let her go her own way.'

'And are you going with her to Belfont House?'

'Lord, no! I have an appointment with my tailor.

Kitty can forward my apologies, not that I didn't make them at the time.'

Andrew left him to finish his breakfast and went up to change into something suitable for morning calls. If Teddy was not going to Belfont House, he certainly was. He dared not let Kitty go on her own.

Livvy and Beth, dressed in simple muslin gowns, went down to the morning room where their mother and the Duchess sat, talking quietly. They were at home to callers and already a stream of people had come and departed, but now there was a lull.

'We are not too late, are we?' Livvy asked. 'Mr Melhurst has not been and gone again?'

'No,' Harriet said. 'But why do you think he will come? He did not say he would. It was only Mrs Melhurst who asked if she might call.'

'Oh, he will come. Did you not see the tender way he looked at me when he thought I was hurt? I am per-suaded he has developed a *tendre* for me and will soon declare himself.' She sat in an armchair and leaned against its back in an attitude of stoic suffering.

In spite of herself Beth smiled. Her sister was such a bright, fidgety person, she could not hold a pose like that for long; she would soon be up and excitedly talking about whatever it was she wanted to do next.

Foster came to announce a caller. 'Viscount Rapworth, your Grace.'

Rapworth came in, almost hidden behind a large bouquet of flowers. He made an elaborate bow to the Duchess and Harriet, followed by shorter ones to Beth and Livvy. 'Forgive the intrusion, ladies,' he said. 'Heard of Miss Olivia's accident, had to come and offer my sympathy. Your Grace, permit me to present this humble offering to the invalid.' He fell on his knees and handed Livvy the flowers. 'I hope you are not too badly injured.'

'How on earth did you hear of the accident?' Beth demanded, speaking for all of them. 'It only happened yesterday afternoon.'

He rose and turned towards her. 'At Boodle's last night, Miss Harley. It's all round town.'

'What are they saying?'

'That Miss Olivia was the subject of a vicious attack by someone using a cricket ball, and I can see that it is indeed the case; the mark of the projectile is plainly visible. I am sorry to see you brought low, Miss Olivia, and if I could meet the perpetrator, then I would seek revenge on your behalf.'

'That will not be necessary,' Harriet said sharply. 'It was an accident.'

'Do the tattlers also name the culprit?' Beth asked.

'It was hinted that it was Lord Melhurst's grandson.'

'Which grandson?'

'Oh, there are two. Forgot that. But it couldn't be Teddy, he's a mild, indolent man who wouldn't hurt a fly. But you must know if you were there.'

'Indeed,' the Duchess said. 'But, as I have said, it was an accident and we apportion no blame to either gentleman. I assure you the ball was not in Mr Melhurst's hands, nor in Mr Edward Melhurst's. If you hear any more about it, I beg you to disabuse the speaker of that idea.'

'Certainly, I will, though the rumours are very strong.' He turned to Livvy. 'Miss Olivia, we were contracted to go riding tomorrow, but I shall wait impatiently until you are better.' He bowed and withdrew.

'How do such rumours get about?' Harriet asked as soon as the door closed on him. 'We have only to sneeze and the whole *ton* knows of it.'

'I think,' Beth said, 'that, in spite of what Uncle James has said, we have a spy in our midst.'

'And one who adds his own embellishments,' Livvy added.

The footman, having admitted Kitty and Andrew as he let the Viscount out, returned. 'Mrs Melhurst and Mr Melhurst, your Grace,' he announced.

Kitty swept into the room and curtsied to the Duchess. 'Your Grace, I am come as I promised. How is the invalid? Oh, I see she is up and about. Oh, you poor child, how your poor head must ache. I have sent a little chicken broth round to the kitchen by my coachman. Perhaps the chef will heat it up for you. It is my special receipt.'

'Thank you,' Livvy said, looking not at her, but at Andrew, and managing a faint smile. 'Mr Melhurst, you are here too.'

'I am,' he said, bowing. 'I wanted to see for myself that you have sustained no lasting injury.' The invalid had a nasty bruise, that was true, but she was not unduly pale and her eyes were as bright and sparkling as ever. He concluded she was milking the situation for all she was worth.

'The bruise will fade in time,' she said. 'A day's rest and I shall be right as ninepence and able to go riding again. Is that not so, Beth?'

Thus appealed to, Beth found Andrew's eyes on her and felt her face grow warm. It had been purgatory to watch him bending over the injured Livvy and displaying every sign of loverlike concern, but now his blue eyes were looking her up and down, it was worse. Did he know how she felt? Could he tell by her blushes and her shaking hands, that she was far from indifferent to him? Could he not see that Livvy was playing with him? And how could he be so brazen as to come to Belfont House if what they were saying about him and his cousin's wife was true? 'I think my sister is being very brave, sir. The doctor has said she must rest for a week. Undue exertion might make her swoon.'

'Did he really say that?' Livvy asked, abandoning her languid pose. 'I did not hear it.'

'You were in pain and perhaps not fully aware, dearest,' Harriet put in. 'But I assure you that is what he said.'

'Then I cannot go riding for a whole week.' She slumped back against the cushions.

'The time will soon pass.'

'We shall visit you often,' Mrs Melhurst put in, reminding everyone she was still there. 'My husband would have come with me today, but he had a business appointment. He asked me to convey his sincere regrets and begs forgiveness.'

'No doubt I shall contrive to amuse myself,' Livvy said in a flat voice.

'Oh, my lady, may I offer myself,' Kitty said, turning to Harriet. 'I feel responsible in so many ways for Miss Olivia's misfortune and I am sure I can contrive to amuse her.'

Andrew looked as though he would like to run her through, but it was Harriet who answered. 'Thank you, Mrs Melhurst, but a lady as popular as you are must have a great many calls on her time, and it has come to a pretty pass if I cannot look after my own daughter.'

'Of course, my lady, I had thought only to relieve you.'

'It is not a task from which I seek relief, Mrs Melhurst, but I thank you for your kind thought.'

Even Kitty caught the coldness of Lady Harley's tone and immediately remembered a pressing engagement and took her leave.

Andrew was trying to suppress a grin, Beth was letting out her breath in relief and Sophie was laughing aloud.

'I am sorry for that, Mr Melhurst,' Harriet said. 'That was uncivil of me.'

'Please think nothing of it, my lady. If you had not given her a put-down, I most certainly would have and not in such polite terms. It is I who should apologise, not only for today but yesterday. I would like to assure you that when Mrs Melhurst suggested an outing to Hampstead Heath, I had not the smallest notion you would be there.'

'Or you would not have ventured anywhere near,' Beth said crisply.

'I would not for the world have embarrassed you.' They were both thinking of her abrupt dismissal of him and they both knew it. There was an atmosphere of tension between them that was evident to them, if not to the whole company.

'Lord Gorsham, your Grace.' Foster was back again, standing aside to admit Henry.

The young man bowed to everyone and fell on his knees beside Livvy. 'Dear Miss Olivia, I had hoped to find you fully recovered, but I perceive it is not so. Your poor face! I could willingly crack Teddy Melhurst's head open for doing that to you.'

She laughed and held out her hand to him. 'Oh, please do not do that, my lord, I should hate to see his brains spilled out.'

'If he has any,' murmured Andrew.

'You are in spirits at any rate,' Henry said, kissing the back of her hand and taking his time to release it.

'Yes, but I do not know why I should be. I have been forbidden to ride for a whole week.'

'Oh, you poor thing! I cannot think of anything worse. But never mind, I shall eschew getting on the back of a horse until you are fully recovered. That will be my punishment for not looking after you better.'

'You could not have prevented it.'

'I could have thrown myself between you and the missile.'

She laughed. 'Then you must have been able to fly, you were too far away.'

'Nevertheless, I shall not ride until you can do so again. It has lost all its attraction for me. Please allow me to come and bear you company while you mend.'

'He is besotted,' Sophie whispered to Harriet behind her fan.

'Do you think it is wise to encourage him?' she whispered back.

'Might take her mind of Mr Melhurst.'

Livvy was laughing. It made her bruise look less disfiguring. 'We could walk in the garden, my lord, if you would not find that too tame.' Beth, her senses heightened, noticed the sideways look her sister directed at Andrew.

'Too tame? In your company, Miss Olivia, nothing is too tame,' he said gallantly, making Andrew roar with laughter, which made Henry turn towards him. 'You may laugh, Melhurst, but I do not notice you paying nice compliments.'

'Alas, I have never learned the knack,' he said. 'I shall have to ask you to instruct me.'

'Compliments without sincerity are meaningless,' Beth said.

Henry was affronted. 'I assure you, Miss Harley, I was never more sincere.'

Beth, who not been thinking of his lordship, but wondering if a compliment could be sincere if it had to be learned, retracted hurriedly. 'Oh, I did not mean your compliments, my lord. I was thinking of someone else entirely.'

Harriet swiftly changed the subject. Having arranged for Lord Gorsham to return the following afternoon at two o'clock, both men took their leave. Andrew was thankful that he had been received politely in spite of Kitty, but he had wanted to speak to Beth alone and there had been no opportunity. Judging by her attitude towards him, she still wished him gone. He simply had to get to the bottom of it.

'I cannot believe there is anything wrong in him,' Sophie said after he had gone. 'He is too open in his manner and too discreet. You could tell it by his attitude to everyone, including his cousin's wife, who is a toadeater of the first water.'

'Well, I for one, will not believe ill of him,' Livvy said. 'If there are any rumours, they are occasioned by jealousy. It's probably that awful Mrs Melhurst.'

'You are probably right,' Harriet agreed, remembering that her younger daughter had not been privy to the discussion about Andrew the evening before, nor the exact nature of the gossip.

'Why would Mrs Melhurst spread tales when they are bound to reflect badly on her own character?' Beth asked.

'I don't know, do I?' Livvy retorted. 'I am tired of the whole subject.'

'And so am I,' Beth said with feeling.

'I wish Dr Spencer had not said I might not ride.'

'You would not wish to go out looking as though you had gone three rounds with Gentleman Jackson, would you?'

'No, but Zephyr needs exercising, she will get fat and lazy if she is not ridden.'

'I will exercise her, if you like,' Beth said.

'Will you not find her too spirited?'

'I can manage her, if you will trust her to me.'

'Of course I do, so long as you do not put her to any fences.'

'You can be sure I shan't do that.'

'Then I think Grimble can be spared for an hour or two, to accompany you,' their mother said.

'Perhaps we should ask Viscount Rapworth to ride with you,' Livvy said mischievously.

'Heavens, no!'

'Or Lord Gorsham.'

'No, he is contracted to keep you company. I shall manage perfectly well with Grimble.'

Lord Gorsham arrived on the step at two o'clock the following afternoon, just as Grimble came round the corner leading Zephyr and a cob on which he intended to accompany Beth. She came out as soon as she heard the clop of hooves, meeting his lordship as he climbed the steps to the door. He touched the curly brim of his hat. 'Going riding, Miss Harley?' he queried, stating the obvious.

'Yes. Zephyr needs the exercise.' She smiled at him and continued down the steps and waited for Grimble to hold out his clasped hands to help her mount. Once in the saddle she set off at a walk. The streets were busy with carriages, phaetons, tilburys, carts and drays, not to mention pedestrians wanting to cross the road, street vendors and beggars standing in the gutters. Grimble was forced to drop back a little. It was not until she turned into the gates of Green Park, that she became aware of another rider almost beside her and that it wasn't the groom.

'Miss Harley, good afternoon.'

She turned in her saddle to find herself looking straight into the cornflower-blue eyes of Andrew Melhurst. 'Where have you sprung from?' she demanded.

'I have not sprung from anywhere. I saw you were alone and decided you needed an escort.'

'I have one. My groom is only a few paces behind me.'

'Too far behind to be of any assistance, should you need it.'

'Why should I need it?'

He shrugged. 'One never can tell. I would not like to think that any ill luck should befall you if I were in a position to prevent it and did nothing. Allow me to ride with you. I will not trouble you with conversation, if you do not wish it.' He wondered if being seen with her might fuel the gossip, but how else was he to have any private conversation with her? He had ridden with Henry to Belfont House, intending to pay his respects and hoped that if all four wandered in the gardens together he might manage a moment alone with her. He needed to talk privately to her, away from that scheming sister of hers, to explain things that needed explaining, to try to remedy the wrong impression that bungled proposal had given her. When he saw her coming down the steps dressed for riding, he had hastily changed his plan.

She looked behind her and saw Grimble hurrying to join her again. Smiling to let him know she was not in trouble, she turned back to the man beside her. Should she agree or give him a put-down and send him on his way? Her longing to be with him, however hopeless her case, did battle with her determination not to be beguiled by him and her longing won. After all, what harm could it do? She was chaperoned and here, in Green Park, which was not so frequented by the *ton*, she had seen no one she knew. And why should she worry about gossip when her uncle clearly did not?

'I cannot stop you riding alongside me, sir,' she said and started forward at a dignified walk.

'Why did you decide on Green Park?' he asked, falling in beside her.

'It is less crowded than Hyde Park and there are trees…'

'Oh, I see, you wish to examine botanical specimens?' She knew he was teasing and it made her relax and smile a little.

'My sister will be disappointed she has missed her ride.'

'Yes, but I am glad her injury is not serious and she will soon be on a horse again,' he said, knowing that Miss Olivia Harley had been most put out when she discovered she could not ride out, though why she would want to with an eye the colour of a lowering storm cloud, he did not know. 'No doubt Henry is amusing her. He is very taken with her, you know.'

'I hope he will not be too disappointed.'

'You do not think she will entertain an offer from him?'

'I do not know. It depends…'

He laughed. 'On what other offers she has, I expect. She is very young.'

'And very determined.' The conversation was beginning to stray beyond her control and, unwilling to continue it, she put her horse to a trot. The sun was warm on their backs and the trot became a canter as she struck off across the grass, easily avoiding other riders and walkers, strolling in the sunshine. He realised that she rode well; perhaps not as dashingly as her sister, but she had a good carriage and had no trouble controlling the spirited mare. He followed, allowing her to dictate the pace.

Beneath the shade of a copse of trees, she slipped from the saddle. He jumped down and joined her, letting the horses crop the grass, watched over by Grimble, who wisely stayed out of earshot, smiling to himself.

'Ah,' she said, peering up into the branches. '*Quercus durmast.*' Then turning away from him to look at another tree. 'And *fagus sylvatica.*'

He laughed. 'Oak and beech. No doubt you know the Latin names of all the trees in this park.'

'No, but I'll wager you do.'

'Do you want to talk about trees?'

'Why not?' She did not turn to face him, she dared not. He would see her bleak longing writ large on her face. 'You could no doubt teach me a great deal I do not know.'

'About arboriculture?'

'Yes.'

'I would do it gladly at any other time, but now I would rather speak of something else. Will you listen?'

'I am listening.'

He paused, wondering how to begin. 'I had no idea you were going to be on Hampstead Heath.'

'So you were at pains to tell us yesterday, but I think Mrs Melhurst did.'

'She assures me she did not. It was coincidence. I would not for the world have embarrassed anyone, least of all you. You had told me plainly enough to go away and from that I assumed my person was abhorrent to you…'

'That was uncivil of me and I am sorry for it. I was upset…'

'By me?'

'Something I heard.'

'May I know what it was?'

'No.'

'Ah, now I begin to see. You have been listening to gossip.'

'It is not something I would willingly listen to, sir, but when people speak so loudly in my hearing I can only suppose I am meant to hear.'

'I am sorry for it. I cannot have been as successful as I had hoped. It was dark and the interior of the coach was unlit and I had supposed no one saw us.'

She turned to face him. She was truly remorseful for what she had done only because it had worried and upset her mother and put her aunt to no little inconvenience, but that was as nothing compared to what he was being accused of and she surely need not be cowed by him. 'I do not refer to the manner of our first meeting, Mr Melhurst, though I am told that is also the subject of speculation.'

'Our first meeting was perhaps not propitious, I agree, but that need not be a barrier to a greater understanding. I certainly do not think of it as such. What is a greater encumbrance is whatever it is you have heard against me. I beg you to enlighten me.'

'I am sure you know already and I wonder at you wanting to speak of it to a lady.'

'If we are not entirely honest with each other, Miss Harley, how are we to go on?'

'Go on, sir?'

'You know well enough what I mean. If you have been swayed by something you have heard…'

'I have not, sir. I make up my own mind.' Which was not exactly the truth, though she owned it ought to be.

'Then it is something I have said or done. You laughed at my clumsy attempt at a proposal…'

'That was uncivil of me, sir, and I regret it.'

'Regret laughing or regret turning me down?'

'Regret laughing.' She paused. 'Mr Melhurst, I think we have said enough on the subject.' She turned away, intending to remount and continue riding, but he seized her arm and swung her back to face him.

'You will hear me out,' he said through gritted teeth.

She struggled from his grasp. 'Sir, you are hurting me.'

'Then I am sorry.' He relaxed his grip, but did not release her. 'I am making a poor hand of this, but if you would only listen to what I have to say, then you may turn your back on me if you wish. We need never meet again.'

'How can that be? My sister would…'

'What has she to do with it?' He stopped suddenly as enlightenment dawned. 'Oh, dear, you thought… But why? I have never shown her anything more than common courtesy.'

'She is convinced that you have.'

'She is a child, Beth, a delightful, mischievous child.'

'She is only two years younger than I,' she said, noting his use of her given name, but deciding not to take him to task over it. It sounded sweet on his tongue and her heart gave a sudden lurch.

'But infinitely younger in maturity. She is not for me. How could she be when I have already proposed to you?'

'Only because you felt it was expected of you. I did not take it seriously.'

'So I recollect,' he said drily.

'Oh, must you always remind me of my errors?' she demanded. 'Is it not enough that I feel bitterly ashamed of them?'

'You are too hard on yourself, my dear.' He took her chin between finger and thumb and lifted her face to his and was taken aback to see tears standing in her eyes. She was not as indifferent as she would have him believe. 'I am sorry I do not have the knack of pretty compliments, but deeds speak louder than words, so I am told.' He smiled and bent to kiss her. It was a bittersweet moment for her and she was deaf to the inner voice that told her she was being foolish, gullible and weak—weak, not only in sense but in her limbs. She felt her knees buckling under her and had to hold on to him for support, which only made him kiss her harder and longer. When he released her she was panting for breath and unable to speak.

'Forgive me,' he said. 'I gave way to temptation.'

She pulled herself together with an effort. 'I am not aware that I tempted you, sir. I certainly did not intend to. And if you think that just because I was so foolish as to travel alone to London and fall into a coil over it means I am easy prey to a rake, then let me disabuse you of that idea immediately. I begin to think that what they say about you might be true.'

There were two bright spots of anger on her cheeks, and her eyes, normally so limpid, were flashing sparks of fire, so intense he took a step back. As soon as he had done so and there was air and space between them, she felt bereft, almost as if she had been abandoned, thrown aside. The heat of anger left her and she found herself shaking uncontrollably with mortification. Once again he had managed to make her feel awkward and ashamed.

Before he could think of a suitable reply, a loud

cough from Grimble alerted them to the approach of other riders and she disguised her agitation by picking up the trailing skirt of her habit and walking from the trees with her head in the air. He followed, cursing himself. He had bungled it a second time and he did not think she would give him a third chance.

'There you are!' Livvy called gaily from the back of Lady. 'His lordship said you would make for Green Park. We had a guinea wager on it and I lost.'

'Livvy, what are you doing here?' Beth demanded, noticing that Livvy had swathed a length of net about the brim of her riding hat and pulled some of it down to form a short veil that hid her eyes. 'You are not supposed to be riding. How did you persuade Mama to let you?'

'I didn't persuade her. She went shopping with Aunt Sophie and it was easy enough to give Miss Andover the slip. She fell asleep on the seat in the garden.'

'Then I am surprised at you, Lord Gorsham.' Beth turned on the unfortunate man, who was forced to bear the brunt of her misery without knowing the reason. 'You were supposed to be keeping my sister company, not encouraging her in her naughtiness. Indeed, I would not be surprised if you did not instigate it.'

'I did not, never would have,' Henry protested. 'Can't gainsay Miss Livvy when she has the bit between her teeth. Had to come, couldn't let her come alone. And she would have.'

Beth recognised the truth of this and softened her tone. 'I am sorry I scolded you, my lord. Now we will all ride back together and hope there is no harm done.' She risked a glance at Andrew, who was staring fixedly at something in the middle distance, his jaw set tight. He strode to pick up Firefly's trailing reins while Grimble came forward leading Zephyr.

'I'll ride her,' Livvy said, dismounting by the simple expedient of loosening her foot from the stirrup and jumping lightly to the ground. 'You can ride Lady back, Beth.'

As Lord Gorsham had not dismounted, there was no one to help her to mount but Andrew. 'Mr Melhurst,' she said.

He turned at the sound of her voice and came speedily to help her into Zephyr's saddle. She rewarded him with a winning smile. 'As soon as Lord Gorsham told me you had ridden to Belfont House with him and had not entered, I guessed what had happened,' she said. 'You have too fine a sensibility, sir.'

'Sensibility?' He was puzzled.

'Why, yes. Seeing Beth about to set out, you must have decided you could not let her ride alone, especially as she was on Zephyr, who is really much too lively for her.'

'You are half-right,' he said, smiling. 'But I discovered that Miss Harley did not need my assistance, after all.' He turned to help Beth into Lady's saddle, noting with grim satisfaction that the barb had gone home and then immediately regretted it.

She settled herself into the saddle and took the reins he offered her without so much as looking at him. Then she clicked her heel and Lady moved off. Livvy followed suit and came up behind her. The two men followed with Grimble a little further behind and thus the cavalcade returned to South Audley Street.

The two men dismounted to escort the ladies to the door, but declined refreshment. 'Don't fancy a jobation from her ladyship,' Henry said, bowing over Livvy's hand. 'Call tomorrow, if I'm still welcome.'

'Of course you are,' Livvy said, then to Andrew. 'Will you come, Mr Melhurst?'

'Alas, no,' he said. 'I find I am otherwise engaged. Good afternoon, Miss Olivia. Miss Harley.' His blue eyes, Beth noticed, were cold as ice and pierced her heart.

She did not wait to see the men return to their horses, but went inside and climbed the stairs to her room, where she sat on the bed and stared fixedly at a picture which hung on the opposite wall. Her brain was numb; she did not hear the clop of departing hooves, nor the front door shutting with a bang, nor feet running up the stairs; could not hear, could not see, could not feel anything but the ice gathering round her heart, squeezing the life out of it. The door burst open.

'What happened, Beth?' Livvy was standing in front of her, blocking the light from the window.

'Nothing.' The word was no more than a murmur. To have spoken aloud would have shattered the blessed numbness.

'Something did, I know. You have not spoken a word all the way home. And what were you doing off your horses, skulking in the trees?'

'We were discussing arboriculture.'

'Beth, do you take me for a flat? Something happened. You were as red as a turkey cock and Mr Melhurst could hardly be civil. I know! You confronted him about those rumours and made him angry. Oh, Beth, how could you? We had all decided there was nothing in them. Now he will never come near us again.'

'I wish he would not.'

'How can you be so unkind when you know how I have set my heart on marrying him.'

'To do that you have to be asked.'

'I know that, silly, but he would have done, if you had not given him a disgust of us.'

'Him! Disgusted with us!' Beth began to laugh and once started could not stop and then the laughter turned to tears, great heaving sobs of misery. Livvy looked on in dismay and was heartily relieved when their mother came in, having heard the unnatural sound from the hall as she arrived home from her shopping expedition.

'Whatever is the matter, Beth?' She sat down beside her elder daughter and put an arm about her shoulders. 'Hush, dearest, tell me what has happened.'

'I hope she may,' Livvy said. 'For she will not tell me.'

Harriet looked up at Livvy. 'What are you doing in your habit, Livvy? Have you been riding?'

'I went after Beth. I thought she might need me. She is not used to Zephyr.'

'Go and change at once. And stay in your room until I come to you.'

Livvy reluctantly obeyed and was not privy to the halting, disjointed tale Beth poured into her mother's sympathetic ear.

'It was indeed reprehensible behaviour, dearest,' her mother said when the recital came to an end. 'But I am sure Mr Melhurst will say nothing of it and neither will we. Nor will we let it ruin our Season.'

'But I am so ashamed that I could have been such a goose as to allow myself to be alone with him. I begin to believe that what is being said about him is true, and he is a rake of the worst kind.'

'No doubt you told him that.' Beth's head was bowed so she did not see the smile that fleetingly crossed her mother's face.

'Yes, I did. He thinks I am influenced by rumours about *me* and I am sure he was going to repeat his offer—' She stopped when she realised she had not told her mother of his offer the day Livvy galloped off by herself and left them alone. 'I know he made one to Uncle James, but I am sure he only did it out of a misguided sense of chivalry and, if he were to repeat it, then it must be because of the rumours. I could not let him do it.'

'Quite right too. Not the way to go about it at all.'

'And he says he doesn't wish to marry Livvy, either.'

'I never thought he did.'

'But what will Livvy say?'

'I think, my love, we will not tell Livvy. She would not believe it if we did; better to let her find out for herself.'

'Is that not cruel?'

'No, for I am persuaded she will find herself mistaken in her attachment and save herself from humiliation.' She stood up. 'Now change for dinner, Beth, and no more will be said. If Mr Melhurst should decide not to return to Belfont House for a few days, I am sure that will be no bad thing.'

'Yes, you are right. I shall not break my heart if he goes back to Newmarket and never comes near us again.'

Harriet patted her hand and smiled at what she

easily recognised as a whisker, knowing it was occasioned by pride. She did not think she need intervene. Not yet. But it might be advisable to find out if James had discovered what lay at the heart of the rumours and who was spreading them. Much as she disliked Mrs Melhurst, she did not think it could be her.

In the next few days, Beth discovered that by keeping busy and occupying her hands and head, she could forget Mr Melhurst for several minutes at a time. Reading and studying were best, especially reading to young Jamie, who had a lively curiosity and asked her one question after another, which required thoughtful answers. Shopping and visiting her aunt's friends also served, as did a visit to the British Museum, which put the man from her mind for a whole half-hour. Going to evening parties and routs was difficult because of the fear that he might be there, but once she had established he was not present, she was able to relax a little and take part in the conversation, albeit in a more subdued manner than formerly. Sewing was worst; it left her mind to wander and in wandering returned again and again to what had happened and asking herself how she could have handled it differently.

Her sister did not help; she blamed Beth for the non-appearance of Mr Melhurst and the fact that she had been given a jobation by her mother. 'If you had not turned into a watering pot, I should have had time to change before she came home,' she told Beth. 'And she would not tell me what ailed you. It is excessively provoking of you not to confide in me, Beth. We have always told each other everything.'

That was quite true and Beth felt very badly about it, but what could she tell her except that her idol had feet of clay? Lord Gorsham came every day, bringing flowers or sweetmeats, paying Livvy pretty compliments and, at the end of the week, when the bruise had all but disappeared, Harriet agreed Livvy could ride out again. This put her in transports of delight and she told Beth that in her opinion a man who would not come near her because she did not look her best was not to be espoused. 'He has been seen out riding with Lucinda Masterson,' she told Beth. 'And she is no great beauty.'

'Who is Lucinda Masterson? Do we know her?'

'Yes, you remember, we met her at Mrs Melhurst's musical evening.'

Beth did not remember; her memories of that occasion were blurred and most figured unseen voices and Mr Melhurst coming to her and being sent away in a most uncivil fashion. 'Do you mind?'

'Good gracious, no! He is welcome to her.'

Whether this was true or simply bravado, Beth

could not be sure. Even if Livvy was not breaking her heart over Lord Melhurst, it did not mend her own, but that was something her sister did not know and must never know.

On one occasion, he was present when she and Livvy went to a reception given by the dowager Viscountess Rapworth, intending, so Livvy believed, to further her son's chances with her. Beth did her best to carry on conversing with her friends and ignore him, but found it impossible. He seemed always to be in her line of vision, though he appeared to be unaware of her as he chatted to a group who included Viscount Rapworth and Miss Masterson. When he suddenly turned towards her, she found herself looking straight into mocking blue eyes. He bowed. She inclined her head. They both turned away and carried on talking to their companions.

Unfortunately Livvy had seen him and dragged Beth over to speak to him.

'Good evening, Miss Harley, Miss Olivia,' he said, bowing.

'Mr Melhurst, you have been neglecting us,' Livvy said. 'We have not seen you in a se'ennight. Where have you been hiding yourself?'

'Hiding, Miss Olivia? I hope I have no need to hide from you.'

'Of course not, but we have seen nothing of you.

And if you have had a falling out with my sister, then I beg you to make it up, for I have missed you.'

'Livvy!' Beth exclaimed, wishing the ground would open and swallow her.

'If we have had a falling out, then I am very sorry for it,' he said, looking at Beth. Her cheeks were bright pink and her eyes betrayed her embarrassment. He felt like putting Olivia over his knee and spanking her like a naughty child.

'There you are!' Livvy said in triumph. 'I knew it was something and nothing. Now we can all be friends again. Perhaps you will call at Belfont House again or we shall meet in the Park when we are out riding.'

'Perhaps,' he said guardedly. 'If our paths should cross.'

'Drew, come and settle an argument,' Miss Masterson called to him and he bowed and left them.

'Livvy, I am seriously displeased with you,' Beth said as they moved away. 'Why did you say we had quarrelled? I was never more mortified.'

'You did quarrel, didn't you? And I wanted you to make it up. How am I to engage his attention if he avoids us because he is out of sorts with you?'

'How do you know he has been avoiding us? I am sure he has other calls on his time.'

'Yes, so I noticed. Lucinda Masterson. But I cannot

think he is serious about her. He is simply paying attention to her to make me jealous.'

It was no good, her sister would never change; Beth gave up.

Chapter Eight

Kitty was as mad as a hatter with Andrew. He had cut off her entrée to the Belfont household and she wanted to know why. 'I cannot believe you would stop going of your own free will,' she told him. 'So you must have been barred. What have you done?'

As usual she had cornered him at breakfast time; he took care to be out of the house during the day and most of the evening, even if it meant spending more time than he liked at his clubs and escorting other young ladies to the various functions to which he had been invited, which was how he came to be at Lady Rapworth's reception. It gave the appearance that he was on the town and going about his normal pursuits. It did not stop him thinking about Beth, one minute cursing himself for his ineptitude and the next blaming her for being so stiff-necked. She had been angry with him and he supposed kissing a single lady who had been strictly brought up was reprehensible, but she had not seemed averse to it and ought to have accepted his apology, especially as he meant to follow it with a proper proposal and would have done if her foolish sister had not turned up just at that moment. He had not seen her again until last night and it was apparent she had not forgiven him.

He had wondered if it had anything to do with the gossip and quizzed Henry about it as they walked home together.

'Don't listen to tattle as a general rule,' Henry had said. 'But couldn't fail to hear.'

'Then tell me.'

'You will not like it.'

'No, I do not suppose I will, but tell me anyway.'

'Word is that you have taken up with Mrs Melhurst where you left off seven years ago and your grandfather has ordered you to offer for Miss Harley to silence the gossip.'

'The devil it is!' He turned and grabbed his friend's arm, his face working with anger.

'Steady on, old fellow,' Henry said, detaching Andrew's hand from his coat sleeve. 'You did ask.'

Andrew released him. 'Sorry, but you must know it is a dastardly lie. Who is saying it? I'll call him out.'

'Course I know it is a lie, do you take me for a muckworm? Don't know who started it, but you know how these things grow and grow, a bit added with every telling. You would have a job to pin it on anyone, considering it is the latest *on dit.*'

'Do they know this at Belfont House?'

'Couldn't fail to hear it, could they?'

So Beth had heard it! No wonder she had been angry. She must have thought he had inveigled his way into the Duke's good books by delivering her out of her bumblebath, had the infinite bad taste to introduce his paramour to her family, invited them to his own house where the lady in question was staying under the same roof and with her husband too, and then added insult to injury by kissing her! 'They will be saying next that George is mine,' he said bitterly.

'Couldn't be,' Henry said flatly. 'You were out of the country.'

'Thank God for that.' He paused. 'If they have heard the slander at Belfont House, when did they hear it? And what have they made of it?'

Henry shrugged. 'Don't know when or even if the whole of it reached their ears; the Duchess and Lady Harley wouldn't talk to me about it, would they? Miss Olivia said they had decided that someone bears you a grudge.' He paused. 'You sure it ain't Mrs Melhurst?'

'Why would she? She is too much of a social climber to beggar her own chances with the Duchess. Must be someone else.'

He turned to Kitty now, feeling almost sorry for her.

'I have not been barred, Kitty, I decided not to embarrass them with my presence any longer.'

'Embarrass them? Why would you do that? Have you offered for one of the girls and been turned down? Is that it?'

'It is my affair.'

'You have ruined everything I have been working towards. Why could you not have married the chit straight away, then no one would have said a word against it. Instead you let it rumble on…'

'Let what rumble on?'

'The rumour about picking her up at the docks when she was determined to run away to sea in boy's clothes, that you recognised her and took her back to her uncle in order to gain a reward.'

'Is that all?' He began to laugh, though there was little to laugh about. Of the two stories, she had seized on the lesser one, which persuaded him she had not heard the one that involved her.

'All? Is it not enough? If the Duchess cuts me dead, I do not know how I am to come about.'

'The best way you could come about is to go back to the country until it blows over.'

'What! Run away with my tail between my legs just as you did seven years ago? How will that serve? Better you go back to Heathlands and let me try and mend it.'

He considered her suggestion seriously and was

almost inclined to follow it, but he was not a quitter, whatever she thought, and it was up to him to do whatever mending was to be done. He considered inserting a notice in the newspapers denying the calumny and threatening anyone who spread it with legal action, but decided against it. As Henry had pointed out, it would be almost impossible to nail the instigator and he could hardly take the whole *ton* to court. Besides, it would draw attention to the rumour instead of putting an end to it. He could almost hear the biddies saying, 'No smoke without fire.'

'I'll ride it out,' he said, knowing his chance of ever marrying Beth was gone and that he must concentrate all his efforts on restoring his good name.

'Does that mean you intend to go to Lady Myers's ball on Friday?'

'Why not? Lord and Lady Myers are friends from my Indian days and they have invited me. It would make matters look worse if I did not go.'

'Her ladyship is also a good friend of the Duchess.'

'I am aware of that,' he said, draining the cold dregs of his coffee and leaving her to her grumbling.

He was not the only one bothered about the ball. Lady Myers was in a quandary and had come hurrying to Belfont House to ask the Duchess what she should do. She was received in Sophie's boudoir where Sophie was resting with her feet on a footstool. Harriet was sitting nearby, sewing ribbons on a bonnet, and Olivia was idly flicking over the pages of the latest copy of the *Ladies* magazine while she waited for Lord Gorsham to arrive to take her riding. Beth was in her room reading Mr John Hawkesworth's book, *Cook's First Voyage*, which she found interesting because of its different perspective on the same story she had been reading to Jamie. She heard the door knocker and voices in the hall, but that was an everyday occurrence and she took no notice, not even lifting her head.

'Oh, dear, I hardly know how to go about this,' Lady Myers said as soon as the maid had brought refreshments and left the room. 'It is all on account of rumours I have heard about Mr Melhurst…'

'Do not trouble yourself on our account, my lady,' Livvy put in. 'We know all about them.'

Her ladyship gave Livvy a startled look. 'Didn't come here to spread tittle-tattle,' she said sharply and then turned back to the Duchess. 'I do not believe it for a minute, but the gossip is so strong that I thought I had better seek your advice.'

'On what score, dear Lady Myers?' Sophie asked.

'On whether he should come to my ball. I invited him weeks ago, when I knew he was back in London, but I am sure he would understand if I explained that you found you could not be seen at the same function as him.'

'Why should I do that?'

'Oh, dear, perhaps you have not heard what is being said about him.' Again that look towards Livvy, but the young lady had returned to the perusal of her magazine and appeared not to be listening.

'Indeed I have and very disturbing it is,' Sophie said. 'But you said you did not believe it.'

'I do not. I have known Andrew Melhurst since he first came out to India for the East India Company at the end of the war, when Lord Myers was attached to the Embassy. He was always the epitome of good manners and good sense. He worked hard and made several very profitable business transactions and there was never a whiff of scandal about him. He seemed to enjoy pottering about in the garden more than anything and went exploring in the high Himalayas. He was, so I believe, instrumental in introducing some new plants to the Calcutta Botanic Garden. I will not believe he is so lacking conduct as to… No, I cannot say it in present company.' This speech was a long one for the plump middle-aged lady and she stopped more from lack of breath than because she had nothing more to say.

'Dear Lady Myers, I hope you do not feel you must withdraw his invitation on our account. If you wish it, I could offer an excuse for us not to attend—'

'Oh, Aunt, please don't do that,' Livvy put in. 'I have been looking forward to going and so has Beth and no one who matters believes such dreadful things about Mr Melhurst and we must show that we do not.'

Harriet smiled. 'My daughter has not yet learned the value of silence, my lady, and I apologise for her. Nevertheless, she has voiced the sentiments of all of us. I should like to bring both my daughters to the ball. And please do not think of barring Mr Melhurst. To do so will compound the trouble he is in and, in some measure, I feel responsible for it.'

'You mean Beth is,' Livvy said. 'I do not see why I should forgo the ball because a lot of old gabble grinders with nothing better to do have decided that Mr Melhurst is a rake.'

'Livvy! How could you?' her mother reproved. 'I was referring to the theory we hit upon that it is someone who bears Mr Melhurst a grudge.'

'Sophie?' Lady Myers looked towards the Duchess, unable to believe they could be so calm about it. She supposed they had not heard the worst and wondered whether it was her duty to enlighten them, but as she most decidedly did not believe it, she would be wicked to repeat it.

'I agree. We will all come.'

There was a little more general conversation before her ladyship took her leave and Livvy was able to excuse herself and dash up to her sister's room. 'Beth, you will never guess…'

Beth looked up from her book. 'I see no need to, since you are about to tell me.'

'We are going to Lady Myers's ball.'

'I know that.'

'And Mr Melhurst is to be there.'

'Is he?' She pretended indifference. 'It is not to be wondered at, considering he has known Lord and Lady Myers for some time.'

'Yes, but Lady Myers has just been to ask Aunt Sophie if she should cancel his invitation.'

'And Aunt Sophie said she would not hear of it.'

'You have been listening at the door.'

'Not at all. It is only good sense. The ball is to be a big occasion with a great crush of people and there will be no need for us to speak to the man. I certainly shall not.'

'What is the matter with you, Beth? I never saw such a Friday face. Mama says I am not to ask you, but that only makes me more curious. Was Mr Melhurst very angry when you confronted him over the gossip? Lady Myers says she does not believe a word of what is being said. And neither do I, and it is unkind in you to keep him from visiting, when you know how much I want him to.'

'I have done no such thing. If he chooses to stay

away, it is not my fault.' She was aware that it was not quite the truth, but she could not tell her sister he had kissed her—her face burned whenever she thought if it. Nor could she tell her that he had said Livvy was not for him, especially as her mother had advised against doing so. She wished her sister would see that Lord Gorsham was altogether a better match for her. He had a title, he was wealthy and he undoubtedly adored her. 'Now, go and change or you will not be ready when Lord Gorsham comes to take you riding.'

'Are you not coming too?'

'No, take Grimble for an escort.'

Livvy flounced out and Beth tried to return her attention to the printed page, but it was no good, the book fell from her hands. Tomorrow she would see him again, tomorrow she must summon up all her courage, all her hauteur, all her self-discipline to pretend nothing was wrong and she was enjoying herself. She would enjoy the ball. Why should *that man* spoil everything for her?

The girls' court dresses were made over for the occasion, which meant removing the trains and the long sleeves in favour of short puffed sleeves. Each girl would carry a colourful beaded reticule in place of the plain white ones they had taken to Carlton House, an embroidered fan and different shoes. At any other time, Beth, surveying herself in the mirror, would have been pleased by what she saw, but the dread, which had been growing on her all day, would not let her feel any pleasure. Before she went down to join the others, she pinched her cheeks fiercely until they hurt and fixed a bright smile on her face.

Her unease had nothing to do with the gossip. Her uncle had made a point of speaking to Henry on the subject and that young man had explained how Mr Melhurst had been constrained to leave his native shore and seek his fortune elsewhere, which had quite eased His Grace's mind on the subject. 'Young pup got himself in a coil over Lady Haysborough,' James told Sophie and Harriet. 'But took himself off when it looked like becoming public. Nothing more than youthful experimenting, but the tattlers are making a meal of it, more than they ever did at the time. It is a great pity that we have become involved.' He did not explicitly blame Beth, but she blamed herself.

'Lady Haysborough?' Sophie queried. 'Who is she?'

'She is the present Mrs Edward Melhurst.'

'Oh, I see. At least, I think I do. But I cannot think there is anything more to it, for Mrs Melhurst is most particular in her devotion to her husband and son and Mr Edward appears to be on terms with his cousin.'

'Then you do not think we need absent ourselves from the ball?'

'Not the least need, my dear. If everyone else is bent on ruining the man's character, there is no need for us to do so.'

And so here she was, going to a glittering ball, dressed in all her finery, supposed to be on the look out for a husband, and she wished she were dead, not because of the gabble grinders who had nothing better to do than blacken people's characters, but because she had not cured herself of love. There was no cure, she decided, and what could not be cured must be endured.

She was right about it being a glittering occasion. Lord and Lady Myers were very popular and famed for their hospitality and everyone of any standing was there. The decorations to the ballroom, the music provided by a large orchestra, the wine, champagne and cordials being served, the food laid out in an adjoining room were all of the highest quality. As was the company.

Hundreds of candelabra lit a scene that drew gasps from Livvy and Beth. Ladies in evening gowns in all the colours of the rainbow, jewels glittering around their necks and in their hair, feathers, sashes, gossamer shawls draped about bare shoulders, hardly eclipsed the gentlemen in the colourfulness of their attire. Some wore plain black evening suits, others were in breeches and stockings, some in uniform, their decorations competing with the jewels of the ladies in their sparkle.

Having been welcomed by their host and hostess, the Belfont party moved forward into the room to find seats. Sophie recognised many of her friends and there were people that Lady Harley knew and others that Beth and Livvy had met since coming to London and their progress was slow as they were greeted and exchanged civilities. Lord Gorsham was soon at Livvy's side, closely followed by Viscount Rapworth, both eager to stake their claim to a dance. Beth, while allowing them to write their names on her card as well, looked about her, unwilling to admit that there was only one person she wanted to see.

She knew he would stand out in the crowd, being so tall and fair, but though she scanned the room, she could not see him. She had danced several country dances and a quadrille before she spotted him. He was standing just inside the door, talking to Lord Gorsham, dressed in impeccable black evening suit and white shirt, waistcoat and cravat, surveying the scene through a quizzing glass. Her steps faltered and her partner was obliged to grip her hand tighter to steady her, but she recovered quickly and, apologising for treading on his toes, she favoured him with a brilliant smile that almost knocked him sideways. He held her hand high so that she could step elegantly round him; when she came back to her starting point and looked towards the door again, her tormentor had gone.

* * *

Half an hour later she had just executed a flowing curtsy to another partner at the end of a cotillion when she saw him again. He had just returned his partner to her seat and turned from her to find himself face to face with Beth.

'Miss Harley, your obedient.' He inclined his head.

Unsure how to respond, she hesitated. Her erstwhile partner looked from her to the handsome man whose demeanour evinced the assurance of one with a prior claim, excused himself and left, leaving her to face Andrew alone. It was too late to cut him and, besides, common courtesy forbade it. 'Mr Melhurst, good evening.'

'Good evening, Miss Harley. I trust you are well?'

'Very well, thank you, sir. And you?'

'Improving by the minute,' he said, offering her his arm. 'Shall we promenade?'

She was in a quandary. It was one thing for her mother to say she did not believe he was a rakeshame and they ought to be polite to him, but quite another to parade openly with him. Far from giving the lie to the tattle it would confirm it. He was going to offer for her because he must.

'You had better say something,' he said. 'Or everyone will think we have quarrelled. Again.'

This struck her as very funny and she began to laugh.

He looked down at her and his own lips twitched. 'A joke, yes, of course. How foolish of me. I should remember that you have a strange sense of humour.'

She stopped laughing as suddenly as she had begun. 'Mr Melhurst, I beg you will not put me to the blush.'

'I beg your pardon.' He bowed and walked away, leaving her standing alone and unsure whether to cry because he had left her or be angry that he had even had the temerity to speak to her at all.

'Miss Harley, I believe this is my dance.'

She had been unaware that the orchestra had begun a minuet and turned to find Henry Gorsham at her elbow. She offered him her hand and he led her back on to the floor. They had been dancing for a full minute in silence before he spoke. 'It is good to see Miss Olivia looking so lively, Miss Harley.'

'Yes, indeed,' she said, trying very hard to pay attention. 'We are all very thankful to have her back to her usual good spirits.'

'I was never more shocked than when I saw her struck down. I would have done anything to have prevented it.'

'It was an accident, my lord. There was nothing you or anyone could have done.'

'No, though I have wondered why Teddy thrashed at the ball so violently.'

'I expect he did not think.'

'Yes, that must be it, simple thoughtlessness.' He was silent for a moment, apparently concentrating on the steps of the dance. 'You must know how I feel about Miss Livvy.'

'I believe I do.'

'Do you think I might have a chance of an acceptance if I should make an offer?'

She smiled. 'Why don't you try it and see?'

'Would the Duke allow it?'

'Why should he not?'

'Mr Melhurst is a good friend of mine.'

'Ah, I see, you think she is hoping for an offer from him and do not wish to stand in his way?'

He smiled. 'You mistake my meaning, Miss Harley. If Miss Olivia were serious about him, I might say you were right, but I am persuaded it is all a game to her and, if it is only a question of horses, I think I can please her on that score. My own stables are not inconsiderable. It is another matter that concerns me. There has been unsavoury and dastardly talk about Mr Melhurst and perhaps my association with him might make me unacceptable to your family. I understand I need to apply to the Duke.'

'I think it is wrong to judge a man on the company he keeps, my lord, though I am aware it happens all too frequently. I cannot speak for the Duke, of course, but I am persuaded he would agree with me. There is no scandal attached to Livvy and none to you.'

He fell silent again for a moment or two while she dipped and swayed to the music. 'Mr Melhurst is an honourable man, Miss Harley. A fine friend I would be to deny him.'

'Your loyalty does you credit, my lord.'

He opened his mouth, shut it again, then decided to take the plunge. 'Nor would he make an offer to any lady in order to silence his critics.'

'I am sure he would not,' she said. 'I am convinced he is indifferent to what is said about him.'

'Not indifferent, Miss Harley. Indeed, he is mad as fire, especially when the calumny is so ill deserved and because it so closely connects to your good self, which above everything has angered him. He considered taking legal action, but against whom? We do not know. I wish I could uncover the source of it for him and the reason behind it.'

'I, too, would like that,' she said. 'My sister puts it down to jealousy on someone's part.'

He chuckled. 'She may very well have the right of it. Let me say at once that, in rising above it yourself, my admiration for you and your family knows no bounds.'

Having got the little speech off his chest, he appeared to relax. He had used the dance to make his point and it left Beth's mind in turmoil again. Mr

Melhurst would not make an offer to silence his critics, he had said. Then why had he made the offer at all? Could it be to silence hers? It was more than she dared hope that he had any true feelings for her. If he had, he would surely have told her so, not blurted out that blunt proposal, which she had dismissed as insincere. And that kiss, oh, the memory of that kiss! She wished she could forget it, but then paradoxically savoured its memory.

Did he realise how cruel it was to tease her in that fashion? Could he guess that she had lain awake night after night thinking about it and wondering how she could have behaved differently? She had not invited it. Or had she? Had she by some look or gesture or something she had said led him to believe she would welcome such an advance? It was that foolish prank of hers, dressing in her father's old clothes and taking herself off to the docks to find Toby which had made him think she was easy prey for a rake. Was he a rake? It would be easier if she could convince herself that he was, but when she tried, she found herself in tears. If only…

She had been doing the steps of the dance automatically, in a kind of trance, but now the music came to an end and Henry was bowing before her. She pulled herself together, curtsied to him and took the arm he offered to escort her back to her mother and reality.

She could not put time in reverse, what was done was done and she was obliged to live with it.

They found Mr Melhurst, standing a little behind her mother and sister, deep in conversation with the Duke. Seeing Beth, he bowed to everyone and took his leave and Lord Gorsham led Livvy off into a waltz. A minute later Viscount Rapworth came to claim Beth.

Andrew decided to go for a walk. He wanted to clear his head before returning home to Teddy and Kitty, who would undoubtedly want to know who had been at the ball, what everyone was wearing, if he had heard any more gossip and whether the Duke and his family had spoken to him, and he did not feel like being quizzed.

Beth had sent him away again. How many times could a man risk that and still call himself a man? But it was his own fault and he could hardly blame her. He had been agreeably surprised that the Belfont family as a whole had not slighted him. The Duchess and Lady Harley had bowed and smiled, Livvy had blushed and the Duke had engaged him openly in conversation.

It had been a conversation very much to the point. 'I like to think I am a fair man,' the Duke had said, after they had exchanged civilities and moved a little way off to be private. 'Condemning a man behind his back is not the way I go about things. Normally I would take no note of gossip—'

'My lord Duke, you could hardly fail to do so, since your niece is also named and I offer my sincere apologies for that. I assure you I have kept my word and nothing of Miss Harley's little adventure has passed my lips.'

'I accept that, Mr Melhurst. And because I believe you to be an honourable man I have not forbidden my family to speak to you. On the contrary, I have suggested that they treat you with the courtesy they would any other gentleman of their acquaintance.'

'Thank you, your Grace.' He had thought fleetingly of Beth at that. Was their relationship to progress no further than cold politeness? Once it had been better, especially when they had been talking after his lecture and going round Kew gardens. How long ago that seemed now.

'But there still remains the question of who is responsible for blackening your name and linking it with my niece. That I should like to discover.'

'So would I.'

'Naturally you would. I suggest we put our heads together to come up with a solution. Do you know of anyone who bears you a grudge?'

'Your Grace, I have been out of the country since I

was twenty and I must suppose any grudge would be at least seven years old. I felt myself obliged to leave England to save my grandfather embarrassment. I was young and foolish and allowed myself to become embroiled with a married lady…'

'I am aware of that, Mr Melhurst, but can that have any bearing on the present situation? The lady is Mrs Melhurst, I believe.'

'She was Lady Haysborough at the time. She married my cousin after Lord Haysborough died.'

'And is there any ill feeling?'

'None at all on my part and I do not think on theirs either. My cousin and I were never very close, but that often happens in families and we rub along tolerably well.'

'And what are your future plans?'

'I can have no plans until my name has been cleared.'

'Then I suggest we contrive to bring that about. You have said nothing of how you met my niece and none of my family would do so, but between us the story has leaked and become so embellished as to be unrecognisable as anywhere near the truth and I am inclined to think the source lies within our own doors, with your servants or mine. If you have reason to suspect any of yours, I wish you would tell me.'

Andrew had remembered Simmonds talking to his coachman when both arrived back in Heathlands and

Simmonds telling Kitty. When had he done that? Teddy and Kitty did not live at Heathlands, although their home was not above five miles from it. Never off the doorstep, his grandfather had said of them.

'The only people who witnessed the scene on the docks were two of my grandfather's servants who had come with me to collect my baggage, and the coach driver who took us to Belfont House.'

'Have you questioned them?'

'No, your Grace, because they are at Heathlands and not in London and as far as I know are not in communication with anyone in town, certainly not with members of the *beau monde*. How could they be?'

'Lord Gorsham?'

'No, I would trust him with my life. I know he has been doing his best to deny the rumours.'

'Mr and Mrs Melhurst?'

Andrew had smiled at that. 'They are too busy climbing the social ladder, your Grace, and no more welcome the gossip than I do. It would kill Mrs Melhurst's aspirations stone dead. She is already blaming me.'

James returned his smile. 'Then we are at a stand.'

'Your Grace, may I suggest a little trap, a sprat to catch a mackerel, so to speak?'

'Go on.'

'It is plain that the rumours are growing and that is

unusual. Given nothing to feed on, they usually die a natural death. Supposing we provide sustenance, something known only to you and me? Then we might pin the culprit down and silence him for good.'

Surprisingly the Duke had entered into the spirit of the scheme, but had insisted it must not be something to reflect shame on anyone at Belfont House, and Andrew himself did not want to add to his own infamy. A crowded ballroom was hardly the place to continue the discussion and so it was arranged that they would meet the following afternoon. Today, he corrected himself, hearing the church clock strike one. It brought him back to the present and he wondered for a moment where he was. He had been walking a long time without paying any attention to his direction and he realised he was some way from the usual haunts of gentlemen and in a less salubri-ous area of town. It was not the place to be dressed in ballroom finery and unaccompanied at that. He turned swiftly and set off for the Strand where he knew he would find a cab.

It deposited him outside Melhurst House half an hour later and he hurried indoors, still musing on his conversation with the Duke. Could they succeed in catching his detractor? It must be the originator, of course, because everyone thereafter had had a hand in its embellishment. And having found him, what was to be done with him? A servant could be dismissed and the reason for his dismissal made public, but if it were not a servant, but a gentleman? Would he call him out, fight for his honour? Have him up before the bench and try to prove his guilt? Supposing it was a woman? He racked his brains to think of anyone. Apart from Kitty, whom he believed to be innocent, there was no one. Certainly not in this country. But abroad? He had not led the life of a monk, but neither did he believe he had treated any lady ill.

Supposing he was not the object of the ill will, but the Duke himself? Serving the King as he did, he must have attracted enemies. Someone in the Queen's household, perhaps? It was a comforting thought. But then he thought of Beth, who was the innocent victim in all of this. Beth, whom he loved. Surely it could not be her sister out of a fit of jealousy? Olivia was giddy and selfish, but not malicious, and he believed she had a genuine affection for her sister.

The doorman took his hat, just as two servants passed through the hall and up the stairs; a footman with a covered tray and a chambermaid carrying a bed brick wrapped in flannel. He looked from them to the doorman, one brow raised in enquiry. 'Lord Melhurst has arrived, sir,' the man said. 'Two hours ago.'

'Good God!'

'He has gone to bed, but Mr and Mrs Melhurst are in the small parlour, sir.'

Andrew strode across the hall, past the door of an elegant withdrawing room, past another that led to the dining room, and down a passage beside the staircase. Here were more doors. He made for the far one and threw it open. Teddy was standing by the empty hearth and Kitty was sitting on a sofa, sipping a glass of wine. They both looked up when he entered.

'Drew, there you are!' Kitty said. 'Grandfather is here. He arrived just as we were going to bed. We have only just done with seeing he is comfortably settled.'

'So I have been told. How is he? Why did he come? The journey must have knocked him up.'

'Indeed it did. He was all out of breath and went straight to bed as soon as it was made up.'

'He was mad as a fire.' Teddy put in. 'If he hadn't been all in, I think he might have dashed out in search of you. We told him you had gone to a ball and so he calmed down and said you were to attend him at eleven in the morning.'

'Did he say what brought him to town?'

'No, but ten to one it ain't good news.'

Andrew bade them goodnight and climbed the stairs to his bedroom where, Tollbank, his valet, waited to help him out of his coat. It was on his mind to ask the man if he knew anything about the rumours; after all, a man could have no secrets from his most personal servant, but decided against it. It would be best for their plans if no one knew that he and the Duke were plotting to unmask the culprit.

After the man had gone, bearing away his coat and trousers to be pressed, he stood by the window in his nightshirt and gazed out on the moonlit street, as if the scene might furnish him with inspiration. A chaise drew up at a door further along and deposited its occupants at the door of one of the houses; a cab rattled by; a couple of drunks staggered up the middle of the road, leaning on each other for support; a cat stalked along a wall, intent on something the other side of it. A dog barked and the wind whistled through the trees in the gardens. There was nothing out there to inspire him and he turned and climbed into bed.

He woke a little after nine, dressed and ate breakfast alone, since neither Teddy nor Kitty put in an appearance, and promptly at eleven presented himself at his grandfather's door and was admitted by the old man's aged servant. 'He is tired,' the man said in a whisper. 'I told him it would not serve, but he would come. Pray, do not overtax him.' Then he took himself off into an adjoining room.

His lordship was sitting in a stuffed armchair beside a fire, dressed in an ancient quilted dressing gown and a nightcap. The room was excessively hot. 'Come over here,' he commanded. 'And sit where I can see you.'

Andrew obeyed. 'Grandfather, I am surprised to see you here—'

'I'll wager you are. Haven't been up to town in years. The place is more crowded and dirtier than ever. You know as we topped the rise at Hampstead, it looked like one smoky orange glow beneath us. New roads and new houses everywhere. There soon won't be any countryside left.'

Andrew sat and waited for this diatribe to finish, which it did eventually when his lordship demanded that Andrew pour him a glass of cognac. Having done this, he resumed his seat. 'Grandfather, why are you come? It cannot be good for you to travel all that way…'

'It ain't good to sit at home wondering what the devil you are up to either,' he said. 'What's this I've been hearing about you and Kitty and that Harley girl? Dashed smoky, if you ask me.'

'It is all unfounded gossip, Grandfather. If I could nab the perpetrator, I'd thrash him within an inch of his life. And how has it come to your ears?'

'I may be old, but I'm not deaf. Heard it from the dowager Brandon, not that I like her any better than I like her daughter. She came over especially to tell me and crowed in the telling.'

Kitty's mother, from whom she had learned her

toadying ways, lived with Teddy and Kitty. Sometimes she visited with them, but as Lord Melhurst never welcomed her, she did not come very often. To arrive alone was unheard of.

'What did Lady Brandon have to say?'

'That you had landed yourself in a coil over one of the Duke's nieces…'

'What sort of coil?'

'You tell me. That is why I am here.'

Andrew began hesitantly, but little by little, prompted by his grandfather, he told the whole story.

'I care nothing for gossip,' he said. 'And this has become so twisted in the telling that even the gabble grinders are contradicting themselves, but something must be done. Some are saying the Duke insists on me marrying Miss Harley and some that I have been banned from the house. Still others say I used Miss Olivia's injury to inveigle my way back in and still more are saying you have ordered me to marry Beth.'

'Beth, eh?' He grinned knowingly. 'Never met the gel, so why would I do that?'

'You want me married.'

'So I do, but not in that fashion. What do you want to do? Marry her sister?'

'Good heavens, no!'

The old man chuckled. 'What's wrong with her? Cross-eyed? Fat? Nothing to say for herself?'

'None of that. She is pretty and has an enviable figure and she has more than enough to say for herself. She is also a prodigious horsewoman. You would like her.'

'But you don't.'

'I like her well enough, but she is not for me.'

'Then it must be the one you call Beth.'

'Miss Elizabeth Harley, yes. But how can I offer for her with this cloud hanging over us?' He paused, remembering how he had made the suggestion she should marry him, but that had hardly been a declaration of love and she had laughed him to scorn. Better not to mention it. 'She is proud and if she believes I am asking in order to save her reputation or mine, she will not have me. And I do not blame her. What sort of beginning is that to a marriage?'

'Then you must do something about it.'

'I intend to. The Duke is of the same mind and we are hatching a plot to tempt the culprit to reveal himself.'

'I see. A false trail. You could be hoist on your own petard.'

'Yes, but it is worth the risk.'

'Well, go on. Tell me about it.'

'I am meeting with the Duke this afternoon to discuss it.'

'Then we will go together. I'll have the carriage brought round.'

'Is Jerry Lubbock driving it?' Andrew asked, suddenly remembering that the man had driven him to the docks and taken him and Beth to Belfont House. The puzzling thing was that he could not have known what transpired inside the house and yet he had told Simmonds who had told Kitty.

'Yes, who else would I have to drive me?'

'Then by all means, let us drive to Belfont House together. I think we might have a glimmer of an answer.'

Chapter Nine

Beth, who was in her room endeavouring to write up her botanical notes and finish some sketches of the wild flowers Jamie had picked on Hampstead Heath, looked up as Livvy rushed into the room in a flurry of petticoats, her cheeks pink, her eyes alight. 'Beth, leave that boring stuff and come down to the drawing room. Henry has arrived.'

'Henry, Livvy?' Beth queried, eyebrows raised.

'Lord Gorsham. Though why I should be so formal when we are to be married I do not know.'

Beth put down her pen. 'I thought you were set on marrying Mr Melhurst?'

'I changed my mind. I have decided I shall be happier with Henry. He adores me.'

'And what about you? Do you love him?'

'Oh, yes. I only realised it last night when we were waltzing together and he told me of his feelings and asked if he might speak to Uncle James and Mama. I suddenly imagined how I would feel if I turned him down and he went away and I never saw him again and I decided I would pine away and die of a broken heart.'

Beth found herself smiling, remembering their mother's comment that Livvy's heart was robust. 'Then I wish you happy.'

'Do you think Uncle James or Mama can have any objection? They would not forbid it, would they?'

'I can think of no reason why they should if you are both set on it.'

'But everyone says you should be married first…'

'It is not a hard and fast rule, Livvy, and I would not dream of keeping you from your heart's desire.'

'Can you not bring yourself to encourage any of the young men we have met this Season?'

'No, I cannot, and who would have me?'

'They would if you would only make a push, but you hold yourself so aloof they are put off from the start.'

'The respectable ones are put off by disagreeable gossip and I have too much pride to toady to them in the hope they will make allowances for my notoriety. As for the rakeshames among them, they think I am fair game for their amorous advances…'

'Goodness, Beth, you never told me that. Who has been making amorous advances? Do tell.'

'I did not say anyone had. I was speaking generally.'

'Beth, you are the most provoking person I know.

Could it be Mr Melhurst? Is he really as wicked as the tattlers are saying?'

Beth felt the colour flood her face. 'You are as bad as everyone else, Livvy, giving credence to gossip.'

'Something happened when you rode Zephyr for me, I know it did. But you have spoken to Mr Melhurst since then, not only at Lady Rapworth's but I saw you in conversation with him at last night's ball and you seemed to be on easy terms.'

'It was hardly a conversation, simply a polite exchange. There is no reason why we should not be civil to one another. After all, that is what Uncle James advised.'

Livvy looked meaningfully at her sister, but Beth, refusing to meet her eye, picked up her pen, dipped it in the inkwell and began writing rapidly.

'Oh, do put that pen down, Beth, and come to the drawing room. I am sure Uncle James must have done with Henry by now. I thought he would not be here when Henry called, he was out all morning, but he came back only two minutes before Henry arrived and they went straight into the library. They have been there for ages and I am in a fever of impatience.'

She had hardly finished speaking when Miss Andover bustled into the room. 'Livvy I have been looking everywhere for you. Your uncle wants you in the library.'

'Oh, they have done! I must go at once.'

'Not before you have tidied yourself and let me do your hair.'

'Oh, no, I cannot stop for that.'

Beth laughed. 'Lord Gorsham is not going to go away, Livvy, unless Uncle James has given him a rightabout.'

'Oh, he wouldn't, would he? Oh, I pray he has not. Hurry, hurry, Nan, I cannot wait to find out.' And with that she ran from Beth's room to her own to be prettied up, leaving Beth thoughtfully chewing the end of her pen.

She wished fervently that she could experience half her sister's happiness, but knew there was no hope for it. The only man she would have entertained as a husband had proved himself ineligible. She looked down at what she had been writing and found the drawings she had so carefully made were covered with his name scrawled over and over again. Andrew Melhurst. Andrew. Drew. Drew. Hastily she screwed it up and then, not knowing what to do with it, stuffed it in the bottom of the drawer in the desk beneath her notepaper. Then she sighed, tucked a strand of hair that had fallen from its comb back where it belonged, and went down to the drawing room.

The Duchess and her mother were sitting together on one of the sofas, the Duke was at a table superintending the opening of a bottle of champagne, which the butler had just fetched. She curtsied to her uncle and moved to sit on one of the upright chairs in the window that looked out on to the garden. It was a riot of summer colour and she regretted staying indoors, pretending to study, when she could have been on her knees among the flower beds.

'They are taking their time,' Sophie said. 'How long does it take to make a proposal and receive an answer?'

'I rather think it depends on how you go about it,' Beth said, thinking of Andrew Melhurst's abrupt 'Marry me' and her subsequent, almost hysterical reply. Thirty seconds at the most that had taken.

'Should we interrupt them?' queried Harriet.

'Oh, let them have their few minutes of pleasure,' Beth said. 'It is a moment that will not come again.' Oh, how true! *He* would not ask again and even if he did, his motives would not have changed and love did not come into it, only the saving of his good name. She would not marry him on those terms.

Harriet looked at her a little sharply but did not comment, and a few moments later Livvy came into the room, clasping Lord Gorsham's hand. She was pink with excitement and his face was bright red. 'Mama, felicitate us. Henry has offered and I have accepted and we are so happy.'

Harriet rose and embraced her daughter, followed

by Beth and Sophie. The Duke shook Henry heartily by the hand, then nodded at the butler who had filled a tray of glasses with champagne for a toast. In the middle of all this, Foster arrived and announced Lord Melhurst and Mr Melhurst were in the vestibule requesting to see the Duke.

'Lord! I had forgotten Melhurst was coming,' James said. 'And with his grandfather—I had not expected that.' Then to the footman, 'Ask them if they would like to join us, Foster.'

The footman left and in a moment was back to announce the newcomers. In the flurry of introductions, explanations and congratulations, Beth was able to compose herself and by the time the two gentlemen had come round to her, she was able to speak calmly.

'My lord,' she said, curtsying to the older man. He was thin, his face well lined, his hair almost white, but he held himself upright and there was a twinkle in his faded blue eyes that reminded her of Andrew when she first met him.

He lifted his quizzing glass and surveyed her through it for what seemed an unconscionable time. 'Miss Elizabeth Harley,' he said, at last. 'I am pleased to make your acquaintance. I have heard of you.'

She smiled crookedly. 'Everyone has heard of me, my lord, my name is a byword.'

'For beauty and intelligence and composure,' he added gallantly.

Andrew chuckled, making his presence felt, and she was obliged to turn and face him. 'Mr Melhurst.' She could not for the world have uttered more. His intent gaze was unnerving her, making her heart beat erratically and her legs feel as if they could not support her. It was how she had felt when he kissed her and it had the mixed result of making her wish he would kiss her again and at the same time stiffening her spine against him.

'Miss Harley, I trust I find you well?'

She found herself saying, 'Very well, sir. You are in time to felicitate Lord Gorsham and my sister.'

'So I have heard. A good match, I think.'

'Oh, yes, we are all very pleased.'

'Drew, you will be my groomsman, won't you?' Henry's cheerful voice interrupted their study of each other and brought them both back to earth.

'With the greatest of pleasure but are you sure you want me, considering my notoriety?'

'If you think I would be influenced by tattle, then you do not know me, my friend.' He stopped suddenly. 'Unless, of course, his Grace has an objection…'

'None in the world,' James said. 'A man should not repudiate his friends.'

Beth was suddenly confronted with a picture of

Andrew Melhurst at the wedding of her sister at which she was bound to be one of the bride's attendants. She could see them standing side by side in church, listening to the words of the service, taking part but somehow not a part, and it was all she could do to stifle a sob.

'When is the wedding to be?' Lord Melhurst asked.

'The day after Christmas. Afterwards, if the weather is not too inclement, we are to go to Leicester for a se'ennight—Henry has a hunting lodge there— and then back home to Norfolk.'

'You will find Lord Gorsham keeps a good stable, Miss Olivia,' Andrew said.

'Nothing like the Melhurst stables,' Henry put in. 'But I mean to expand.'

'Then I shall have to look to my laurels,' Lord Melhurst put in. 'Eh, Drew?'

'You promised us a visit to Heathlands,' Livvy reminded Andrew. 'Do not think that, just because I have accepted Henry, you are to be let off. I want to go to the races.'

'Then so you shall,' Lord Melhurst said. 'And I hope to entertain Lady Harley and Miss Harley too.' He bowed towards Harriet, who inclined her head, but did not speak. 'Besides the stables, the gardens are worth inspection. I believe you are a gardener, Miss Harley?'

'It is one of my hobbies, my lord.'

'Miss Harley is uncommonly knowledgeable,' Andrew said, smiling. 'She can quote Latin names by the yard as easily as any botanist.'

'You exaggerate, Mr Melhurst, I am all too conscious of my shortcomings.'

'Then you should certainly visit Heathlands,' his lordship told her. 'My grandson has made a fair garden for exotic species. The glasshouses are extensive and everything carefully arranged. I don't understand the half of it, being more interested in horses…'

'How long are you planning to stay in town?' the Duchess asked him.

'A few days, no more. The hustle and bustle no longer suit me. As soon as my errand is done, I shall go back to Heathlands.' He turned to James. 'My lord Duke, I believe we have business to discuss, if the ladies will excuse us.'

'Yes, let us retire to the library. Gorsham, you can come too, if you wish. If you are to be family, it concerns you.' Then to the footman, 'Foster, see that Lord Melhurst's driver is given refreshment in the kitchen. We will send word when his lordship's carriage is needed.'

The four men trooped out, leaving the ladies looking at each other in puzzlement. 'What are they up to?' Harriet asked.

Sophie shrugged. 'I have no idea. I did not realise James was acquainted with Lord Melhurst.'

'I think our father knew him well,' Harriet said. 'Though why he should suddenly renew the acquaintanceship I have no idea.'

'Course you have,' Livvy said, put out that she had ceased to be the centre of attention. 'He has come about those rumours and he wants to see the cause of them.'

Beth, who understood very well what her sister was implying, was appalled. 'That means they have got as far as Newmarket,' she said. 'And if that is so, they are likely rife in Sudbury too.'

'We cannot know that,' Harriet said. 'News from London is often slow in reaching the country, especially when it is only talk. And Lord Melhurst might have come on quite another matter, something to do with his estate or his horses on which he needs to consult James.'

'Fustian!' Livvy exclaimed. 'Lord Melhurst knows a deal more about horses than Uncle James. I'll wager he has heard these tales and has come to determine the truth of them and decide whether to banish Mr Melhurst back to India or make sure he marries. No doubt he has someone in mind, though I hope, for his sake, it is not Lucinda Masterson; she is a fribble and will bore him to death.'

Beth was inclined to that view too and wished for the thousandth time she had never climbed into that coach in Sudbury. If only it were possible to put the clock back! If only she were safely working in her garden at Beechgrove and the last few weeks had never happened. Would the calumny follow her back there? And was it fair that her foolishness should deny Mr Melhurst his birthright?

Harriet, looking at her elder daughter, smiled in sympathy. 'Beth, are you at all inclined to take any of the young men who have been dancing attendance on you since we arrived in London?'

'No, Mama, I am not. And I wish you would not press the matter.'

'I was not going to. But it occurred to me that once we have announced Livvy's engagement and had a little reception for her and Lord Gorsham, we could return to Beechgrove. London is becoming altogether too crowded with everyone arriving for the coronation. Half the population seems to be making their way here and some of it not at all civil. I think, too, it would relieve the Duke of the burden of looking after us when he has so much to do.'

'You are not a burden,' Sophie said. 'Never say that.'

'No, perhaps not, but you must own James is fully occupied at Carlton House with the coronation only a month away, and if any of the gossip should reach the ears of the King, it might not sit well with him. I would not, for the world, cause James embarrassment.' Harriet turned to Beth. 'What do you think, dearest? Would you like to return home?'

'Oh, Mama,' wailed Livvy. 'I want to see the procession.'

'You could come back for that,' Sophie said. 'It is not that I wish to see you go, but it might help the scandal to die down if you are not here for a month.'

'I should like to go home,' Beth said, giving up the last vestige of hope that Mr Melhurst might forgive her for bringing this trouble down on his head. 'Livvy can come back if she wishes. I shall content myself with the garden.'

'Then that is what we shall do.'

The gentlemen rejoined them, but, if the ladies were hoping to be enlightened about the business they had discussed, they were disappointed. Refreshments were ordered and brought and the conversation returned to Livvy's engagement. Harriet told her brother what had been decided about their return to Beechgrove. 'We thought an announcement in the *Gazette* and a small reception before we leave,' she said.

'Nonsense! We will give a ball and make the announcement then.'

'A ball!' Livvy exclaimed, clapping her hands. 'Oh, I should like that above everything.'

'James, it is not in the least necessary,' Harriet said. 'A ball takes time and money to arrange and we thought something quiet—'

'You may have thought it, but I am surprised at Sophie

agreeing. Never let it be said the Duke of Belfont is lacking when it comes to launching his nieces.'

'One niece,' Beth reminded him.

'Oh, I have not given up on you, my dear,' he said airily. 'You may yet find someone to set your heart racing.'

She could not help it; she risked a glance at Andrew, only to find he was looking at her, his mouth turned up in a quirky smile, and hastily turned from him.

'When shall it be?' Sophie asked her husband. 'You are so busy…'

'I think I can find time to attend a ball in my own house. I have already spoken to the King and obtained leave to be absent for the occasion. At one time, nothing would have kept him away himself, but he does not go about much now.'

'Too fat to stir himself,' Sophie said, laughing.

'But you did not know about the betrothal before today,' Livvy said.

'I would have suggested the ball in any case,' James told them. 'But the announcement of an engagement will set the seal on it. One week from today…'

Harriet gasped. 'Surely it cannot be arranged so soon? Sophie, tell him he is asking too much of you, especially now.'

Sophie gave her a meaningful glance, meant to remind her that her condition was meant to be a secret, and smiled. 'Now is the best of all times. I have been thinking about it myself and have already put some of the arrangements in hand. A week it shall be.'

Livvy rushed from Henry's side to embrace her aunt. 'Thank you, thank you,' she cried. Then, remembering whom she truly had to thank, she curtsied low to the Duke.

Beth managed a smile, knowing there was nothing for it but to look pleased. Indeed, she was pleased for her sister. Lord Gorsham was a bluff, straightforward man, a perfectly suitable husband for her madcap sister, and she wished them happy with all her heart.

The Melhurst carriage was sent for and Lord Melhurst and Andrew took their leave, but not before Andrew had promised to attend the ball. If he had had any idea of pleading another engagement, he found it impossible to do so when Henry insisted he needed him at his side for the ordeal of the announcement. 'Can't abide fuss,' he said. 'Need you to field some of it.' And the Duke added his urging in a tone that brooked no argument.

'Then I shall be delighted,' he said with a bow, contriving as he straightened to look across at Beth. She was gazing out of the window at a thrush busily cracking open a snail.

'Well, Drew, will it serve?' Lord Melhurst asked, as they were driven away.

'I sincerely hope so.'

'So do I. And we have the Duke to thank for it. I always liked his father and he is cast in the same mould; a real gentleman with none of the arrogance so often to be found in men of his rank. Lady Harley is a fine woman too. I wonder why she has never married again.'

'Did you know her husband?'

'No, he fell at Corunna, I believe, leaving her with the two girls to bring up. Handsome chits, ain't they?'

'Yes.'

'Is that all you have to say? Henry has snaffled the younger, but you could do worse than fix your attention on the elder. I'll go so far as to say you could hardly do better.'

'She will not have me, no one will, while this cloud hangs over me. And over her. She blames me for the gossip, though for the life of me I cannot see what I could have done differently, short of leaving her on the docks to be tormented by those sailors.'

'It was not the rescue that sits so ill with her, but her own mortification,' his lordship said with a smile. 'Wait until she comes to Heathlands, she will not be able to resist the gardens.'

Andrew laughed. 'You think she will come?'

'Yes, because her sister will insist on it. I have Henry's word.'

'Grandfather, you old meddler. But I am not sure I

want her if the only thing I have to commend me in her eyes is a garden.'

'Then you must pray the Duke's scheme improves her eyesight.' He paused, but when Andrew did not comment, went on. 'I think I will return to the country tomorrow. If I am to be out of countenance with you, it would be better done at a distance.'

'Very well. I shall join you after the Belfont ball. I never meant to be away so long and it is about time I attended to the garden. I left Simmonds with instructions for looking after my botanical specimens, but I need to know that he is following them.'

'By all means,' his grandfather said complacently. 'But you will be expected back in town for the coronation.'

That was nearly a month away and he looked forward to it with mixed feelings.

Sometimes it seemed that the next week dragged by, at others it sped along so fast, Beth was breathless. Sophie left much of the arrangement for the ball to Harriet and Beth, who found herself so busy she had little time to brood during the day, but with the night came misgivings and these were mixed with a wild hope. Would the ball and Livvy's engagement be enough to give the gabble grinders something else to turn their tongues around and make them forget to link her name with Mr Melhurst's in a way that did credit to neither of them? He was a rake and she was a hoyden and they deserved each other, so it was said.

How far were they right? And did the fact that Lord Melhurst had come to London and made a point of calling at Belfont House confirm the story going round that the old man had ordered Mr Melhurst to marry her? No wonder his proposal had been so brusque; he had wanted a refusal. So be it, she had given him what he wanted, but that made his subsequent kissing of her even more despicable. She did not know whether to look forward to the ball or dread it. Most of the time, when she remembered that dreadful gossip, she dreaded it.

Livvy could talk of nothing else but the ball, her wedding and what she and Henry planned to do when they set up home together. She dragged Beth round to the dressmaker to have new gowns made for them both and to the Bazaar to buy accessories. She had to be dissuaded from choosing a scarlet taffeta for her ballgown and gently steered towards forget-me-not blue sarcenet, trimmed with cream. Beth herself chose pale peach silk, knowing it would set off the richness of her chestnut hair. Let them talk, she decided, she would not be cowed. And if Mr Melhurst should ask her to stand up with him, then she would do so and smile while she danced, though her heart would be breaking.

Livvy went riding with Henry nearly every morning, with Grimble trailing behind them to observe the proprieties, but they frequently managed to lose him. Each day she came back full of things Henry had said, plans they had made, people they had seen. On one occasion she returned with the news that Lord Melhurst had gone back to Heathlands in a miff and had threatened to disinherit Andrew.

'How can that be?' Harriet asked. 'They were here together only a few days ago and there was no sign of any discord.'

'I am only telling you what I heard.'

'What did Lord Gorsham have to say on the matter?'

'He would never say a word against his friend, but he did not deny it. How could he when Viscount Rapworth said he had it from Mr Edward Melhurst himself? He said no one could take the title away from Mr Melhurst because he is in direct line, but the estate is not entailed and Lord Melhurst has promised Mr Edward that Heathlands will be his.'

'I collect Mr Melhurst is still very wealthy in his own right,' Beth said.

'It is not the same as owning Heathlands, is it?'

'I am surprised at Lord Melhurst, if it is true,'

Sophie said. 'He did not impress me as someone who listened to scandal.'

'We listen to it,' Beth pointed out. Every time Mr Melhurst's name was mentioned, she felt as though she died a little. She longed to hear it, longed to hear good, not ill, longed to have him come to her knowing there was no shadow hanging over them, nothing in the way of their happiness. But she did not see how that could ever come about. There was always gossip and usually it died down and was forgotten when something else caught the scandalmongers' attention, but this seemed to regenerate with every telling. And because it had its beginnings with her foolishness, she did not see how he could ever forgive her.

'How can we fail to hear it?' Livvy said. 'When it is all over town.'

'There is no need for you to repeat it, Livvy,' Harriet said.

'I never would.'

Repeat it or not, the story gained momentum and the morning of the ball, Livvy returned home bursting with more news.

'You will never guess the latest *on dit*,' she said, finding the Duchess, her mother and sister in the small parlour, going over the last-minute arrangements. The food had been bought and was in the process of being prepared by a battery of temporary staff under the direction of the Duke's French chef; the wine had been chosen and the butler was even now counting the bottles; the flowers had been ordered and would be arranged by Beth as soon as they arrived; the housemaids were busy polishing the ballroom floor, the musicians had been booked and the invitations sent on cards embossed with the ducal crest. It was to be a grand occasion; because an invitation from the Duke and Duchess of Belfont was much prized, almost all had been accepted, notwithstanding the short notice. There were many disappointed hosts and hostesses whose guests had suddenly discovered they could not come. Sophie recompensed them where she could by inviting them too.

They looked up as Livvy burst into the room, still in her habit and riding boots. 'You will never believe it,' she announced. 'The King is creating a whole batch of new peerages to mark his enthronement and Mr Edward Melhurst is to receive a viscountcy.'

'Livvy, where did you hear that?' Sophie said. 'Honours like that are supposed to be a closely guarded secret until they are gazetted and an official announcement has been made.'

'Then you know about it?'

'Not at all, I was simply making an observation. Tell us, where did you hear it?'

'From Mrs Melhurst. We were riding along the Row and she came up in her carriage and stopped to felicitate us. Then she told us it was not the only event worth celebrating because her husband was expecting a great honour. Henry quizzed her and she pretended reluctance to say, but then she swore us to secrecy and admitted he was to be made a viscount.'

'Why would the King honour him?' Beth asked. 'He has done nothing of any import. Why, if it had been Mr Andrew Melhurst it would be understandable since he has been of value in the cause of botanical research.'

'That is a silly reason for giving a man a peerage,' Livvy retorted. 'According to Mrs Melhurst, it is because Lord Melhurst is going to leave Heathlands to Mr Edward and an estate as large as that needs a peer at the head of it. She was gushing all over the place and saying it was all down to Uncle James. I never knew he had so much influence with the King.'

'I doubt he does,' Sophie said, 'though his Majesty might have asked his opinion.'

'I refuse to believe Uncle James would have recommended the man,' Beth said. 'He knew perfectly well why Mrs Melhurst was emptying the butter boat and would never have succumbed to it. And why a viscountcy? It would elevate him above Lord Melhurst, above Mr Andrew Melhurst when he comes into his lordship's title. It is all a hum.'

'Surely Mrs Melhurst cannot have made it up?' Harriet asked.

'Who knows?' Sophie said. 'But I think I had best inform James about it. If it is true, it could well result in the honour being withdrawn and James will be in bad odour with the King.'

'Then we must do nothing to make matters worse,' Harriet said. 'Livvy, you will not repeat the story to anyone else, do you understand? You will forget you ever heard it. If it is true, we must wait until it is gazetted.'

'I shall say nothing, Mama, but if the story is already about town, what difference does it make?'

'All the difference in the world. I am sure the Duke will want to track down the source and the fewer people there are to suspect, the better.'

'But it must have been Mr Edward Melhurst himself,' Beth said.

'Would he risk having the honour withdrawn because he spoke too soon?' Harriet queried.

'No, but his wife would, she is the silliest of women.'

'True,' Sophie said, smiling. 'But we must say nothing, even if we are asked to confirm or deny it. Now, let us put it from our minds. It really does not concern us. Let us rather think about the ball.'

'Yes, go and change, Livvy,' Harriet said. 'Then you may help Beth write out the dance cards.'

Beth, who had spent the time since Andrew kissed her in vilifying him to herself, trying hard to convince herself that he was a rake who was not worth breaking her heart over, found herself feeling sorry for him. Because of her and the scandal she had attracted, he had lost his birthright and would have his cousin lording it over him. And what would happen to the gardens he had so carefully created if he had to leave Heathlands? She was very angry with Lord Melhurst. How could he do it? Why could he not see that none of it was Andrew's fault? She was even angrier with the gossips, whoever they were, for ruining a man's character without any more evidence than that he had rescued a foolish woman from her own folly.

The King could give honours to whom he chose, but a viscountcy to that worm who was not fit to lick Andrew's boots was the outside of enough! From being Andrew's detractor, she was now his champion. She saw nothing inconsistent in her musings and would have been outraged if anyone had pointed them out to her.

The ladies of Belfont House rested all afternoon in order to be in fine form for the ball and at five thirty had tea and light refreshments before beginning the long and careful process of preparing themselves. Baths were brought up to their bedrooms by toiling chambermaids and filled with warm scented water. They lay and soaked until it was almost cold and then underwear was put on and powder gowns donned while they had their hair dressed by a specialist who came to each one in turn.

Livvy was looked after first as the ball was in her honour and she could not for the life of her sit still. When she was ready she came to Beth's room to sit and watch her being got ready and to chat on and on, until Beth, normally a very patient sister, wanted to scream at her. Beth's agitation was due entirely to the knowledge that Andrew Melhurst would be at the ball and she would see him and it would be the first time since that revelation about his cousin's peerage. Would that have changed him? Would he blame her more than ever? She was laden with guilt. How could she tell him how sorry she was and make him believe her?

'Beth, I do believe you have not heard a word I have been saying,' Livvy complained. 'What have you been daydreaming about?'

Beth pulled herself together. 'I was not daydreaming. I was simply sitting still in order that *ma'mselle* can do my hair. And you are talking enough for two of us. Pray, do calm down or you will never last the night.'

They were ready at last and made their way down to the ground-floor ballroom where the Duke and Duchess and their mother were already gathered. It was a huge room, with a row of pillars and archways on one side that formed an overflow area which could be used if the company were large and tonight it would certainly be that. Flower arrangements, made by Beth, decorated the pillars and window ledges. At one end was a dais on which the orchestra were tuning their instruments. Later, it would be used by James to make the announcement of the engagement.

The girls had hardly been inspected and complimented on their appearance before the sound of horses and carriage wheels heralded the first arrivals. They moved out to the anteroom to greet their guests. Lord Gorsham was the first, closely followed by dukes, earls, lords, ladies and commoners, important people and those of little importance, but whom the Duke and Duchess counted as friends. And almost everyone the girls had met during their stay in London were included, some of whom were nursing a disappointment that Miss Olivia Harley had made her choice and they had been overlooked. Others were prepared to overlook hoydenish behaviour and try for the sister in order to have a duke for an uncle.

Beth looked in vain for Mr Melhurst, though his cousin and Mrs Melhurst were among the early arrivals. Beth wondered why they had been invited: Mrs Melhurst was overdressed and overloud in her praise of the Duke and her husband smirked visibly when James bowed to him. Was that why Andrew had not come, because he could not bear to have his humiliation made public?

Lady Myers's ball had been a grand affair, but the Belfont ball far surpassed it in the splendour of its setting, the size of the orchestra and the sumptuousness of the repast that was laid out in an adjoining room. If there was any gossip, it was subdued, perhaps in deference to the Duke and Duchess, perhaps because there was nothing left to talk about. There could surely be nothing to add to a disinheritance and a viscountcy!

Beth had half-expected to be left to languish on the sidelines, but she found herself standing up with one young man after another. They talked about nothing at all and paid lavish compliments, which she answered with a smile, though half the time she did not hear them. Her mind was on other things. Where was he? She longed for him, longed to be able to tell him how sorry she was, not only for his disappointment, but because she had unwittingly been the cause of it.

He arrived an hour late and nearly everyone was dancing, but his entrance was noted and a low murmur ran round the room. Beth did not wonder at it. Andrew Melhurst looked magnificent. He wore a deep blue tailcoat with covered buttons. Its sleeves were gathered into the shoulder and flared a little at the cuff to reveal the flounces of his shirt sleeves. His shirt was pleated down the front and a black cravat was intricately knotted about his throat. His breeches were a pale blue, his stockings white and his dancing shoes black.

He stood a moment surveying the company, as if searching someone out, then strode over to the Duke and Duchess. He bowed to Sophie and shook hands with James. Beth, watching surreptitiously, almost fell over her partner's feet and was obliged to apologise.

'No, no, the fault was mine,' he said gallantly. 'I see Melhurst has arrived.'

'Has he? I hadn't noticed.'

'Oh, I am sorry, perhaps I should not have mentioned him in your company.'

'Why ever not? He is a great favourite with all our family and a friend of Lord Gorsham.'

'I beg your pardon. I thought he was—' He stopped in embarrassment.

'Are you acquainted with Mr Andrew Melhurst?' she asked, while still having one eye on the look out for the gentleman in question. But he had disappeared from view.

'Only by hearsay.'

'Then I suggest you pay less heed to hearsay. Mr

Melhurst is a fine, honourable gentleman. I hold him in the highest regard.'

'Oh, quite,' he agreed. 'Top-of-the-trees Corinthian.'

She was glad the dance had ended and curtsied in reply to his bow, but he was never given the opportunity to escort her back to her seat because Andrew was there beside her. 'Miss Harley. The next dance is mine, I think,' he said, bowing to her.

It was not. His name was not on her card at all, but she smiled and took his hand and went docilely with him into a waltz, while half the population of the upper echelons of London society looked on.

'You do not need to defend me quite so hotly,' he murmured, as they danced.

'Why not? It grieves me to see a man ruined by gossip, especially when it is undeserved.'

'You think it is undeserved?'

'I know it is. It is all my fault and I am truly, truly sorry. If I could make amends…'

It was on the tip of his tongue to say 'marry me' again, but he thought better of it. When he asked her again, it would have to be when all shadow of scandal had been lifted from him. He smiled. 'What has brought on this change of heart? Two weeks ago I was out of favour. You went as far as to say my infamy was deserved.'

'That was when—' She stopped suddenly, feeling the heat flood her face and knew it must be scarlet.

'When I kissed you.' He smiled. 'If I distressed you by it, then I beg your pardon, but I am not sorry I kissed you. It was a delightful experience.'

'How could you?'

'Easily, since it was something I had been wanting to do ever since I met you.'

'I meant remind me of it. That was uncivil of you.'

'Are you still so angry with me?'

'No, I am not angry with you. I am sorry for you.'

'Oh, dear, I am not sure which I find most humiliating. Why are you sorry for me?'

'According to gossip, your grandfather has disinherited you and is bequeathing Heathlands to your cousin.'

'How very interesting. I should like to know who said that.'

'It was your cousin's wife who told Livvy and Lord Gorsham when she met them out riding.'

'Did she now?'

'I cannot believe Lord Melhurst would do anything so unjustified and, if it is not true, why do you not publicly deny it?'

'Because I do not chose to.'

'Oh, Andrew, then it is true.'

He smiled. Hearing his given name on her lips was very pleasant and gave him hope. This was a very different Beth from the firebrand who had called him a rake; it was the Beth with whom he had first fallen in love. 'You do care,' he whispered, whirling her through one of the archways, away from the mass of dancers.

'Of course I care.' She hardly noticed where they were and would not have protested if she had. 'I blame myself. If I had not gone to the docks to see Toby…'

'Mr Kendall—I had almost forgot him. I collect Miss Olivia saying you were missing him.'

'She had no business to say that.'

'Is it not true?'

'I would feel his absence if I were at home tending the plants because we have always done that together, but not here in London. He was a friend and companion of my childhood, but we all outgrow childish things in the end, though I would like to think he remained my friend.' She paused, but when he made no comment, added, 'If you are sent away from Heathlands, what will you do?'

'If I am sent away from Heathlands, then I shall have to start again elsewhere.'

'I cannot bear to think that you must leave your garden and your plants, everything you have worked so hard for. Will they transplant?'

'Some might.' He stopped dancing and stood looking down at her. 'Why are we talking about plants?'

'It is an interest we have in common and something we both care about. If you wish, you could bring them to Beechgrove. I am sure we could find room for them and, when Toby comes back, you could work together.'

'Oh, Beth, you are a treasure.' He laughed.

'Sir, I think we should continue dancing,' she remonstrated, but she was heartened by his use of her name. But how could she be a treasure?

They resumed waltzing, but he was in no hurry to emerge from behind the foliage into the main area. She danced well and having her in his arms, even at the required twelve inches' distance, was a pleasure he was reluctant to bring to an end. One day, God willing, he would do more than dance with her, he would make love to her—resisting the temptation to tell her so was taking all his restraint.

The orchestra brought the music to an end and they stopped and faced each other. He bowed, but did not immediately offer her his arm. 'Beth, do you think we could set aside whatever it is that separates us and be friends?'

Friends, he said, friends just as she and Toby were friends. It was not what she wanted at all. She wanted more, much more, but how could she tell him that? 'How can you want me for a friend when through my foolishness, you are being denied your birthright? Surely it must give you a disgust of me?'

'Your foolishness is only that you appear to believe what you are saying. It is not your fault, nor mine either. I have made an enemy who delights in seeing me brought low, and it is unfortunate that he heard of the manner of our meeting and used it to try and ruin me.'

'You know who he is?'

'I do now.' He lifted a hand and used his finger to lift her chin. 'I think we shall yet come about, sweet Beth, but I need you to trust me.'

'Naturally, I trust you.'

'It is all I ask.' He paused and added, 'For now.' He stopped again and, taking her hand, raised it to his lips, before offering his arm. She laid her fingers upon it and they walked together out into the main ballroom and promenaded round the circumference of the room, as many other couples were doing. 'You return to Heathlands soon, I believe,' she said, trying to pretend they were only exchanging civilities, when every word, every nuance, every look, meant so much more.

'Yes, I have had my fill of London and my garden beckons.'

'As does mine.'

'God willing, we shall meet again very soon. If you would like it, that is.'

'Oh, I should like it very much.'

He found himself grinning as he handed her over to her mother and bowed to them both. Almost immediately, James, who had mounted the dais along with Livvy and Henry, called for silence and made the announcement of the engagement. In the general chorus of felicitations and toasts, he slipped away.

Chapter Ten

Beechgrove was a haven of peace. The garden was at its best and Toby's plants, under the care of young Pershore, were, for the most part, thriving. Beth was soon dressed in her father's breeches again and working on the soil. Here she felt at ease, here she could reflect on all that had happened in the last two months and dream and wonder and sigh. It seemed an incredibly short time for so much to have happened.

That Livvy seemed deliriously happy pleased her and, if only for that, the Season had been a success, but she was glad to be home. She had made a complete ninny of herself, had become the subject of gossip and fallen in love. She went over her last con-versation with Andrew again and again. It had seemed to promise so much and yet had promised nothing at all. Except friendship. Must she be content with that? She had not seen him again before they left town and had been told he had left for Heathlands the very next day. Had the gossip continued after their departure or had their absence silenced it?

It seemed a dreadful indictment of society that a man's reputation and his future prospects could be ruined by scandalmongers. Did those people who loved to gossip ever stop to think of the effect their words were having? Not only had Andrew been vilified, so had she. If she had been serious in seeking a husband among the eligibles on the town, she would have been sadly disappointed; none would have a woman with a scandalous reputation. It was as well that she was able to stand aside from that. Except… Except…

Had he meant it when he said they would meet again soon? Did that mean he would obey his grandfather and ask her to marry him? Again. And if he did, could she hold out against him, even knowing the reason behind it? Kneeling among the flower beds pulling up weeds, she smiled to herself, remembering the day Henry proposed to Livvy and saying, 'It depends how you go about it.' She had been thinking of Andrew Melhurst then. She could not stop thinking about him now. He filled her thoughts.

When she saw a particularly fine botanical specimen, she imagined talking to him about it; when one wilted, she asked him in her head what ailed it; when she tried to think of the proper botanical name for a tree, she remembered that ride in the park and the time he had kissed her. He had apologised and then added that he did not regret it because it had been delightful. She remembered the cricket match, spoiled because Livvy had been hurt, but that had been the beginning of Livvy's realisation that she loved Henry. And now a wedding was being arranged. But not her own.

Livvy and Mama had gone back to London to buy wedding clothes and view the coronation procession, leaving her with Miss Andover. It was a peaceful time in which she came to terms with what had happened and resigned herself to remaining single. Oh, she might go to London for another Season, but she could not envisage a time when any other man might win her love. Her heart had been given and, once given, could not be taken back and offered to another.

She looked up as Miss Andover hurried towards her along the narrow path. 'Elizabeth, the London newspapers have arrived and there is a report of the coronation. Leave that and come in for tea and let us read it together. No doubt, the Duke, your uncle, will be mentioned.'

Beth rose and followed Nan into the house by a side door where she changed her shoes and scrubbed the soil from her hands before going up to her room to change into a gown and brush her hair.

* * *

Half an hour later the two women were sitting in the small back parlour over tea and cake, and Nan was reading the report aloud.

It gave a full account of the King's coronation robes, which had a red velvet train twenty-seven feet long and a crown glittering with diamonds. His retinue, almost as splendid, was extensive and included the Royal Dukes and other high-ranking aristocrats, among them the Duke and Duchess of Belfont. The Abbey, when the procession reached it, was filled to capacity with invited guests: foreign royalty and heads of state and as many members of the peerage as were able to attend and who were not out of favour with the monarch. A long list followed, among them newly created peers, but only one name stood out as far as Beth was concerned and that was Viscount Melhurst of Newmarket. So, it was true after all. Andrew's cousin had been elevated above him. It must have been gazetted days before, but she had missed seeing it.

She felt acute hurt and disappointment on Andrew's behalf and wondered at the duplicity of her uncle in sponsoring him. But perhaps he had not, perhaps it was not Mrs Melhurst's toadying but Mr Edward Melhurst's own efforts in other quarters that had borne fruit. Her guess that Andrew knew the rumour was true had been correct. It was why he had not denied it and why he had left town. She hardly heard the rest of the account, being too wrapped up in wondering how he was taking it and wishing she could let him know how truly she sympathised with him. But perhaps he did not care for the title, though it brought advantages with it, but he must care very much about losing Heathlands. Was the rest of the gossip about Edward inheriting that also true? The new Viscount had chosen the name of Newmarket, which seemed to suggest it was.

'Good heavens!' Nan said, unaware that Beth was not attending. 'There is another report here about the Queen. She tried to get into the Abbey and was barred from entering and then she went to Westminster Hall where a banquet was held after the ceremony in the Abbey and was turned away because she did not have a ticket. Oh, how could they do that to the poor lady? She is still our Queen.'

'What? Oh, I do not know what goes on in the heads of those who should be above petty squabbles. No wonder the country is in such a muddle when undeserving people get honours and those who do good remain unrecognised.'

'Were you thinking anyone in particular, Miss Elizabeth?' Nan asked mildly.

Beth felt her face grow warm. 'No, no, I was speaking generally.'

Miss Andover folded the paper and laid it aside to drink her tea. 'No doubt Miss Olivia will have much to say about it when she comes home. His Grace will have made sure she and your mama had a good view of proceedings from some convenient window.'

Harriet and Livvy arrived two days later and Livvy could hardly wait to get in the door and divest herself of her bonnet before she was describing everything she had seen. 'Oh, Beth, you should have been there, really you should. We had a magnificent view from a first-floor window in Whitehall. The procession was miles long and it was fun to guess who everybody was. Afterwards we had a huge repast while we waited for them to return from their banquet. But the King did not come back the same way because the road was blocked by two over-turned carriages. Uncle James told us afterwards that they chose a route through some dreadful back streets and he feared they might be waylaid. And then they had to cross a foul ditch by a rickety bridge that creaked and groaned as the carriage went over it and he thought at any minute the whole equipage would be hurled into the filth and the King drowned, for as sure as anything no one would have been able to haul him out…'

'Livvy, do wait until we have changed our clothes and had some refreshment,' Harriet said. 'You have hardly greeted your sister.'

'Sorry,' she said, embracing Beth and kissing her on each cheek. 'How are you, Beth?'

'I am very well. No need to ask how you are. You are blooming. Did you finish your shopping?'

'Most of it. When the trunks are brought in I shall show you it all. Come up with me while I change. There is so much to tell you.'

Harriet followed her maid up to her own room and the girls went to Livvy's room, where Beth sat on the bed and listened to her sister chattering as Nan helped her change. 'Henry took me to a coronation ball at Almack's and that was a glittering occasion. I wore a new green silk gown and an emerald necklace Henry had given me as a betrothal gift and everyone stopped to felicitate us and Henry was so gallant and paid me so many public compliments.' She paused and added with a laugh. 'Even if some of them were more suitable for horses. He is coming down in two weeks to escort us to Heathlands…'

'Heathlands?' Beth echoed.

'Yes, you collect Lord Melhurst promised to invite us.'

'I didn't know he meant it. I thought it was simply a politeness. When I left, he had returned to the country—'

'Oh, you cannot have heard. He came back to attend the coronation and called at Belfont House that evening with Mr Melhurst, who has been made a viscount. Just think what that means!'

'I saw Viscount Melhurst's name in the account of the coronation, but I cannot think why you are in such raptures over it. He is a muckworm and I, for one, have no intention of visiting him at Heathlands. And I wonder at you, Livvy, being so taken in as to rejoice that he has been elevated above his cousin.'

Livvy stared at her sister, uncomprehending. 'Beth, how can you be so ungrateful? He risked his reputation to save you from being carried away to sea and ruining yourself over Toby Kendall and he never complained, not even when the *on dit* was that he had compromised your reputation and his grandfather had ordered him to marry you. And now you call him a muckworm. Do not let Mama hear you use words like that; she will lock you in your room and not let you into the garden for a whole se'ennight.'

Beth, who had been looking down, toying with the pleats in her yellow muslin skirt, looked up at this speech. Were they talking about the same man? 'Do you mean Mr Andrew Melhurst?'

'Of course I do. You don't think I meant Mr Edward, did you?' And she went into peals of laughter. 'Oh, then I agree with you, he is a muckworm and I do not care if Mama does hear me say it.'

'The rumours were wrong, then? It wasn't Mr Edward, but Mr Andrew who has been made a viscount.'

'Yes, I just said so, didn't I? There was no point in making him a baronet or even a baron, was there? He would be a lord in any case when his grandfather dies.' She giggled. 'What price the gossip now? I'll wager my pin money everyone will forget the dreadful things they have been saying about him and will be busy singing his praises and saying they never did believe ill of him. And all the young ladies will flock to be noticed. You, my dear sister, will be forgotten in the crush.'

Forgotten in the crush. She would be only too pleased to have her faults forgotten by the busybodies, but to be forgotten by Andrew was enough to send her spirits plummeting. Friends, he had said. That must surely mean he was looking elsewhere for a bride. She had told him she was sorry for him, had offered to house some of his exotic plants and he had known all along that he was to receive a viscountcy. And he had not said a word! How many more times was she to make a fool of herself before him? No wonder he smiled!

'Was Mr Edward in London?' she asked.

'No, he went back to the country with his tail between his legs. Mrs Melhurst is said to be furious.'

'And Heathlands?'

'If you mean the inheritance, that remains to be seen. Nothing was said in my hearing. I believe Lord Melhurst was ill at the beginning the year, but he seems hearty enough now and I doubt the question will arise for some time. We are to go there at his express invitation and I am looking forward to seeing the stables and going to the races. Henry says we can learn much from the way the Melhurst stables go about breeding and training racehorses which will stand us in good stead when we start doing it in earnest ourselves.'

'And will An… Viscount Melhurst be there?'

Livvy shrugged. 'I have no idea. I did not speak to him myself. He looked prodigious handsome in his robe. He is so very tall he stood out above everyone when they all went into the Abbey. All the ladies in our window party were sighing over him, and praising his face and figure and his blue eyes, which I never thought out of the ordinary, and though I'll wager he knew what was happening, he kept looking straight ahead and never smiled.'

Beth refrained from reminding her sister that she had once set her heart on marrying the man. 'It was a solemn occasion and not one for frivolity.'

'Do you know the Queen turned up with her entourage, but her way was barred by two huge men dressed as pages? I felt so sorry for her and so did the crowd who cheered her when she turned about and left. I think Uncle James would have liked to let her be admitted, but the King had overruled him… Beth, you are not listening to me.'

'Yes, I am,' Beth lied, reluctant to tell her sister that her mind had been picturing Andrew in the Abbey, standing upright and unsmiling and wondering if his inheritance still hung in the balance. Was his grandfather still insisting on him marrying? It would hardly be surprising; he would want to be assured that there was another generation to carry on the name and the estate. But there was, she realised. If Andrew did not marry and have an heir, then Mr Edward Melhurst was next in line; if he predeceased Andrew, then his son, George, would come into Heathlands. George would not inherit Andrew's title, not being in direct line, but as he was a great-grandson, he would take Lord Melhurst's title. It was all too complicated and thinking about it made her head reel. 'I read about that in the paper,' she said. 'I am more interested in the bride clothes you have bought.'

This distracted Livvy from the subject and she was all for turning out the trunks that had been brought up to her room by two footmen, but Nan, who had just finished arranging her hair, dissuaded her. 'You can do that after nuncheon, Miss Olivia. Lady Harley will be waiting for you downstairs.'

The two girls descended the stairs together, with Livvy still chattering. 'You should see the gown I have chosen, Beth. It is in pale lemon satin embroidered with gold thread and pearls. It cost Uncle James a fortune, but he said he did not mind. And we bought a length of lovely deep blue silk for you, which Madame Bonchance can make up for you. Mama said it was a colour that would suit you very well.'

'Thank you,' Beth said as they entered the dining room and joined her mother. 'I am sure it will.'

Fortunately for Beth's peace of mind, Livvy was entirely engrossed with her wedding arrangements during the following two weeks and did not mention Andrew again until Henry arrived to escort them to Heathlands. By this time Beth had become resigned to her fate and had determined that if she must go to Newmarket, then she would endeavour to enjoy the garden and not trouble herself too much over its owner. It was easier determined on than carried out.

Heathlands was only a three-hour carriage ride from Beechgrove and they set off one afternoon early enough to be there by dinner time without having to stretch the horses. Lord Melhurst must have heard the carriage because he was standing on the step to greet them as they drew to a halt on the gravel beside the front door. And beside him stood Andrew.

Beth felt herself begin to shake even before she left her seat and was afraid her legs would give way under her when he came forward to greet them. He was everything she remembered. He was just as handsome, his hair just as fair, his eyes the same vivid blue, and his mouth still had that quirky half-smile, as though he were not sure whether to break into a laugh or be formally serious.

Henry had jumped down and was helping Livvy out, so he offered his hand to Harriet. 'Lady Harley, welcome.' He bowed and turned to Beth, while her mother walked towards the door to be greeted by Lord Melhurst. 'Well, Beth, you are here at last.' His hand took hers while his eyes ranged over her face. 'You are very welcome.'

She used the necessity of looking where she was putting her feet to regain control of herself and, once standing on the ground, curtsied to him. 'My lord.'

'Miss Harley.' He bowed and offered his arm to escort her into the house, somewhat disappointed by the formality of her greeting and her unsmiling countenance. He had hoped a little time apart and the news that his elevation had silenced his detractors might have mellowed her a little, especially after the last time they had talked. He could not have told her of the honour that was coming to him, but he had tried to hint that all would be well and they would talk again. Surely she was not still angry with him over that kiss? He was going to have to tread carefully if he were to dispel her distrust of him and convince her that he loved her and that love had nothing to do with gossip or who she was or who he was, no connection with any obligation she mistakenly felt he had towards her, nor with his new title. Nor, more importantly, with anything she may have heard about his grandfather ordering him to marry her.

There had always been gossip and, given the nature of humankind, there always would be, but the scandal that had attached itself to him and to her had been particularly malicious and had puzzled him for a long time. Was he really the object of it or was Beth being used to discredit the Duke? It was not until he had spoken to his Grace that he realised he had in him a staunch ally, as determined as he was to get to the bottom of it. He had had no idea at the time that he was to be honoured for his work as a plant finder, but the Duke, who knew of it, had, with the King's approval, come up with the idea of using it to spread a little false gossip and trace its route to the gabble grinders. They had been emerging from the Duke's library and had spoken loudly enough for the waiting footman to hear their words. The footman had told his grandfather's coachman, busy filling his stomach in the ducal kitchen, who had told Teddy, who was conceited enough to believe it and not question why he had not yet heard it officially from the King's office. Teddy had told Kitty and Kitty, all delight, had told Livvy. Livvy had told Beth and thus it had come back to him.

The Duke had questioned his footman, his grandfather had questioned his coachman and, on pain of losing their positions, it had all came out. Teddy's whole aim had been to discredit Andrew to such an extent that Lord Melhurst would banish him again and this time for good. After the first juicy morsel of learning how he and Beth had met, his cousin had hit upon the idea of paying the servants to listen to what went on in South Audley Street. He had picked up a little here and a little there to give it a certain veracity and embellished it with titbits of his own, then paid them again to pass it on to the servants of other members of the *beau monde* who would enjoy telling their employers' wives. It was too easy, but just for good measure, he had added that he believed Andrew was cuckolding him. That was the part Andrew had found impossible to ignore. Poor Kitty! She was a foolish and greedy woman, far from discreet, but she did not deserve that. And he had had the devil of a job persuading his grandfather there was no truth in it.

Teddy, who had been deliberately encouraged to grasp the wrong end of the stick, had been made a laughing stock when the honours were gazetted, had gone back to his country home in a huff, trailing a resentful wife who still did not know that her husband was the source of the rumours. Andrew hoped she would never learn it.

Now that all that was out of the way, he could concentrate on what most concerned him, persuading Beth to marry him. But, impatient as he was, he must go slowly. She was too proud to capitulate easily and he doubted the prospect of being a viscountess would count for much unless he could offer other less tangible inducements.

He turned to smile at her as he ushered her into the hall. 'I am proud to have you here and it is my fervent wish that you should feel at home,' he murmured as he released her to be greeted by his grandfather.

The old man was still a charmer and knew how to please. He took Beth's arm. 'You do not mind helping an old man along, do you, my dear?' he asked.

'Not at all, my lord.'

'We shall have a little refreshment while your baggage is taken up to your rooms and then you may rest a while before dinner. There will be time enough to look round tomorrow.'

They progressed into the drawing room, where a footman waited beside a side table upon which stood a tray of glasses and bottles. 'There is ratafia or orgeat or cordial for the ladies,' his lordship said. 'Claret or cognac for the gentlemen. Unless you would rather have tea?' This last was addressed to Harriet, who was walking on his other side. Andrew and Henry were close behind with Livvy between them.

'I think I should like tea,' Harriet said. 'I find it is most refreshing when the weather is warm.'

'Tea it shall be.' He nodded to the footman who promptly left the room.

Beth used the time they were waiting to look about her. The drawing room, like the initial view of the house itself, impressed her with its proportions. Heathlands was bigger than Beechgrove, but not as huge as her uncle's Dersingham Park, which had always struck her as an impersonal showpiece, too large and too perfect to be comfortable, though her Aunt Sophie had done much to dispel that impression. Heathlands was solid, comfortable and well appointed. The carpets and curtains were thick and both were designed with scrolls and fanciful birds peeping from strange foliage. The furniture was solid and well cared for, the stuffed chairs echoing the colours of the curtains. A glass cabinet contained porcelain figures and a heavy mantel clock told them it was half past five.

There were several good pictures, one of which was of Lord Melhurst as a young cavalry officer. Another was of a boy just coming into manhood and Beth went over to study it in detail. There was no mistaking the fair hair, clear blue eyes and firm mouth. He stood beside a chair occupied by a lady who was also very fair.

'Is this you, my lord?' she asked Andrew.

'Yes.' He came to stand beside her. 'I was sixteen. The lady is my grandmother. She brought me up. I never knew my mother.'

'I am sorry for that,' she said. 'I cannot imagine being without my mother. She is my rock. Without her I should have foundered.'

'Beth, you are putting me to the blush,' Harriet said. 'Pray desist.'

'I am sure Miss Harley speaks from the heart, my lady,' Andrew said.

Beth, embarrassed, moved away and walked to the window to admire what she could see of the garden. There was a terrace outside the window, which led down to lawns and flower beds, surrounded by shrubs, some of which she did not recognise. On the far side was an archway that looked inviting. She would enjoy exploring that.

The tea was brought in and she turned back into the room and the conversation turned to more general topics and afterwards the guests were shown to their rooms.

Beth found herself in a room with a rose pink carpet, pale cream-and-pink striped curtains and a four-poster bed draped in the same material. The furniture was of a light oak and gleamed with polish. There was a huge arrangement of pink-and-cream roses on a table by one of the two large windows. She went over to sniff their scent and discovered a card lodged among the blooms. 'Welcome to Heathlands,' it said.

She wondered who had put them there. She supposed it was the housekeeper, a plump homely woman, obviously very fond of Andrew, whom thcy had met while they were having tea. She pulled one of the flowers from the vase and held it to her nose as she wandered round the room, which had a double aspect. On one side the view was of the park and drive down to the gates on to the road. To the other side were informal gardens that led to a small copse, a summer house and a glimpse of sparkling water.

She turned from the window as a maid brought her hot water and asked if she could help her dress. 'Your maid is helping the other young lady,' she said. 'I am Martha.'

Beth thanked her and was helped out of her carriage dress and into an evening gown of taffeta striped in three shades of blue. It had a fitted waist, fell over her hips in a smooth line and flared out a little at the hem. The neck was boat-shaped and it had large puffed sleeves. Her hair was dressed very simply and held by a matching ribbon. She had hardly finished her *toilette* and dismissed the maid when Livvy came running in to her.

'Oh, good, you are ready. Is it not a lovely house? I can see the stables from my room and a paddock with the most magnificent horses. I cannot wait to get close to them. Tomorrow, I shall prevail upon his lordship to lend us mounts.'

'He won't let you ride his racehorses.'

'No, but he must have others. I want to show off my new habit. It is the colour of burgundy. We bought it in London. When we go to Leicester on our wedding trip, I mean to hunt every day and shall need at least three habits. Come on, let us go down. I heard Mama go ages ago.'

Dinner was a cheerful affair, with two fish dishes, roast beef and boiled ham, all in appropriate sauces. There were meat pies and several kinds of vegetable, which his lordship assured them had been grown in their own gardens, as had the fruit that followed: pippins, plums, peaches and oranges.

These gave Beth the opportunity to ask Andrew about the growing of them, and what could have been an uneasy silence between them developed into a lively debate, only brought to a conclusion when Livvy asked about the horses. The evening was finished off with a hand of whist and some music, with Harriet playing the accompaniment for the girls to sing. Livvy sang a duet with Henry and, after that, Beth, after much urging by everyone, agreed to sing 'Polly of the Plain' with Andrew. He had a strong baritone voice that blended well with hers and she forgot her nervousness as they sang. Only when they had finished and he took her hand and put it to his lips did she begin to tremble. His open gaze as he looked into her eyes over her hand unnerved her and she found herself blushing furiously.

'Delightful,' Lord Melhurst boomed, reminding them that they were not alone in the room.

Andrew released her hand reluctantly and she returned to her seat, glad to sit down and hide the shaking of her limbs. So much for her resolve to enjoy the gardens and not allow their owner to trouble her. She was not so much troubled as thoroughly disturbed. Her heart was pounding and all because he had looked into her eyes and seen what she could not hide: her love for him. How could he not have seen it? She could not control it, could not deny him. She was spineless in his company and that was not at all like her. She was usually so sure of herself. Even when he had almost forced her into his carriage on the docks, she had fought him; she had had no hesitation in rejecting his advances in London, had been at her haughtiest when he kissed her. So what was different now?

Andrew and Henry sang a comic song and Harriet played a little Mozart before the evening was brought to a close with a light supper and a promise from Andrew that he would take them riding the following morning. It was all very amiable and civilised, but, as far as Beth was concerned, more unsettling than she would have believed possible. He was so correct in his behaviour, not a word had been said out of place, not a hint of what he was thinking, no gesture that gave her any reason to hope. Friendship, he had said, and friendship he had meant.

The four young people went riding immediately after breakfast the following morning. It was, so Andrew said, the only way to see over the estate. Having viewed the stables and admired the two horses that were due to race the following day, they were taken to see the latest foal, only two days old. 'He's a beauty,' Livvy said, falling on her knees in the straw to fondle the animal, ignoring the fact that she was wearing her new burgundy habit. 'Have you named him?'

'No, perhaps you would like to suggest a name,' Andrew said.

'Blaze,' she said, pointing to the white diamond on its nose. 'Melhurst Blaze.'

'Blaze he shall be.'

Their mounts were being brought into the stable

yard and they went out, mounted and rode out of the yard, walking past the paddocks where several horses grazed, and on through the park. Crossing the road, they came to open heath and here Livvy galloped off with Henry hallooing in hot pursuit. Beth smiled. 'I do not think he will have much success taming her.'

'I doubt he wants to. Her vivacity is part of her charm. Shall we leave them to it and ride round the lake?'

He turned his horse and re-crossed the road and they took a wide grassy path through the trees. They were alone, riding side by side when they came to the edge of a large lake, the path, recently cropped, divided right and left to encircle it. He chose to go left and they continued round the water, which lapped gently against the banks. The sun was shining on their backs, the birds were singing and there was the smell of newly mown hay on the air. Neither spoke for some time and the only sound was the clop of their horses' hooves. She could not make up her mind if he was brooding over something or merely thoughtful.

'I have yet to congratulate you on your elevation to the peerage,' she said when the silence became unbearable.

'Thank you. Ill deserved though it is.'

'You are too modest, my lord. I have heard you have done sterling work in the cause of botanical exploration. But why did you not tell me you were expecting it when we last talked in London? You let me think… Everyone was saying…'

'Such honours are secret until gazetted.'

'You did not trust me.'

'Oh, Beth, it was nothing to do with not trusting you. I would trust you with my life. It was all to do with that gossip…'

'You mean everyone saying it was Mr Edward who was being honoured. How could that have come about? Surely Mrs Melhurst did not make it up?'

He laughed. 'No, it was down to the Duke.'

'My uncle?' she asked in surprise. 'I cannot believe he would spread gossip.'

They had come to a fallen tree trunk, which had been fashioned into a bench seat facing the water, and he reined in and dismounted. 'Come, let us sit a little and I will tell you how it came about.' He held out his hands and she released her foot from the stirrup and slipped to the ground and into his arms.

He held her close for a moment, looking down into her upturned face, wanting more than anything to kiss her slightly parted lips. But he held himself in check. The last thing he wanted to do was spoil the rapport they had managed to establish. He would kiss her when that wary look in her eyes had gone. It reminded him of a frightened deer. He released her and walked over to sit on the bench.

Breathless and not a little disappointed, she followed and sat beside him, careful to leave a little of the seat between her spreading habit and his breeches-clad thigh. He half-turned towards her, though she gazed out over the water, pretending an interest in a couple of mallards circling each other in the middle. 'Is it deep?' she asked.

'In the middle, very deep.' So, she wanted to keep the conversation on an impersonal level, he decided, though it was she who had introduced the subject of his peerage. 'My great-grandfather made it by widening a bend in the river that runs through the estate. When I was a boy, I used to row out in a little boat we made and dive into it, trying to find the bottom.'

'And did you?'

'No, it was too murky and full of weeds. I nearly drowned once when I became entangled and Grandfather forbade me to swim there again, so I contented myself with fishing. The best spot was from that island over there.' He nodded towards it.

'You were an adventurous child? Was it that sense of adventure that started you off as an explorer?'

'No, that was being sent from home and being thoroughly resentful over it. I was not a coward and would rather have stayed and faced up to what I had done, but for Grandfather's sake I decided discretion was the better part of valour. I needed something to expend my energy on and the opportunity to go exploring was there. I came home when I heard my grandfather was ill, little realising what was in store for me.'

'Oh.' She had not meant the conversation to lead to that episode and wondered how to turn it about.

Her chuckled suddenly. 'It does not matter what we talk about, it will always return to the gossip. I think I had better tell you the whole…'

'My lord, it is not my concern.'

'I think it is. Will you hear me out?'

'Naturally, I will listen,'

He told her about his student days, the scrapes he got into, the ladies he was introduced to. 'Some were not real ladies at all, but I was not wise enough or experienced enough to tell the difference. I experimented, tried my wings, fell in love with them all…or I thought I did. One lasted a little longer than the rest. Her name was Kitty Haysborough. She was a demirep, though I did not know it at the time, and a married woman, which I own I did know. She made no secret of it, nor of the fact that she had made a man of me. Lord Haysborough, who until then had been quite content to let his wife do as she pleased, suddenly decided I was a danger. He threatened to call me out if I did not cease my attentions to his wife.'

'My lord, should you be telling me this?'

'Does it offend you?'

'No, but it must pain you to speak of it.'

'Not any more. I have put it down as one of life's experiences and made the most of my sojourn abroad by travelling and interesting myself in the plants of the regions I visited. It is perhaps immodest of me to say so, but I have become somewhat of an authority of the trees and shrubs of the Himalayas.'

She smiled and turned towards him for the first time. 'And this country, if not the world, is the better for your knowledge.'

'Praise from you is praise indeed and much appreciated. But it is important for you to know the history behind it because it has a bearing on what happened when we met and I took you to Belfont House.'

'You mean the gossip. I have never understood why it was so quick to spread and so exaggerated. No one that I know ever said you had absconded with me after my lover had abandoned me and yet that is what was being put about. If my uncle had not been who he was, I should have been quite ruined.'

'I know. It was unkind and malicious and once something like that starts it is difficult to eradicate it, but I think it will die down now—'

'Because you have been made a viscount. Livvy said it would do the trick, that everyone will say you are a paragon of virtue and they never believed the gossip anyway. How snobbish people are. As if a title can change what a man really is.'

'Do you mean that, in spite of the title, you still think I am a rake?'

'I never thought that.'

'Oh, but you did. I distinctly recollect you saying you believed what was being said about me.'

'I was upset.'

'With good reason. I did apologise that last evening in London. I understood you had forgiven me.'

'So I did, so I have. It is in the past and should be forgotten. Let us not speak of it again.'

'Then we will not.'

They sat in silence for a minute while each tried to return to the ease they had had before. He cursed himself for mentioning that kiss and she regretted that she had ever believed ill of him. It wasn't fair to blame him when she had wanted him to kiss her and had been so lost to propriety she had allowed it to go on. Being angry afterwards had been hypercritical. 'You did not finish telling me how you managed to staunch the gossip,' she said, endeavouring to put matters right. 'If it wasn't the viscountcy, what was it?'

'It was not that I was given a title, but the fact that Teddy was not...'

'Yes, how did it get about that he was? Mrs Melhurst herself was convinced...'

He laughed. 'That was the Duke's doing. He decided to spread a little false gossip in order to trace it back to its source…'

'And?' she prompted.

'I am afraid it was my cousin Teddy. He wanted me banished for good and when he heard about our meeting on the docks from my grandfather's coachman, he seized the opportunity to discredit me and embroidered the tale more and more. I am more sorry than I can say that you were the innocent victim.'

'Not so innocent. If I had not been so foolish, you would not have been obliged to rescue me.'

'Then we would never have met. And that I do not regret.'

'But why would he do such a thing? And surely he did not start the rumour about his wife and…' She stopped, confused.

'He thought it would give him credence and gain him sympathy.'

'And your grandfather believed it?'

'What made you think that?'

'He came up to London. Word was that he had ordered you to marry to scotch the rumours.'

'He wants me to marry, I agree, but he knows better than to order me. I am not good at taking orders and, besides, I shall marry when I choose to do so and I shall choose my own bride—' He stopped. Was he going too fast? Should he declare himself? Would there ever be a better opportunity?

She was trembling all over. Why was he telling her all this if he did not mean to propose? But perhaps he was simply preparing her for disappointment. She took a deep breath and sat on her hands to stop them fluttering about as if they had a life of their own, and gazed out across the water so that he could not see into her eyes. The mallards had been joined by two swans, majestically dipping their heads into the water and occasionally spreading their wings.

'Beth, listen to me.' He took hold of her forearms and brought her hands from under her so that he could take them in his own and make her face him. 'I…'

He got no further. The sound of galloping hooves was followed by the arrival of her sister and Henry. 'There you are!' Livvy cried, slipping from her saddle and hurrying to join them as Beth hastily retrieved her hands. 'We have been looking for you everywhere. Why did you slink off like that? I thought you were behind us, but when we drew up you were nowhere to be seen. Anyone would think—' She stopped suddenly and turned to Henry, who was dismounting behind her. 'Have we interrupted something, do you think?'

'I rather think we might have,' he said, grinning.

'Oh, do not be so silly,' Beth said, trying not to cry. 'The only thing you have interrupted is the story of how Mr Edward Melhurst came to believe he was to be given a peerage.'

'Oh, that! Henry has told me all about it. Shall we go back to the house? I am prodigious hungry.'

And back to the house they went, Livvy chattering excitedly about going to the races on the morrow, Henry humouring her with a laconic reply now and again and the other two silent as the grave.

Chapter Eleven

Newmarket, once a nondescript little village, was a town dominated by horse racing. Everything needed by horses, their owners and their riders could be found in its environs: stables, blacksmiths, saddlers, farriers, harness makers, boot makers, clothiers specialising in jockey's colours, breeches and jackets, together with hotels and inns, where, according to Henry, most of the business of the town was done. Not only did the racing fraternity gamble on the races, he told them, there were a great many hazard tables, where a gamester might take his choice between loo, quinze, *vingt-et-un* and whist.

Lord Melhurst and the ladies had arrived in his lordship's carriage and joined the mêlée of coaches, chaises, phaetons, gigs and tilburys making their way into the town. Henry and Andrew rode. Having found a suitable place to leave their carriage and horses, they walked to the area where the horses were being prepared for the first race, among them his lordship's Melhurst Sunburst, a three-year-old colt.

'Stay close together,' Andrew advised them, as he led the way through the growing throng. 'The races attract all sorts and there are pickpockets and undesirables about.'

Beth was quiet, had been ever since the ride the day before had given her so much to think about, but Livvy more than made up for that. She was in her element, running her hand down Sunburst's neck and over his shoulders, making the horse snicker and ripple his muscles in pleasure. She walked to its hind quarters and it stood docilely while she felt its haunches and legs and fired questions at Lord Melhurst, who answered good-humouredly.

'He is magnificent,' she said. 'He cannot fail to win.'

'I have high hopes of him,' his lordship said.

'I wish I could ride him.'

'Livvy, don't be foolish,' her mother chided her. 'The animal is a racehorse and highly strung.'

'I recall Miss Olivia stating she could win a race as easily as a man,' Andrew said with a chuckle.

'So I could if I were allowed to.'

'Then I am glad you are not. You could be injured or even killed and that would be unbearable for us all. You have all your life before you and so much to look forward to, not least a wedding.'

'Quite right,' Henry said. 'I will find you horses to ride, but not on a racecourse. Come, let us look at the opposition and decide which to back.'

'I want to put a guinea on Sunburst,' she said, taking his arm. 'You will put it in for me, won't you?'

They wandered off to inspect the other horses and Lord Melhurst stopped to have a few words with John Tann, his master of horse, and the young lad who was to ride Sunburst. His name was Tom Barker and he was thirteen years old. Andrew offered his arms to Beth and her mother and with one each side of him they strolled back to the carriage, which had been left near the finishing line so that they could use it as a viewing platform.

'Shall you venture on the outcome?' Beth asked Andrew. It was the first time she had spoken directly to him since they had been sitting on the tree trunk by the water's edge. The words they had said, the understanding of each other they had reached, had been replayed over and over in her mind. The whole episode had been bittersweet. Had he been going to propose or had his mind been set on explaining to her that he would not be bullied into marrying her? He had half-said that already. Oh, why, oh, why did Livvy have to come looking for them just then? She had been so tactless too, and that was enough to put any man off his stride.

Since then they had never been alone and everyone else had had so much to say, so much to exclaim over, so many questions to ask about Heathlands, she could not bring herself to instigate a conversation. They had walked in the gardens during the afternoon, but Mama and Livvy had been there too and, besides, she was too full of confused emotions to speak and not even her interest in the shrubs and trees could persuade her to open her mouth. And mealtimes were the same. If anyone noticed her silence, they did not comment.

Andrew had noticed it and wondered. He had been so angry at Olivia's interruption and the knowing wink that Henry had given him, he had ridden home in haughty silence. It had taken courage to get as far as he had; another two minutes and the words, for good or ill, would have been out. She must have guessed what he had been about to ask her, but she had pulled her hands away from his and turned from him, almost as if she were glad of the interruption. Since then she had not, until this moment, addressed a single word to him. He did not want to risk another rebuff, so perhaps he would not try again. But could he live the rest of his life without her?

He turned to look down at her. She was looking straight ahead, her face hidden behind the brim of her bonnet. A very fetching bonnet it was too, of cream straw decorated with forget-me-nots. Forget-me-not, the flower that was supposed to ensure the wearer would never be forgotten by her lover. Had she realised what they were when she put the hat on? In spite of himself, he smiled; she no doubt thought of them as *Myosotis*.

'I will perhaps put a guinea or two on Sunburst,' he said. 'He has done well in training.' He laughed suddenly. 'Gambling is an evil when taken to excess, but it is that which makes the whole endeavour worthwhile, not the prize money, if there is money—it is often only a trophy.' He paused. 'I will put a guinea on for you, if you wish. You may be lucky and come out a winner.'

They had arrived back at the carriage and he helped them in and went off to find a bookmaker. He returned with Henry and Livvy just as the race began. It was the first time Beth had watched anything more than local races with amateurs in the fields about Beechgrove and she found herself carried away by the excitement as the horses thundered away. The colours of the jockeys identified the horse and owner and the blue and silver of the Melhurst stables was prominent in the close-packed group near the front. Beth found herself, along with Livvy, jumping up and down and crying out, 'Come on, Sunburst!' until Harriet tugged on their skirts and made them stop before the carriage overturned.

Sunburst pulled ahead in the last few yards and won by a length. Nothing would satisfy Livvy but she must go to the enclosure and give the horse a pat and collect her winnings and they all left the carriage a second time.

Lord Melhurst was with his horse and they hurried over to offer congratulations. 'I knew he would win,' Livvy said, while Beth stood beside Andrew, who was smiling his own pleasure. 'What a pity the odds were so short.'

'They will be longer on Moonshine,' his lordship said, pointing to a filly who was being walked about by Tom. 'She is only a two-year-old and less experienced.'

'You do not think she can win?' Beth asked.

'She can if she puts her mind to it, but like all females she can be temperamental and may not choose to oblige.'

'Oh, my lord, that is unfair.'

He laughed. 'I say nothing of human fillies, though, from what I have heard of young ladies nowadays, they are no different. In my day young people did as their parents bid them.'

Beth could not be sure but she fancied he looked directly at Andrew when he said it. She risked a glance at him, but he was looking at something else. Following the direction of his eyes, she saw Mr and Mrs Melhurst bearing down on them. 'What does he want?' Andrew murmured.

Edward hurried forward, almost dragging his reluctant wife. 'We are well met,' he cried. 'Ladies, good afternoon.' He bowed and received a formal inclination of the head from Harriet and a slight bob from Beth and Livvy in reply. 'Grandfather. Drew. Henry. Your obedient.'

They greeted Mrs Melhurst, who seemed to have lost most of her animation and stood beside her husband with a smile on her face that did not reach her eyes. Beth was almost sorry for her and wondered how much of her husband's scheming she had known about. She certainly looked uncomfortable.

'What are you doing here?' Lord Melhurst asked, far from welcoming.

'Why, I am come to watch the races and put a guinea or two on the Melhurst nags. Must support the family enterprise. Pity the odds are so short.'

'That is because of the excellence of the breed and the expert training the horses have,' Andrew said. 'It is a reputation to be envied.'

'Oh, quite,' he said. 'Long may it continue.' He paused. 'Haven't had an opportunity to congratulate you on your elevation, Drew. Very unexpected, was it?'

'Such things always are until his Majesty chooses to make them public,' Andrew said meaningfully.

'True, though one is left wondering if his Majesty realises how he is being manipulated.'

Lord Melhurst intervened before Andrew could comment. 'Take care what you say, Edward,' he warned.

Teddy ignored him. 'After all, the Duke of Belfont could not marry his niece off to a commoner, could he?'

Beth gasped and felt Andrew stiffen beside her, and wondered what answer he would give. 'Please, my lord,' she begged. 'Do not answer him.'

Teddy laughed harshly. 'Yes, my lord, do as you are told. You always do.'

Andrew stepped forward, his jaw working, clenched fists raised, and it took the combined efforts of Henry and his grandfather to hold him back, while the ladies looked on in horror. Kitty grabbed her husband's arm. 'Teddy, you promised you would not make trouble. Just friendly congratulations, that's all, you said.'

'And that's all it is.' Knowing he was outnumbered, he stepped back and smiled. 'Let me know when further felicitations are in order, Drew. I will endeavour to provide a suitable nuptial gift.' And with that he walked away with Kitty grumbling beside him.

The afternoon had been spoilt as far as Beth and Andrew were concerned. Andrew knew, with certainty, that Teddy's poison arrows had found their mark. Beth was furious. After the pains he had taken to assure her he did not always obey his grandfather, the doubts had returned; he could see it in her troubled eyes. He would have to talk to her again, to try to put this episode out of her mind and continue the conversation begun by the lake.

'I am going back to the carriage,' Beth said, and plunged into the crowd without waiting for anyone else. Andrew followed and caught her arm. She shrugged him off.

'Beth,' he said, staying doggedly by her side, 'do not let that scapegrace spoil your day. He is not worth your tears.'

'I am not crying,' she said angrily, but the thickness in her voice told him she was manfully trying to hold them back. 'What have I to cry for?'

'Nothing,' he said softly. 'Nothing at all. Beth, I must beg a few minutes to talk privately to you. I need to finish what I started to say yesterday. I cannot let it go unsaid.'

'Then say it.'

They were being pushed and bumped against in the crowd, which was surging in the opposite direction, trying to inch closer to the railings for the next race, and he was fully occupied trying to protect her. 'Not now. When we get home.'

'It will be late. Dinner time. I shall have to go up and change and we cannot leave the company afterwards.'

'Then tomorrow morning. Will you take a walk in the garden with me?'

Her bonnet was knocked off and he stooped to

retrieve it. He held it up and touched the little blue flowers, sadly crushed by someone's foot. 'Forget-me-not,' he murmured as he handed the hat back to her.

She took it by its ribbons, but did not attempt to replace it on her head. 'It has been spoiled.' It was not the bonnet she was thinking of and he knew that.

'Not permanently,' he said. 'It can be mended, I am sure.'

'You think so?'

'Oh, yes. With a little patience. You have not answered my question. Will you take a walk with me tomorrow and let me finish what I started to say yesterday?'

'Very well.'

'Thank you.'

They had reached the carriage, with Lord Melhurst and her mother close behind them. His lordship was still trying to apologise for Teddy's behaviour. 'I would not have had you or your delightful daughters witness such boorishness for the world,' he said. 'Please try to put it from your mind. It was sour grapes, nothing more. I will have a word with him.'

'I think the least said the better,' Harriet told him. 'He is a disappointed man and must learn to accept. Who knows, in the future he might earn the honours he covets so much.' She settled herself in the carriage beside her daughter. 'Beth, I am sure, attaches no importance to his ranting. Do you, dearest?'

Beth managed a smile. 'Not in the least, Mama. But where is Livvy?'

Harriet looked round. 'I was sure she was behind us. Isn't it just like her to wander off.'

'Henry will look after her,' Andrew said, as the roar of the crowd told them the next race had begun. 'She is probably waiting in the enclosure to see Moonshine come in a winner.'

Beth could not work up the same excitement for this race as the earlier one. Her mind was too full of the coming interview with Andrew, wondering what he was going to say. Dare she hope? She stole a glance at Lord Melhurst, who was sitting opposite her, but he was intent on the race. Andrew stood on the step behind them to get a better view.

'My God!' he exclaimed as the horses thundered past. 'That isn't Tom on Moonshine, it's—' He stopped and jumped down, intent on going to the finishing post, just as Henry arrived. 'Is Livvy not with you?' he asked, peering past Andrew at the carriage.

'No, she's on the back of that damned horse.' Andrew ran past him.

Henry gasped and promptly turned to follow. 'We were coming back to the carriage, but were separated in the crowd,' he explained. 'I looked everywhere for her, never dreamed she would go back to the horses.'

'Why did you not keep her close by you? If she is hurt, we'll neither of us be forgiven.'

'I shan't forgive myself.' They heard a roar from the crowd, but could not see what was happening on the course. 'My God, she's fallen.'

Breathlessly they arrived at the finish to find a triumphant Livvy in Tom's livery, dismounting. She saw them coming and called out, 'I won. I told you I could, didn't I?'

Henry grabbed her arm and dragged her into Moonshine's box, where Tom Barker sat on the straw in his ordinary fustian clothes, looking decidedly down in the mouth. 'I won, Tom,' she said, pulling off her jockey's cap and shaking out her long hair.

'Livvy, how could you?' Henry said. 'After all we said. If you had been hurt... Oh, it doesn't bear thinking about.'

'It will make all bets void,' Andrew said.

'No, it won't,' she said. 'Who's to know it wasn't Tom riding? He won't say anything. And please don't be angry with him, it wasn't his idea.'

'Where are your clothes?'

'Over there.' She nodded to a peg on which her gown and bonnet hung. 'Now, if you all go out, I will change and everything will be as it was before. Tom can go and accept the praise for winning.'

They left the box and stood outside, pretending to

praise Moonshine, while Tom set about rubbing her down. 'How could you be so stupid?' Andrew demanded. 'If anything had happened to Miss Olivia, you would have found yourself on a charge of murder. How she managed to persuade you, I cannot imagine. I doubt you will ever be given another ride for the Melhurst stables. And where is Mr Tann?'

'Taking Sunburst home, tha's what 'is lordship told 'im to do. He's coming back for Moonshine. And it weren't my fault. The gen'leman said it were a wager 'e had made with you, that 'e couldn't bring it about…'

'Gentleman, what gentleman?'

'Mr Melhurst.'

'Edward!'

'Yes, sir, I mean, my lord. He said there was a lot of money riding on it and if I did'n' hand over me colours, he'd tek 'em anyhow and tie me up.'

Livvy put her head out of the box. 'Is the coast clear?'

'Yes, you can come out.'

She emerged and handed the colours to Tom, who disappeared into the box to put them on. Henry went to her and took her bonnet from her hand and set it on her curls. 'I never had such a fright in my life. Don't you ever do anything like that again or I shall die of apoplexy.'

She laughed, tying the ribbons beneath her chin. 'But I was good, wasn't I? You never expected

Moonshine to win, you told me so. I'll wager you are sorry you did not put a bet on now.'

'I wonder if Teddy did,' Andrew murmured thoughtfully.

'He said I couldn't win,' Livvy said. 'And I said I could.'

'Then he lost,' Henry said, beginning to smile. 'It won't have improved his temper, especially if he staked a large sum.'

'No,' Andrew said. 'How did you come to be speaking to him about it, Miss Olivia?'

'He heard me talking to Henry about riding in a race as we walked back to the carriage. He grabbed my arm and pulled me into the crowd. Then he asked if I meant it and if I was willing to put it to the test, so I said yes.' Her eyes were shining. 'And so I did.'

'Well, it's done now,' Andrew said. 'And you came to no harm. Let us go back to your mama and Miss Harley. It is time to go home.'

'Yes, I suppose I shall be in for a jobation.' She sighed, then turned to Henry. 'Do not forget to collect my winnings. I staked all I won on Sunburst, so it should be a tidy sum.'

He went off dutifully and Andrew escorted her back to the carriage where her mother was sitting, unaware that it was her daughter who had brought Moonshine home to victory. He looked at Beth as he handed her sister into the carriage and knew from the enquiring look on her face that she had guessed the truth. 'Later,' he murmured in her ear.

The ladies had withdrawn and the men were sitting over their cognac after dinner when the subject of Moonshine's race was brought up by Lord Melhurst. 'What happened to Tom Barker this afternoon?' he asked Andrew. 'And who authorised a substitute?' He laughed suddenly. 'Trying out a new jockey, were you? Am I expected to offer more rides?'

'No, Grandfather, it was one race only.'

'I sincerely hope so. What were you thinking of to allow it? And you, too, Gorsham. My reputation as a trainer will be in tatters if this gets out. Good God! Have we not had enough of gossip this year, without adding to it?'

'My lord,' Henry said before Andrew could reply, 'it was not done with the knowledge or connivance of either of us. Heaven forbid! I am afraid the fault lies at the door of Edward Melhurst.'

'The devil it does. Drew, I will have an account of it, if you please.'

Andrew explained what had happened. 'I fear he must have lost money on the race,' he ended 'From what Miss Olivia told us, he was convinced she could not win and would have laid his blunt elsewhere.'

'Doesn't have any blunt,' the old man grunted. 'Came to me a few weeks ago, begging to be relieved of his debts. I gave him a thousand and told him not to come back for more.'

'How much did he owe?'

'I cannot be sure, but it was a great deal more than that. I think that's why he took himself to London, hoping to borrow more or win more at the card table. I heard he'd been paying his gambling debts with post-obit bills on my life. It was why I betook myself to London.'

'So you did promise him he would inherit?'

'Nothing of the sort! Do you take me for a lobcock? But someone seems to think that I threatened you with disinheritance if you did not marry…'

'So you did.'

'I did not mean it, you knew that, surely? One of the servants must have passed it on and he used it…'

'Another of the rumours and the most damaging as far as I am concerned. A certain young lady is convinced the only reason I want to marry her is because you have ordered me to and that belief was strengthened by what Teddy said today. How I am going to change her mind, I do not know. Poison tongues, like poison arrows, are barbed and, once they have found their mark, difficult to retract.'

'Shall I have a word with her?'

'No, thank you, Grandfather. I should not like her to think I need you to fight my battles for me. But I could willingly strangle Teddy. If his malice had only affected me, I could bear it, but the damage he has done to Beth's reputation and her sense of her own worth is untold. I pray he does not spread any gossip about Miss Olivia's escapade.'

'There I can do something. I'll send for him. He'll come if he thinks I'll stand buff for him again. Now, let us join the ladies.'

They rose and went into the drawing room where Harriet presided over the tea pot. Lord Melhurst was particularly jovial and nothing was said about Livvy's prank. They talked of the races, of Livvy's coming wedding and Henry's plans for them both, of Andrew's travels and the garden, which Beth had not properly examined, anything except Mr Edward Melhurst and what had happened that afternoon. Livvy was more subdued than usual and Beth was more than a little absorbed in thoughts of her coming interview with Andrew.

She broached the subject to her mother when she came to her room that night. Nan had helped her into bed and withdrawn and she was sitting up in bed, with the curtains drawn back to that she could see the clouds drifting across a full moon and see the tops of the trees swaying in the breeze. It might mean that the good weather was coming to an end. Her mother came into the room in an undress gown and sat on Beth's bed.

'Home tomorrow,' she said. 'Have you enjoyed your stay?'

'Yes and no. I will be able to tell you after breakfast tomorrow.'

'Oh, what is to happen at breakfast?'

'Andrew, I mean the Viscount, has asked me to take a walk in the garden with him. He says he has something to say to me.'

'Oh, I see. You think he is going to make an offer?'

'I don't know. I am so confused. And that dreadful man this afternoon brought back all my doubts.'

'He is a muckworm.'

Beth gave a cracked laugh. 'Livvy said you would scold me for using that term.'

Harriet laughed too. 'Not when it is said about him. He undoubtedly has his reasons for saying what he did, but please don't let his malicious tongue influence you.' She reached out and took her daughter's hand. 'The important thing, the only truly important consideration is—do you love Andrew?'

'Yes, but if he is only going to ask me because his grandfather says he must and his inheritance depends on it...'

'And who says he is? Did he?'

'No, he said he did not take kindly to being told what to do and he would make up his own mind…'

'There you are then.'

'No, because he might be going to tell me he has fixed on someone else and it would be dreadful if he is only telling me because he thinks I am expecting an offer he is not prepared to make. I would be mortified if he thought that. It would be as bad as when he found me making a fool of myself on London docks…'

'Oh, my dear, how complicated you make it sound.' She smiled and leaned forward to kiss Beth's cheek. 'You must make up your own mind when you hear what he has to say, but, whatever happens, do not let pride come into it or fear of being put to the blush. There are worse things than that, you know, and one of them is losing what you most desire because you cannot be honest with each other. If you love each other, it does not matter one iota what anyone else thinks about it, especially the gossips who have nothing better to do than tear other people to shreds. Listen to your heart. I am sure Viscount Melhurst is listening to his. Now, try to sleep or you will not look your best tomorrow.' She kissed her again and was gone.

Beth, as usual when her mother gave her one of her little homilies, had felt comforted and settled down to sleep, but she was awake early. The cloud had dispersed and the sun was shining. The day of reckoning had come. Unable to lie in bed, she dressed in a simple spotted muslin, brushed her hair back and secured it with a ribbon and went down to the breakfast parlour.

There was no one there, but a couple of used plates and a cup that had held coffee bore witness to the fact that she was not the first onc down. She supposed Andrew had been there before her and was perhaps already walking in the garden, waiting for her. She ate a slice of toast, drank a cup of coffee and hurried through the house to a side door and on to the terrace. He was not to be seen from that vantage point and she walked down the steps and across the grass to an archway that led into a walled garden. It was sheltered here; peach trees grew against the walls and brilliant red pelagoniums flourished in the borders. The centre beds, divided by a grass walkway, contained roses and lilies of every hue, some waist high. At the far end of the garden was an arbour about which honeysuckle and clematis climbed. She walked to it and sat down to wait.

The effects of her mother's talk were beginning to wear off and she felt nervous and much less sure of herself than she had when she woke up. It was an effort of will to sit still and her hands picked idly at the petals of one of the flowers. He would come. She shut her eyes and breathed in the perfume of roses, lilies, honeysuckle, strong first thing in the morning, contained as they were within the walls of the garden.

She heard running feet and her eyes flew open. It was not Andrew, but a stable lad. 'Miss Harley, come quick, Miss Olivia hev took a tumble.'

She sprang to her feet. 'Where is she? I must find someone to help.'

'No need. Mr Andrew, I mean the Viscount, hev already gone to her, but she want you. I'll tek you to her.'

She had no choice. She followed him. He led her across the park and plunged into the wood, following a narrow path. When they came into a clearing, she realised they were almost alongside the lake and not far from the spot where she and Andrew had talked. The boy stopped. 'There,' he said, pointing.

There was a saddled horse cropping the grass and nearby a pile of logs. Livvy, out for a pre-breakfast ride, must have attempted to jump the logs and been thrown. Beth picked up her skirts and ran forward calling her sister's name.

There was no answer. She ran round the logs; there was no one there. She turned back to ask the boy to show her where her sister was, but he had disappeared. There was no Livvy, no Andrew and now no stable lad. Was this someone's idea of a jest? She thought of Andrew going to the garden expecting to find her and she not there. He would conclude she had no interest in listening to what he had to say and he would never ask her again. But supposing Livvy had really been hurt and crawled away somewhere badly injured? Supposing Andrew had picked her up and was even now carrying her homewards? She ran round and round examining the ground, looking for evidence of someone injured or the presence of a second horse but the ground was bone hard. She called Livvy's name more and more urgently.

'She won't hear you.'

She whipped round to find Edward standing beside the horse, his hands on its bridle, smiling at her. 'Where is she?' she demanded, suddenly feeling threatened. 'I was told she had taken a tumble. The boy said Andrew was with her.'

'He was mistaken. It was I. I'll take you to your sister.'

She was reluctant to go. 'Should we not fetch someone? If she needs carrying…'

'I will see to that after I have taken you to her. You can comfort her while I fetch my cousin and a couple of men with a cart. I was on my way to Heathlands in any case, summoned by the old man.'

She walked beside him along a path and then out of the trees to find herself at the lakeside. There was no one in sight. 'Where is she? How came she so far from her horse?'

He shrugged. 'Adventurous article, your sister. She's over there.' He pointed over the water to the island.

'What is she doing there? How did she get there?'

He pointed to a small skiff, moored at the water's edge. 'She saw a heron and nothing would serve but I must row her over there to see it at close quarters. As I said, I was on my way to the house…'

'And she has been hurt? How did that happen?'

'Come and see for yourself.' He stepped down into the boat and untied the rope. 'Come, she is waiting for you.'

She hesitated, but gingerly stepped into the small craft. If it were not for worry over Livvy, she would never have ventured into it. 'Have you harmed her?'

'Gracious me, no. Why should I do that? I have nothing against the chit at all.' He grinned. 'Except she is too good a horsewoman. I had hoped to clear my debts when Moonshine lost, but instead I am out by a few thousand. No doubt that was why my grandfather wanted to see me. He would want to recompense me for my loss…'

'Or your evil tongue would be at work again, is that it?' She knew she had angered him and ought not to have spoken. She was at his mercy and, though he pulled strongly for the island, he could easily tip her out; she remembered Andrew telling her the water was very deep. She would not put it past the dreadful man to abandon her and Livvy on the island; they would never be able to swim across the lake. But why would he do that? 'If you have nothing against my sister, what have you against me?' she asked.

His laugh did not make her feel any easier. 'Why, my dear, you are my cousin's intended bride and I cannot have him married. If he had stayed out in Calcutta it would not have mattered, but here, once more society's darling, a Viscount no less, married to the niece of a Duke, hc is too much of an obstacle.'

'Obstacle?'

'To my inheritance. All the time he was away and in disgrace I danced attendance on the old man, made myself indispensable to him, and how does he serve me for that? As soon as the prodigal returns, I am cast aside. If Drew marries and has a son, then I am without hope.'

'What makes you think he wants to marry me? He could have the pick of anyone.'

'You, my dear, are the niece of a Duke, great grand-daughter of one too, daughter of a war hero, and my grandfather has decreed it must be you.'

'And you think Andrew will marry me to please his grandfather?'

'He will if Heathlands is at stake.'

'You do not know him very well if you think that.' Even as she said it, her own doubts flew away. She had spoken the truth: Andrew was too independent to be dictated to. But that revelation was as nothing when she thought of him sitting in the garden waiting for her. How long would he wait before he went in search of her? Or would he bother to look, just assume she did not want to see him and take himself off somewhere until she left for Beechgrove, which had been planned for that afternoon? How long before her mother missed her daughters? That would surely not be long and then she would alert everyone and they would search for them. Surely, surely no one would believe she had embarked on another scrape like running after Toby? That was what had begun it all. If she had known…

The boat bumped against the bank on the island and he put up the oars and scrambled out, pulling on the mooring rope to steady it as he offered his hand to help her. She would have liked to manage on her own, but the small craft pitched alarmingly as she stood up and she was obliged to grab the hand and be hauled ashore.

'Now, where is Livvy?' she demanded.

He laughed. 'I don't know. At home in bed, I shouldn't wonder.'

She gaped at him. 'You mean she isn't here?'

'No. As I said, I have nothing against your sister, but I needed to lure you here somehow.'

She was truly frightened, but hid it as well as she

could, seeking refuge in anger. 'And now you have done so, what are you proposing to do with me?'

'Oh, nothing, my dear. You may do as you please. There is the island to explore, but that is only a little larger than the drawing room at Belfont House. There is a small hut that we built as boys when we rowed ourselves over to play shipwrecks. You can see what that holds. There are a few unusual trees Drew planted before he went to India; you can study those if you like. Hours of amusement, don't you agree?'

'And what will you be doing while I am amusing myself?'

'Why, I told you. My grandfather has sent for me and a summons from him is disobeyed at one's peril.'

'Will you tell them where I am?'

'Eventually, perhaps. Perhaps only Drew. I am sure he will rush to your rescue.' And with that he jumped back into the boat and pushed off.

She stifled the plea that came to her lips. She would not beg. Andrew would find her. He would make Mr Melhurst tell him where she was.

Edward had been right about the size of the island. It took less than five minutes to walk its circumference and when she returned to the same spot she saw Edward tying up on the other side. She crossed into the middle of the island, which was really a small hillock, and on the top found the hut made of bits of driftwood and bare branches. There was a mouldy blanket inside, a fishing line and a basket, which had once probably contained food. There was nothing in it now. She remembered she had been so anxious to be in the garden she had eaten only had one piece of toast for breakfast and she was hungry. And thirsty. She returned to the shore and sat down. How long before she was missed?

'Oh, Andrew,' she murmured aloud. 'Believe I was going to listen to you, believe I was tricked into leaving the garden, know that I love you and need you and, if I am given the chance, I shall tell you so. Mr Edward Melhurst will not part us.'

Andrew had paraded the circumference of the garden three times without a sign of Beth. She had said she would meet him and he could not believe she would deliberately snub him. Perhaps she had misunderstood where he wanted to meet her. He went to the glasshouses and walked their length, asking Simmonds who was busy in the heat in nothing but a shirt and breeches, if he had seen her. The answer was in the negative. He went to the stables. All the riding horses were where they should be, even the ones Livvy and Beth had used. The grooms were busy polishing Henry's carriage and grooming his four bays, ready for the return journey that afternoon. No one had seen Miss Harley.

Fuming with frustration, he went indoors, prepared to confront her wherever she was and make her listen to him. Lady Harley and Livvy were eating a late breakfast. Her ladyship looked up as he entered. 'Good morning, my lord.' She smiled, evidently expecting to see Beth behind him. 'I hope you have good news for us.'

'My lady,' he said. 'You knew I was to meet Miss Harley this morning?'

'Yes, though you should have applied to me first.'

'I needed her consent to do so.'

'And have you received it?'

'I have not seen her. As far as I can discover she has not been outside at all. Can she still be in her room?'

'If she is, I will have strong words to say to her, keeping you waiting like this. But it is not like her; she was never impolite and I am persuaded she had determined to meet you. I think I had better go and find out why she has changed her mind.'

She rose and left the room but was back within the minute. 'She is not there. According to Miss Andover, she saw her leave the house over an hour ago. Are you sure you have looked everywhere?'

'Everywhere in the garden. She must have wandered further afield. I will go out again.' He dashed from the room and out of the front door, passing his cousin as he mounted the steps to be admitted. 'Good morning, Drew,' Edward called to the vanishing figure and went indoors, smiling.

Chapter Twelve

Beth's disappearance caused a furore. Everyone, family and servants alike, were sent out on the search, to no avail; she seemed to have disappeared into thin air. It looked more and more as if something dreadful had befallen her and Andrew was almost out of his mind with worry. Even Edward helped with the search for a time, but then said he had better be getting home; Kitty needed him. 'I will keep a sharp look out on my way,' he said. 'And let you know if I hear anything of her.'

It was unlike Teddy to be so helpful, but Andrew was too worried to care. He nodded and set off once again to search across the heath that bordered the estate, though why she should have walked so far, he did not know. By early afternoon his spirit were at their lowest ebb and he could hardly hide his dejection from Harriet and Livvy, who had abandoned all thought of returning to Beechgrove. His grandfather had been overcome that such a thing had happened at Heathlands and collapsed. He was helped to bed by his valet and the doctor sent for. Henry had searched as hard as anyone, but now he was comforting Livvy, who had soaked several handkerchiefs with her tears.

In the middle of it all a young village lad arrived with a note from Edward. Andrew tore it open and scanned its contents. 'It may be a false trail, but perhaps it is worth investigating,' he read aloud to Harriet, Henry and Livvy, who had gathered to consider what to do next. 'The bantling who is bringing this to you told me he had seen a young lady on Heron Island. She must be stuck there because he saw the boat drifting in the middle of the lake. Question him and he will confirm it.'

'Heron Island?' queried Harriet. 'Where is that?'

'It is a tiny island in the middle of the ornamental lake. I must go at once.'

'I will come too,' Henry said.

'No, you harness up the gig and bring it round by the road. If Beth has been on the island any length of time, she will be cold and upset. Put some blankets in it and a flask of something to revive her.' He dashed from the house, leapt into Firefly's saddle and galloped off across the park and into the trees. He emerged near the landing stage and dismounted.

He could see a small heap of white on the island,

which could have been a lady's dress. Equally it could have been a resting swan. He shouted, but the bundle, whatever it was, did not move. He cast his eyes round for the boat. It had drifted a long way down the lake and would soon join the river and be lost. If he swam across, and he had no doubt he could do it, how was he to bring Beth back? He had no idea if she could swim, but in any case would not ask her to attempt it. The middle was deep and full of weeds that could capture legs and pull a body down. It had happened in the past. And that unmoving bundle of white was worrying him.

He raced round the water's edge until he was level with the boat, then stripped off his coat and riding boots and plunged in. It seemed to take an age as the wide water of the lake was funnelled into the narrow opening of the river and increased the current. He reached it at last and scrambled aboard, only to find there were no oars. Had they been left on the island or were they already floating down the river? Unable to propel the boat from the inside, he slipped over the side and pushed it ahead of him.

The last time he had had to exert himself in this manner was on a fast-flowing river in India and he had nearly drowned. He must not drown, he must reach that island and rescue Beth. Too late he realised he should have waited for help, sent someone to find another boat. Now he was committed. He swam using his legs only, pushing the skiff, which seemed to become heavier and heavier with every yard. He could not see where he was going and the weeds, swaying backwards and forwards in the current, were grabbing at his exhausted legs. He kicked himself away from them.

'Beth Harley, I shall spank you when I get you safely home,' he muttered. 'I knew you were head-strong, but I never dreamed you would try this trick. Are you testing me? Shall I live to find out?'

His energy was nearly spent and the shore—both shores—seemed as far away as ever. If he was to survive, he would have to abandon the boat. He looked back to the landing stage and saw, not Henry, as he had hoped, but Edward. He was standing with his feet apart and his hands on his hips and he was laughing. 'For God's sake, man!' he managed to shout. 'Fetch some help. I'm drowning.'

Edward laughed all the more, bent down and picked up the oars and waved them at him. 'Drown, why don't you?'

Andrew's fury was enough to give him the strength to go on. With a monumental effort, he guided the skiff onwards, into calmer water and a few moments later beached it on the island and scrambled after it to collapse face down on the muddy shore, unable to move. It was fully a minute before he found the strength to get up and investigate the bundle. It was a woman's petticoat, tied securely to a bush, but there was no sign of Beth. 'Beth!' he shouted. 'Beth, where are you?' He moved inland a little taking the path through the trees towards his old hideout, shouting her name as he went.

Then she was running out of the hut and straight into his arms. He hugged her to him. 'Thank God you are safe.'

'You saw my signal. I didn't know how else to attract attention.'

His relief was followed by anger. 'What in hell's name did you think you were up to? You have the whole house in an uproar. Livvy is in floods of tears, my grandfather has collapsed and your dear mother very near to it, not to mention the fact that I was out of my mind.'

'It wasn't my fault. I was waiting for you in the garden and a stable lad came to tell me Livvy had taken a tumble and you had gone to her aid and needed me. What was I to do but go with him? I had no reason to be suspicious…'

He had questioned all the stable lads and according to John Tann they had been working in the yard since breakfast and he did not think any of them would have lied. He wondered if it was the young lad who had brought him Teddy's note, who was unknown to him and certainly not one of the Melhurst employees. 'Your sister is safe at home.'

'I did not know that. I had not seen her before I went into the garden and I thought she was out riding, though I wondered at her going without Lord Gorsham.'

'The boy brought you here?'

'No, he took me to meet Mr Melhurst, who told me Livvy was on the island and had had a fall and he would take me to her and then fetch help. I couldn't refuse to go, could I?'

'Teddy! But what did he want you over here for?'

'To lure you over. I think he means to kill you. He as good as told me so. With you gone, he is your grandfather's heir, and he is so pinched in the pocket, he cannot wait.'

'No doubt he thought I would drown coming over here.' His legs suddenly became shaky and he sat down heavily on the grass.

She sank down beside him, noticing how wet he was. His fair hair had gone into tiny curls that sat close to his skull and his shirt was clinging to his body, showing every rippling muscle. But he was shivering and it worried her. 'Do you mean you swam across?'

'Yes, pushing the boat most of the way.'

'Pushing it?'

'Yes. It was drifting and when I reached it the oars were gone.'

'You could have drowned.'

He smiled. 'I very nearly did.'

'Oh, Drew. He must be hoping the shock of your death would kill his lordship too.'

'Then we must endeavour to disappoint him. But not for a moment. I need to get my breath back.'

'Do you think you can manage to get to the hut? It is starting to rain.'

He was already too wet to notice a little rain. 'Is it still there?'

'It is falling down, but it might afford a little shelter.'

He forced himself to his feet and they made their way into the hut where he sank to the floor, leaning back against one of the walls. She shook out the mouldy blanket and wrapped it around him. He grinned. 'It stinks.'

'Better than nothing.' She sat beside him. 'What do we do now? Wait to be rescued?'

'It might be difficult. We have the boat and I do not know where there is another one. Henry would have to go into the village, even Newmarket, to find one. When the rain stops I will see if I can find a piece of wood to use for a paddle, then we can take ourselves across.'

'Are you feeling strong enough?'

'I shall be directly.'

They were silent for a moment, sitting side by side on the dirt floor of a tumbledown hut, wrapped in a filthy blanket, not the most romantic of places, but she was happy. She began to smile; there would never be a better time to take the initiative. 'Drew, we should have been walking in the garden.'

'Yes, I know. I have been thinking that myself.'

'Do you think we should have that talk now?' She chuckled. 'After all, I cannot run away, can I?'

'Do you want to run away?'

'No.'

'Good.'

He was shivering and she lifted the corner of the blanket and crept inside it with him. He put his arm about her and she laid her head on his shoulder. 'This is the strangest place to make a proposal of marriage,' he said.

'Oh, so that was what you were planning?'

'You must know it was.'

'I know nothing of the sort. I am not a mind reader, you could have been intent on telling me you were going to look elsewhere for a bride. I had almost convinced myself of it.'

'Why?'

'Perhaps because you told me you would not marry someone simply because your grandfather had ordered you to…'

'Neither would I.'

'I thought that's what you were doing, that time in London.'

'When you laughed me to scorn. It was enough to make a man less in love than I am give up.'

Her heart was beating fast and her eyes were shining. 'In love?'

'You know it, you tease. I love you more than life itself. I would rather have drowned than live without you.'

'But you did not drown and you do not have to live without me.'

'Is that a yes?'

'You have not asked me yet, not properly.'

He flung the blanket back. 'You would have me on my knees?'

'No, you must keep warm.' She pulled the offensive blanket back around him and settled herself beside him again. 'Just tell me.'

'I love you. I have loved you since I first set eyes on you and, if your uncle had been less careful of you and taken me up on my offer, I would have married you the next day.'

'I don't believe you.'

'So I am a liar, am I?'

'No, no, I did not mean that, but how could you have known?'

'Oh, I did, believe me, but all that gossip got in the way. I was afraid you believed it, especially after I had been so ill mannered as to kiss you. Have you forgiven me for that?'

'There is nothing to forgive. I wanted you to kiss me. You can do it again if you like.'

He laughed and obliged her. It lasted a long time and his lips roamed all over her face and neck, along her arms and into the cleft between her breasts, making her squirm with delight. 'Will that do?' he asked, looking into her eyes. They were swimming with bright tears. Happy tears.

'I am not sure. Perhaps you ought to do it again to convince me you mean it.'

He did. 'No more,' he said, suddenly coming up for air. 'I will not be responsible for my actions if I do. I must contain myself in patience until we are married.'

'You haven't asked me yet.'

'Then, my dearest love, will you make me the happiest of men and marry me?'

'Oh, yes, I think I should like that.'

'Well, we can't do it here, so we had better make a move. There is still the matter of some very deep water to negotiate. Henry should be on the other shore by now. Are you ready?'

'Yes, if you feel strong enough.'

He stood up and looked about him and then started

pulling the hut to pieces to find a couple of planks of wood. 'These will do. Come, my love.'

They ran down to the shore and he helped her into the boat and they set off for the landing stage, where Henry could be seen waving to them. It was hard work, with only a couple of rotten planks for paddles, and his strength had not fully returned. She took one of the planks to help him.

They were less than halfway and nearing the deepest part when the boat began to fill with water. She stopped paddling to bail out with her bare hands, but it was not long before she realised she was making no visible difference. Andrew did not speak, but simply gritted his teeth and rowed the harder. He looked round and shouted to Henry, 'We're sinking. Get help.'

Beth, realising they would be in the water in a matter of seconds, stripped off her skirt, knowing it would hinder her; the next moment the boat had gone and they were in the water. Her immediate thought as she began to swim was that if she drowned she would die happy, but her second was a determination to live, to spend a long life with the man she loved. He was swimming alongside her, ready to support her when she began to flag. Looking back the way they had come, she saw Edward on the island, standing with his hands on his hips watching them.

'Look,' she said. 'He's there. He must have another boat.'

He looked. 'The devil he is. Well, we are not going to satisfy him, are we? Come, my love, keep going. I am here beside you. I will always be beside you.'

It was comforting, but she was not the only one whose strength was spent. Just when she thought they were both being dragged to a watery grave, she realised there were other people in the water beside them: Henry and John Tann and two other men. She felt strong arms under her shoulders and a voice, loud in her ear. 'I've got you. Relax now.'

It was only a minute at the most when she was dragged on to dry land and lay there exhausted, uncaring that she was in nothing but her shift and drawers. 'Drew?' she panted, trying to sit up, but too exhausted to do so.

'Safe and sound.' It was Henry's voice. 'You nearly made it alone, do you know that?'

She turned her head to see Drew sitting beside her, his curls once more plastered to his skull and filthy streaks down his dear face. But he was grinning. John Tann produced a flask and warm blankets that did not smell as if rats had been nesting in them, and they were dosed and wrapped up and taken to the carriage, which waited on the road on the other side of the copse. And thus they returned to Heathlands and were put to bed.

* * *

She woke next morning to find the sun shining in her window and her mother sitting by her bed. 'Oh, good, you are awake. How are you, dearest?'

'I'm perfectly well. Drew?'

'Ah, so it is Drew, is it? Am I to infer that all is well between you?'

'Yes. He asked me to marry him. Has he not asked you for your consent?'

'He has not been able to. I am afraid he has caught a chill. Lord Gorsham fetched the doctor last night and he ordered him to stay in bed.'

'Oh, no. I must go to him.' She flung back the bed covers and scrambled out. 'Help me dress…'

'Beth, I am not sure it is quite proper.'

'Proper! Who cares about proper?' She was throwing on clothes as she spoke. 'We were stuck on that island for ages and I had to swim in my drawers. Proper did not come into it. Oh, I knew something like this might happen. He was in the water a long time and then sat about in wet clothes…'

'Beth, calm down.'

'When I have seen him.'

Decently clad in an undress robe of cream silk, she ran from the room, followed by her mother at a more dignified pace. Without waiting to knock, she burst into Andrew's room. He was in lying in bed, watched over by his Tollbank and Henry, who looked as though he had not been to bed.

She fell on her knees beside the bed and took Andrew's hand. His face, once so tanned, was pale as death. 'Drew, I am here, Drew, please open your eyes. Tell me you are not going to die.'

'Beth.' The lids flickered open and she found herself being scrutinised by a pair of very blue eyes.

'Oh, thank the good Lord. You must get better. I could not bear to have you taken from me now…'

'He is not going to be taken from you,' Henry said. 'The fever broke in the early hours. All he needs now is rest. What he did yesterday was a monumental feat of strength, which would have killed a lesser man, or certainly one less in love.'

Beth turned to him smiling. 'And you have stayed with him all night. I thank you for that. But go and rest now. I shall stay with him.'

'Beth!' her mother remonstrated.

'You may say "Beth" all you like, I shall stay here by his side until he is strong enough to get up.'

'Beth, sweetheart, go away,' Andrew murmured. 'I am going to get dressed.'

'You are too sick.'

'I am nothing of the sort. Now, go away and I shall join you directly.'

There was nothing to do but obey. She went back

to her room to complete her *toilette*, then went down to the dining room for a late breakfast. Finding she was suddenly ravenously hungry, she did justice to it, watched over by Harriet, who was so thankful to have her daughter safe, she could not bear to let her out of her sight. Beth's meal was punctuated with an account of what had happened to her the day before.

She had barely finished when Livvy rushed into the room. 'Nan said you were up and dressed. Oh, Beth, we have had such a time of it. We thought you must be dead, though Henry kept saying he was sure you were not. Everyone was out searching, even Mr Edward Melhurst. And Lord Melhurst had a seizure…'

'How is he?'

'Oh, he recovered when he was told you were both safe, but he is confined to his bed for the moment. Goodness, you never saw such a bedraggled state as you were in when they brought you home. How did you lose your clothes? I am sure if it had been me I should have died of mortification. Did you really swim across the lake?' She fired one question after another without waiting for any to be answered. 'Did you think you would never be rescued? And Mr Melhurst…I mean the Viscount, of course, was nearly out of his mind. You will have to marry him now.'

Beth smiled. 'You don't say!'

'Indeed, I do. You were alone together for hours and you only half-dressed.'

'Is that the only reason you think we should marry?'

'Well, I was hoping you might find it in your heart to like him a little too. If you had seen the state he was in when you were missing, you would not doubt his affections are genuine and nothing to do with everyone saying he should marry you.'

Beth laughed. 'I think we might have overcome that obstacle.'

'You mean he has declared himself and proposed. Oh, Beth, you did say yes, didn't you? You can be so stubborn sometimes.'

'He has yet to apply to Mama and Uncle James.'

'Oh, he spoke to James some time ago,' Harriet put in.

Beth looked at her in astonishment. 'When?'

'When they were discussing how to scotch all those rumours. Your uncle wanted to be sure of his intentions.'

'Oh, Mama!' Beth exclaimed. 'Why didn't you say?'

'It was up to you and Andrew to sort yourselves out first, but I would never have wanted it to happen in the way it did. I thank God, no harm came to you, though I feared for Andrew last night. He was in a raging fever.'

'It is hardly to be wondered at. He was sitting in wet clothes longer than I was and was exhausted as well.'

As she finished speaking the door opened and Andrew came in, properly dresses and shaved. He was still looking pale, but he was smiling. 'Drew!' Beth sprang up to go to him. Are you sure you are fit to come down?'

'Entirely.' He picked up her hand and put it to his lips, looking into her eyes as he did so, wanting to reassure himself that he had not dreamed her acceptance of him. What he saw there served to convince him that all was well. She was looking rosily healthy and her dark, expressive eyes were glowing. He grinned. 'And I am prodigious hungry.'

'Then come and sit down and I will serve you. Are you sure you are sufficiently recovered? Perhaps some gruel—'

'Be blowed to gruel, I'll have eggs and ham and anything else that's going.'

'Livvy,' Harriet's quiet voice called her younger daughter to her. 'I want to speak to you in my room.'

Livvy was about to protest, but noticed her mother's eyes go swiftly to Beth and Andrew and back again, and quietly followed her mother from the room. The soft click of the door told the lovers they were alone. He pulled her down on to his knee.

'I thought you were hungry.'

'Hungry for you. Are you well?' He searched her face. 'No ill effects?'

'None at all. But how you must have suffered. And

I let you sit in wet clothes with that disgusting blanket round you so that I could make you tell me you loved me.'

'I do not remember anyone making me do it. You know how I feel about having my hand forced…'

'Yes, so you told me. More than once.'

'Then you must know I did it of my own free will.'

'Would you have done it if we had not been marooned on a desert island like Robinson Crusoe?'

He laughed. 'That you will never know.'

'Oh, but you must tell me. I shall deny I said yes, if you do not. I shall say I succumbed because you were so wet and bedraggled…'

'Did you?'

'Oh, Drew, need you ask?'

'Need *you*?'

'No. Oh, let us be done with this sparring and cry truce.'

'Why? I was enjoying it.'

'Now you are teasing me.'

'Very well. No more teasing, not at this moment anyway. I cannot promise for the future. And, no thanks to my cousin Edward, there will be a future. When can we be married?'

'As soon as you like.'

'As soon as I like would be tomorrow. No, today. At any rate, as soon as the banns can be read.' He sighed. 'But I suppose I shall have to wait while you do whatever brides have to do before they agree to walk up the aisle.'

'If it were up to me, you would not have to wait long. And Livvy has always said she wants me to marry first. I must talk to Mama, but shall we say November?'

'We shall say November.' He paused. 'Where would you like to go for a wedding trip?'

'I don't know, I had not thought of it.'

'That's a whisker. I collect you telling me the first day we met that if you married a rich husband, you would go plant hunting. I imagine I might qualify.'

'Oh, you don't think… You cannot possibly think that I—'

He laughed. 'Oh, my darling, you are so quick to rise to the bait and I could not resist it. But, seriously, would you like to travel? I could show you some of India. We might even catch up with your friend, Toby.'

'Oh, Drew!' She flung her arms about his neck and kissed him. He laughed and kissed her back. 'But only if your grandfather is well enough to let us go. If, not we must wait.'

'So this is where you are hiding!'

Beth scrambled off Andrew's knee, as Lord Melhurst entered the room. Her hand went up to her face, trying to smooth down the stray curls that had escaped. 'My lord,' she said. He was wearing a burgundy velvet dressing gown and supporting himself with a stick, but otherwise appeared well. 'You have made a good recovery?'

'Yes, but don't you ever put me through anything like that again. Get yourselves married and settle down.' He turned to Andrew who, though he had stood, was unperturbed by his grandfather's untimely entrance. 'I suppose you did make an offer?'

'Yes, sir, and was accepted.'

'About time too. I am sure in my day we did not spin it out so long. Now, if you have finished your breakfast, come into the drawing room. I want to hear what happened. Later we can make plans.'

Smiling broadly at each other, they followed him into the drawing room where Harriet, Livvy and Henry were gathered. The old man was settled into his favourite armchair by the hearth and the story was told again, some of it by Beth and some by Andrew, interrupting each other and smiling at each other in a way that left no doubt in their listeners' minds that all the earlier difficulties had been swept away and, if nothing else, their ordeal had brought them both to their senses. But what an ordeal! That they had not both drowned was a miracle. Edward, having failed to see Drew drown on the way over to the island, had used another boat he had hidden to row over to the island to make sure of them. He had loosened the bung in the bottom of the skiff. He had not bargained on Andrew's superb fitness or Beth's courage when faced with a gruelling swim, but it had been a very near thing.

'It is difficult to believe anyone could be so malicious,' Beth said.

'There was a lot at stake,' Henry said. 'I discovered he had prodigious gambling debts. He heard Livvy say she wished she could ride in a race and he hit upon the idea of persuading her to ride Moonshine. Then he gambled everything he had and more besides, not only that the horse would lose, for which the odds were not great, but that it would never finish the race. The odds on that were long enough to wipe out all his debts if he was right.'

Livvy laughed. 'Really? You did not tell me that. Oh, if I had known I could have told him I would not only finish but stay on to the end and win. Oh, he must have been furious.'

'And desperate,' Henry said. 'But I never dreamed he would go so far as to attempt murder.'

'What happened to him?' Beth asked. 'The last I saw of him he was on the island.'

'And that's where he stayed,' Henry said. 'I rowed over after we had you safely back. I am afraid...' he paused '...I am afraid he hanged himself on one of the trees.'

'Hanged himself! Oh, no, poor Mrs Melhurst,' Beth said. 'She had nothing to do with any of it, did she?'

'No,' Andrew said.

'I'll look after her,' Lord Melhurst said. 'Think no more about it. Now, tell me your plans. I assume there is to be a wedding?'

'Two weddings,' Livvy put in.

'Oh, yes. Forgot. Two weddings.'

They spent the rest of the morning talking and planning and in the afternoon Beth and Andrew took their walk in the garden, but they hardly looked at the shrubs and trees Andrew was so proud of. They were too busy looking at each other and stopping every now and again when they were out of sight of the house and the gardeners to kiss and laugh and say 'I love you' over and over again so that neither was left in any doubt.

They spent two more days in the idyllic surroundings of Heathlands to give Beth time to recover fully, it was said, but she had felt no ill effects from her ordeal and it was simply her mother's gentle understanding that allowed her to have a little more time with Andrew. While Henry and Livvy went riding, Beth and Andrew wandered about the garden, the glasshouses and conservatory, talking about every subject under the sun. They laughed a lot, teased each other unmercifully and occasionally argued hotly, which always ended in them kissing each other until they were both breathless.

The time inevitably came when they left Heathlands for Beechgrove and from there returned to London to give the Duke the good news and tell him there was another wedding to arrange. To give him his due, he was delighted. They shopped for a second lot of wedding clothes, expressed sorrow at the death of the Queen only three weeks after her husband's coronation, and returned to Beechgrove from where they were married on a misty day in November. By then Sophie had been delivered of a healthy daughter, named Elizabeth Olivia, after her two cousins. She was brought in to the wedding breakfast for everyone to admire, which quite put Jamie's nose out of joint until Beth gave him a hug and promised to write a journal especially for him while she was on her travels.

Andrew watched her with the boy and his heart swelled with pride that he had at last made her his bride. After they came back from their plant-hunting trip, which he had decided would not be prolonged or even slightly hazardous, he would start a family of his own. He had no doubt at all she would make the best of wives and an excellent and loving mother. His Viscountess. He smiled; she was far too animated for that title, but he supposed she would grow into it, though he would never want to change her. She was perfect as she was.

'Well, my boy, I am persuaded all's well in your world.'

He turned towards his grandfather, looking better than he had for a long time. 'Yes, Grandfather, all is well.'

* * * * *